Praise for
Charming

Beast

Charming Book Two

Jade Linwood

SOLARIS

First published 2025 by Solaris
an imprint of Rebellion Publishing Ltd,
Riverside House, Osney Mead,
Oxford, OX2 0ES, UK

www.solarisbooks.com

ISBN: 978-1-83786-447-8

10 9 8 7 6 5 4 3 2 1

A CIP catalogue record for this book is available from the
British Library.

Designed & typeset by Rebellion Publishing

Printed in Denmark

MIX
Paper | Supporting
responsible forestry
FSC® C104608

To Dave, best of husbands, always.

The Lost Prince

T HE STORY BEGINS, as so many do, with a man, on a horse, in a forest.

Jean-Marc Charming Arundel, frequently though not exclusively known as Prince Charming, glares into the gathering darkness and drags a hand through his tangled hair. Though the moon is up, and full, only fragments of light manage to pierce the thick cover, teasing the eye with moving glimmers but providing little actual visibility.

"Forests," he mutters. "Poets are always going on about forests. How green, how pretty, how romantic... What they are is dark, inconvenient and full of brambles. And branches that knock your hat off. I *liked* that hat."

The horse huffs.

"Stop complaining, it's not my fault we're lost. That was a perfectly good path. Until it wasn't."

The horse shakes its head, and huffs again.

* * *

"YOU KNOW WHAT?" Charming said, "I almost miss Roland. At least he usually knew where we were. Although you aren't as annoying. And you smell better."

As though to disprove this, the horse whickered, and shifted, and suddenly and noisily emptied its bowels.

Charming sighed. "Still not as bad as Roland. Come on, get a move on, let's see if we can find somewhere to—"

A howl cut through the night, a cold and primal shriek. Charming barely had time to swear before the horse's entire body hunched under him and it bolted.

Charming was an excellent horseman, but even he was hard put to cling on, almost flat to the horse's withers, as branches whipped his sides and snatched at his hair.

Finally, the hard-breathing beast began to slow, and Charming let out a breath, started to sit up. The horse skidded on a muddy slope, reared again in a panic, and Charming hit the ground. The horse twisted, tore the reins from his hands, and skittered off into the darkness.

"Oh, wonderful," Charming said. He got to his feet and stood very still, listening.

Shufflings and creaks and cracks which might have been the horse—wretched ungrateful beast that it was—or might have been something else. Such as a very large wolf. And all its friends. Or any of a number of unpleasant creatures wandering the woods in the middle of the night, and just in the mood for snacking on a tasty royal morsel such as himself.

He rubbed his sore hands together, brushed at the seat of his breeches, grimacing at the feel of mud, and considered.

Well, he was surrounded by trees. That was something. He scouted about until he found one with branches low enough for him to reach, and scrambled up to a crook that he could probably contrive not to fall out of for a few hours.

He took off the harness that held his sword across his back, looped it around a couple of branches and stuck his arm through it, wedged his bruised backside against the trunk and braced his feet. It wasn't exactly safe, and it certainly wasn't comfortable, but it would have to do. He stared up at the moon, bright and cold in the star-pricked sky.

He was hungry, and his provisions were in the saddlebags, now halfway to who-knew-where. Maybe the horse would avoid being eaten for long enough to be caught by someone—but whoever found it would probably regard it as a convenient windfall, and either stable it or sell it, rather than put together a search party for its previous owner.

Well, previous *rider*. It wasn't exactly Charming's horse, any more than the sword he carried was officially his sword. He had simply acquired them on the road. People shouldn't carelessly leave things unattended if they want to keep them, that was his opinion.

At least it was August, he reflected, squinting at the sky, and still reasonably warm.

Even as the thought crossed his mind, clouds drifted over the face of the moon. The night darkened to pitch. A casual spitter of rain hit the leaves, increasing to a drenching rush.

Charming mumbled curses on faithless horses; even more faithless servants; three—no, *four* interfering women without whom he wouldn't be in this position in the first place; his father, who was to blame for it all anyway; paths that took you in the wrong direction; and everything else he could think of, as the rain snuck its chilly way down the back of his neck.

Another wolf howled, perhaps complaining about the downpour, and was soon joined by a chorus. "Oh, shut up," Charming mutters. "Go eat the horse."

The Four Impatient Ladies

EANWHILE, NOT SO very far away as the crow flies or the sparrow gossips, in the Kuchenmeister, a guest-house of old-fashioned style but adequate comfort, four women are gathered, waiting.

"He isn't coming," Princess Marie Blanche de Neige declares, without looking up from the rather impressive gutting knife she is sharpening. She has dark bronze curls, eyes of such deep brown they are nearly black, and strong, muscular hands. She encountered Charming when he rescued her from a poisoned apple, a coma in a glass box and an evil stepmother. Unfortunately, he then absconded with a large portion of her treasury—and a good deal of her faith in humanity.

"Must you do that?" Queen Ella de Braise, otherwise known as Nell, says before taking a bite of the vast slab of bread and cheese she is holding. She is a slight woman, with large, liquid brown eyes and a look of fragility that is entirely deceptive, dressed in fawn velvet which emphasises her doe-like appearance, and a matching whimsical feathered concoction of a hat tilted over one eye. Charming rescued her from a life in the kitchens. And from the unfortunate fate of inheriting a wealthy kingdom. She'd already possessed a healthy dose of cynicism, but he probably added to it.

Marie Blanche raises her eyebrows. "This is my best knife, I am not trusting its care to anyone else."

"It's not that you're *sharpening* it, dear," Nell says. "It's that you do it in such a *threatening* way. As though you were just waiting for the right stabbable person to walk through the door."

Marie Blanche snorts. "I have promised not to stab him. *If* he turns up. I keep *my* promises."

"He will." Bella Lucia dei' Sogni turns from the window. Even that small movement sings with grace. The morning sunlight dances gleaming among the dark cascades of her curls. She is, in a room of exceptionally handsome women, astonishingly—one might say supernaturally—beautiful, and manages to make a simple doublet and breeches look as though they had been designed for her by the most talented of seamstresses. Charming rescued *her*, too. And broke her heart.

"And *no*," she says, "I don't think that because I'm still in love with him, you needn't say it, Marie Blanche, I saw that look. But whatever else he is, he isn't stupid. If he misses the meeting with Mephistopheles, he will die. Unless he's found a way around the curse. Could he do that?"

"A curse set by one of the lords of Hell?" Doctor Rapunzel, seated at a table covered with maps, instruments, quills, and ink pots shakes her head. She has striking features, hazel eyes and long clever hands slightly stained at the fingertips from her years of working with potions. As always, she wears a headdress that entirely covers her hair. Today it is a rich forest green, stitched here and there with tiny gold daisies. And yes, she too has encountered Charming. Her rescue involved a tower, and a sorceress, and losing a great many useful and magical objects. How it left her feeling, she keeps to herself. She keeps a lot to herself.

"HE IS CLEVER, certainly," Rapunzel continued, "but few people—or any creatures—are clever enough to do that. I know where he is, to a degree." She tapped the map in front of her. "He went into the Scatovald. But it is a place thick with magic, and I cannot scry anything more than that he has gone in and not, so far as I can tell, left."

"Why in the name of Goose would he go into the Scatovald?" Marie Blanche said.

"Possibly he was attempting to shorten his journey, though why he thought plunging through dense forest would be easier than a perfectly good road I cannot fathom." Doctor Rapunzel tapped the map again and it curled up neatly and slotted itself back into its case. "We still have time. Bella Lucia, your men with the gold—I am assuming they can be trusted to wait?"

"I spoke to them myself," Bella said. "They'll wait."

"Of course they will," Nell said, rolling her eyes, but with a grin.

Bella blushed, and responded with a slight, self-deprecating grin of her own. It quickly dropped away and she turned to the window again. "Do you think he's in trouble?"

"Almost certainly," Doctor Rapunzel said drily. "When is he not? And without him the gold will do no good. I should not want the King, or your men—or, let us be frank, ourselves—to suffer the consequences of failing to fulfil Mephistopheles' demands to the letter. At best, we lose the gold. At worst..." She let the sentence hang.

"At worst, if Charming fails to turn up to hand the gold over personally, Charming's father dies, *Charming* dies, Mephistopheles decides to pay us back for our interference by cursing us all in a variety of inventive ways, *and* we lose the gold," Marie Blanche said.

"If Charming fails to arrive," Bella said, "I will send the men away, and stay there alone with the gold. I will not risk my men's lives, and there is no need for you to risk yours."

"My dear," Doctor Rapunzel said, "that is a noble thought, and very like you. But even *your* gifts are unlikely to work on Mephistopheles."

"Or they could work *too* well," Nell said. "I mean Charming is undoubtedly a cad, a traitor, a conman and as selfish as the day is long, but I daresay having a *demon* take a fancy to you could be worse."

Doctor Rapunzel closed her eyes briefly, and shuddered. "Do not, please, say such things."

"Charming never did take a fancy to me," Bella said. "It was all a trick, I'm perfectly well aware of that. So what do we do?"

"I suppose we must go after the wretched man." Doctor Rapunzel rubbed her eyes. "I really am rather tired of following him about. But first, we must find out more about the Scatovald. 'Shadow Forest'—the name does not bode well, does it? And I am not setting foot somewhere *that* riddled with magic without knowing more. Nell, would you be so good as to talk to the staff here? They are local, and can probably tell us something, at least. Marie Blanche…"

"I have overheard a little from the birds already. I will sniff about."

"What about me?" Bella said.

"Talk to the townsfolk, please. See what you can discover about the forest, and if anyone has had sight or sound of our wandering prince."

The House of Roses

ORNING FOUND CHARMING cold, stiff, wet, and grumpy, with moss in his hair. He had not really slept, but occasionally fallen into an uneasy doze, full of howling, and images of glowing, predatory eyes, before jolting back to awareness as he felt himself, or imagined himself, slipping from his perch towards waiting teeth.

The morning air shimmered with birdsong. The clouds had cleared, and sunlight filtered green and gold through the canopy. Charming unhooked himself, reslung his sword, and climbed further up the tree, to see if he could find his bearings. Balanced on the highest branch that looked as though it would hold his weight, he peered over the apparently endless landscape of the forest.

Nothing but trees, in every direction, and in the distance, the blue hint of mountains. *That* was where he was supposed to be headed, but he was, if anything, further away than when he went off the road. He shook his head. Normally his sense of direction was a good deal more reliable.

Then he caught a glimpse of something, just lit by the rising sun, that looked the wrong shape for a tree.

It was a chimney. He was almost *certain* it was a chimney. It was definitely not a tree. And he thought he could see the gleam of windows amidst the greenery below it.

It was slightly out of his way, but he needed food, and directions.

He fixed the direction in his mind and climbed down.

In sharp contrast to the night before, today the forest seemed inclined to help Charming on his way, with the easiest route frequently going in just the right direction. Near midday, the trees thinned in front of him, to reveal a path.

It was overgrown, but it was unmistakably a path. In fact, *path* was hardly adequate. It was wide enough for two carriages to pass each other. Further off it was gravelled, raked and lined with well-kept orange trees, and swept up to the steps of an impressive manor house. He could see no sign of any occupants.

He paused.

Charming had experience with impressive, well kept, apparently empty buildings. It had made him wary.

As he watched, a curl of smoke rose from the chimney. At least someone was about. With any luck he could find the servants' entrance, charm some form of portable meal out of whoever happened to be around, and get those directions. Maybe even a ride on a cart. Anything other than more hours of walking in these ill-fitting boots—so long as 'anything' didn't include any eligible ladies in unfortunate circumstances. He had had his fill of those, and then some.

He dragged his fingers through his hair, brushed off as much mud as he could reach, and limped his way up the path, through a pair of very fine wrought-iron gates that stood welcomingly open, and around the side of the manor to where he hoped the kitchens might be.

THE GRAVEL CRUNCHED under Charming's feet and bees hummed past his head, occasionally pausing to investigate his golden if slightly mossy locks for pollen. Late-blooming roses climbed the walls of the mansion and crammed every flowerbed, filling the air with sweetness. They ranged from the snowiest white through peaches and yellows and mauves to a lush and midnight crimson. Some were a single shade, others stippled and flecked and striped as though they had been flinging their colours at one another in a cheerful game.

Charming, not a man much interested in gardening at the best of times, headed towards the clatter of pots and dishes and sniffed appreciatively. *Bacon.* Far more appealing, at this precise moment, than the most fragrant of roses.

The kitchen door stood open. "Hello?" he said. "I say, the house? I am but a poor harmless traveller, lost in the woods, and would beg your hospitality. And directions."

He poked his head around the door, armed with his best smile. Well, possibly his second-best smile. He was tired.

The kitchen stood empty. Pots bubbled on the stove, fresh loaves stood on the table, their aroma and that of the bacon crisping in a pan making Charming's stomach twist with hunger. "Hello?"

He edged into the kitchen. It was a fine place, with long wooden tables scrubbed and piled with vegetables ready for the chopping, and a couple of sleek fat rabbits waiting to join them in a hearty stew. The oven pumped out heat and the enticing smell of baking, and a cauldron over the fire gave off savoury steam. The floor and walls gleamed, the utensils were ranked like soldiers, and everything was as clean and wholesome and well organised as could possibly be imagined.

Charming blinked as a knife, gleaming in the sunlight, floated into the air. "Oh, *no*," he said, and backed towards the door.

Then a loaf drifted weightlessly towards the table, and the knife bit into it.

A plate emerged from a cupboard. Thickly cut bacon cooked to perfection, ripe yellow cheese, blush pink apples, creamy butter, deep red jam and pristine cutlery assembled themselves. Small beer and milk appeared in charmingly rustic jugs.

A chair edged invitingly away from the table.

Charming looked over his shoulder at the door, then back at the plateful of food. He was *extremely* hungry.

"Well, this is all very nice," he said. He sat down in the chair and regarded what was on offer. Not the apples, at least not to start with. But cheese, surely, was about as unmagical a foodstuff as you could get. Even if it floated itself to the table. He cut a cautious sliver, placed it on his tongue and waited to see if he would start turning into something.

It was *very* good cheese. Nothing unpleasant seemed to be happening, and his stomach was yelling at him to stop messing about and get on with breakfast.

He shrugged, made possibly the largest bacon sandwich ever seen in that kitchen, and proceeded to stuff his princely face.

"You know what," he said, between mouthfuls, "I could get used to this. All of the service and none of the moaning. What a marvellous idea. I suppose this wonderful house belongs to someone, though."

A speculative glint appeared in his eye, then he sighed. "I need directions to the road to Floriens."

He thought for a moment. "Ah. Can you talk? Or otherwise indicate where I should go? No? Bother. Well, I should appreciate a bath. I am sure such a splendid house would have no trouble providing me with that? Oh, and also, possibly, some boots that actually fit."

A towel appeared by the inner door, hanging in the air. He followed it to a room of gleaming marble, where there stood a vast wooden tub, sealed with pitch, full of steaming water smelling of sweet herbs. Charming flung aside his clothes, sank in with a groan and ducked his head under.

When he emerged, his clothes were gone—along with his sword. This worried him, but only slightly. A place like this was bound to have weapons lying about, and at worst, there were knives in the kitchen.

He spotted a bottle of rosemary-infused oil and a comb and leapt upon them with delight, easing tangles out of his hair until it was once again, a handy mirror assured him, a magnificent golden mane instead of a leaf-and-mud-matted disgrace.

New clothes had been laid out for him. He frowned slightly at the sight of them. Not that they were ugly— in fact, they were princely. Silken hose; a shirt of fine cambric, foaming with lace; satin breeches and a satin coat in a deep blue that might have been chosen specifically to match Charming's colouring (though, to be fair, most things did). Not really *travelling* clothes.

But the house was doing its best. And, wonderfully, there were boots, glossy as fresh-fallen conkers, that fit so perfectly his abused feet almost burst into tears.

Sunset light fell richly through the windows as he left the bathing room, a towel still wrapped around his hair. A door opened, and he peered in to see another room that looked almost too inviting, all deep cushions and velvet curtains and crackling fire and tempting decanters.

A small marquetry table next to one of the chairs bore a glass of what smelled like extremely good brandy. Next to it lay a single, perfect rose, just out of bud, unfurling its crimson petals in the warmth of the room. "How delightful," Charming said, settling himself in and raising the glass.

"Now, my former man... accomplice... *servant*, Roland, would probably have necked this"—he took a sip—"this really *excellent* brandy before I got a look in and pretended it was for my own good. Making snarky remarks the while. This is *so* much nicer. I can probably stay just one night. I mean, you've provided such splendid service, House. And a decent night's sleep will set me up for the journey. But after that, alas, I must get on. Places to go, demons to pay off. I shall definitely be back, though. I can promise you that."

The sun sank. Lanterns bloomed to life. The fire danced. Charming fell into a comfortable doze, until something jolted him alert.

The hairs on the back of his neck were standing up like soldiers on parade. He sat, wide-eyed but still, scanning the room. The fire had sunk to a glow, only one lantern still cast a flickering light. He felt surreptitiously for his sword, but of course, it wasn't there. The door stood slightly ajar, showing a fragment of corridor, lit with moonlight.

Something shuffled. Something brushed the wall. The fragment of corridor disappeared except for a small section at the top. Whatever lurked was well over seven feet tall.

Charming could see fur, a furtive gleam that might be an eye. His hand stole out for the brandy decanter and closed around the neck.

Then the shape moved away.

Charming waited for a few minutes, swore heartily if quietly, got up, and went looking for a sword.

The Young Men of Felendstadt

 ARIE BLANCHE PAUSED outside the guest house, shoving her hands in her pockets as she looked up at the warmly lit windows. She had spent the afternoon listening to the birds chatter and gathering what she could from such beasts as she could coax to her. Missing her own dogs fiercely, she spent perhaps more time than was strictly warranted with the local dogs, who, while happy for her attention, could not tell her much. She only knew as much of their language as any human who spends a great deal of time with them might do.

Through the window she could see the other women bent over the maps. What would happen after the demon's bargain was fulfilled? Would they all go their separate ways? She had come to think of them as friends—even Bella, now the girl had, for the most part, come to her senses. Marie Blanche would hate to lose the first friends she had made in her adult life, but they all had lives and responsibilities to return to. As did she.

The thought of home weighed on her. All those people, depending on her. Her household, her infant half-brother, her father, the entire kingdom. All coming to her for help and advice and guidance. And who was *she* to turn to, when she went home?

Put your hands to what is in front of them. Her mother's saying, though Marie Blanche could no longer remember how her voice had sounded. She straightened her spine, and walked into a room ringing with laughter.

NELL, EYES SPARKLING with mischief, was back in servants' clothes, with her hair in a kerchief. Bella, her tumble of black curls up in a respectable snood, in a plain green travelling dress that entirely failed to look plain on her, was laughing at something—something not entirely polite, judging by Bella's blush and Nell's grin.

Doctor Rapunzel was waving a long, slightly green-tinted finger at Nell. "Ah, Marie Blanche! Good, a little *sensible* conversation will be welcome. What have you found?"

"Less than I would like. I have discovered that there is a wolf clan that claims half the forest. Led, it seems, by a human woman: one Little Red Cap."

"That sounds… unusual," Doctor Rapunzel said.

"It sounds absurd," Marie Blanche said. "Nonetheless, she exists. She has a fearsome reputation, but how much of it is true, and how much is exaggeration—that is hard to tell. She is popular with the crows, that I do know."

"Popular with… oh. Ugh," Bella said.

"It may mean nothing. But it suggests that where she is, there is dead flesh to be had. Possibly she, or her beasts, are simply wasteful hunters."

"I know this one," Nell said. "I went to the kitchens. You bung on an apron, walk in, pick up a knife and start chopping and people just assume you're meant to be there. Amazing what they'll tell you over a pile of carrots. What they told *me* was that people don't kill wolves any more, hereabouts. Anyone does, and next day they're likely to find one of their prime beasts slaughtered and hung on a fencepost, not touched by anything but crows."

"Interesting," Doctor Rapunzel said. "Anything else?"

"Bears," Marie Blanche said. "A clan of bears, *also* led by a woman. This one a witch."

"Seems to be the fashion," Nell said. "The locals mentioned her. Goldlöckchen."

"Bless you," Marie Blanche said.

"That's her *name*," Nell said. Then she made a face. "Oh, hah hah."

"Sorry," Marie Blanche said.

Nell snorted. "No, you're not. Look at you, making jokes. You *have* loosened up."

"Like a dog, I can learn a trick or two, given time and patience," Marie Blanche said.

Nell laughed. "And we're testing the good doctor's. Sorry, doctor. The name was all I got. Everyone's scared stiff to even mention her, never seen so many signs against the evil eye. And so much salt thrown over people's shoulders it was like being at sea."

Doctor Rapunzel was drumming her fingers on the tabletop. Little blue flickers danced between her nails. "Goldlöckchen. Goldlöckchen. I *know* that name, or something like it. I have read it. Anything more?"

Nell shook her head.

Marie Blanche said, "It seems that until five winters ago the wolves and bears were hardly aware of each other's existence. Now, for some reason, they are crossing into each other's territories. Normally that would not present much of a problem—they don't even hunt the same prey—but they do not behave as bears and wolves should." She shook her head. "Still, if they are led by humans, why would they? There is aggression every time they meet. No deaths, yet, but I doubt it will be long."

"What happened five winters ago?" Rapunzel said.

"That I don't know. Even the starlings didn't know—they were happy to guess, little gossips that they are, but one can usually tell with them if it is purely speculation. Whatever happened, it is still ongoing. It was not one thing that could be apologised for and repaid."

"That is unfortunate," Doctor Rapunzel said. "Bella Lucia?"

"There is something," Bella said. "I got chatting to the baker."

"Wondered where those nice cinnamon buns came from," Nell said.

"She insisted. A year or so ago her son went missing for some days, and returned apparently unharmed, but with no memory of where he'd been. I wouldn't have made anything of it, if I hadn't heard similar stories from the candlemaker"—Nell glanced pointedly at the fine wax candle standing on the table—"and the draper."

"Lovely bit of wool, that," Nell said. "Just your colour."

"You're welcome to it, Nell. It would suit you just as well," Bella said.

"Nothing would, dear," said Nell. "But go on."

"Yes, please do allow her to go on," Doctor Rapunzel said.

"Sorry, doctor." Nell made a token effort to look apologetic.

"In the draper's case, it was his grandson," Bella said. "I spoke to the boy, too, but he had no memory at all between going into the fringes of the wood after mushrooms, and wandering out again about a month later. He said his bed felt very hard, once he got back, and he thought that was odd, since he must have slept on the forest floor. And he no longer eats mushrooms."

"A mushroom that could make one forget everything for a *month* would be potent indeed," Doctor Rapunzel said. "I don't know the flora of this area as well as I should. I shall check my books. In the meantime, perhaps it would be safer to avoid any fungi. Now, I have some other research to pursue."

The Doctor, the Imp and the Bargain

OCTOR RAPUNZEL'S RESEARCH was interrupted by the appearance of a face at the window. As the window was on the second floor, this should perhaps have been alarming, but Doctor Rapunzel, after flicking her fingers in a quick spell to ensure that she was actually seeing what she thought she was, opened it.

"*Roland?*"

"Wotcha."

Roland, which was the name he was currently using, mostly passed for a small, and somewhat whiffy, human, though he tended to give the casual observer the feeling that he wasn't put together in quite the standard way. He climbed in and sat on Doctor Rapunzel's desk, scratching himself. "So, how's things?"

"Roland, what are you *doing* here?"

"Thought I'd drop in, see how you ladies are doing. Don't suppose you've got a bit of sausage about you? My stomach thinks my throat's been cut."

She pushed over a platter. "These are called heathen cakes."

"Hah." He took one and chewed. "Not bad," he said, eventually. "Not bad at all. Eggs and bacon and apples, I like it. Not sure about the beef. A bit more pepper wouldn't go amiss."

"Nor would fewer crumbs. *Please.*"

He snorted, but brushed a few crumbs off the mound of papers next to him. "What're these, anyway?"

"Magistrates' rolls."

"What are they when they're at home?"

"Records of court cases."

"Bor*ing.*"

"Roland…"

He peered at the papers. "Some of these go back *years!* What d'you need these for?"

"We have mislaid Charming."

"Have you indeed. Slippery as always, eh? Still don't know why you need a lot of old court stuff, though."

"Because the Scatovald is largely unmapped land, disputed by no fewer than *three* lords—a prince and two archdukes—all of whom claim feudal authority and the right to levy taxes across the area. Since, officially speaking"—she raised an eyebrow—"there are no subjects in the forest to rule or tax, the matter is largely considered moot. But I thought it wise to familiarise myself with any past troubles that might have bearing on our search. I have, however, noticed something odd. There are gaps. Missing years, missing papers… Local court records are not always the most efficiently kept or stored, but there appears to be some sort of pattern, affecting the last few years, and I cannot spot it."

"I'm not surprised," said the little man, flicking

through the sheets. "They're a bit rubbish at their jobs, some of 'em. Look at this one: two kiddies gone missing in the forest, magistrate declares them dead and closes the case. Seems like no one barely bothered looking."

He caught Doctor Rapunzel's look.

"What?"

"I did not expect the fate of two children to be of concern to you."

"I'm not *concerned*," he growled. "Just think it's interesting, that's all. Thought you lot cared about your spawn."

"Some people care more than others, I'm afraid. Now, not that I am sorry to see you, but why exactly are you *really* here? I assume you want something?"

"Not as *such*," he said.

"That means, yes, you want something, but you're going to take a long time getting to it. Please, don't."

"I just want your help with something. And I've got something useful for you in return." He looked over his shoulder—rather farther over his shoulder than should be possible for anyone who wasn't an owl, and then back at Rapunzel. His expression of anxious sincerity sat very oddly on his face. "But you got to keep my name out of it. *Both* my names. You got to *vow*."

"I can make no vows without more information." Doctor Rapunzel had been dealing with the infernal, when she had to, for a number of years, and had survived this long by being extremely cautious. It isn't paranoia if an unwary promise really can result in your soul being yanked out through your ears.

"Roland, tell me what you want. You have been of great help to me, and I am grateful, but I really do need to know what I might be getting myself involved in."

"Well, thing is, I was by way of doing a little sort of private sniffing about. 'Cause His Lordship The Biggest Cheese likes to know what's going on in his Domain."

"Roland, I am aware that you were one of the Eyes of the Thousand-Eyed."

Roland grimaced. "Well, it's usually around nine-hundred-and-eighty-something, more like. It's a job with prospects, being an Eye, but they ain't always *nice* prospects. See, how it works down there—well, it's a lot like court up here, so far as I can tell. Favour here, bribe there, a bit of information in the right ear, and you get a chance to move up a bit. *Wrong* information, *wrong* ear, you're more likely to end up on the *wrong* end of something spiky. Yes?"

"So I understand. But I have not personally spent a great deal of time at court, since I was locked in a tower for much of my life. Which you should remember, since you were also there."

"So I didn't keep up with where you went *after,* did I? Talent like yours, you could have been Court Magician of Macqreux, or Chief Sorcerer to the Emperor of Chitan, or whatever, by now."

"But, as you know perfectly well, I am not. Is there a point to this rampant flattery?"

"Ain't flattery if it's true, is it? *Anyway,* point is, His Lordship suspected that maybe someone was getting a little too big for their boots. Well, he always does, I mean, 'paranoid' isn't in it. So muggins here gets sent to have a sniff. Well, he didn't send me *himself*—that would be beneath him—but anyway, I get sent.

"So I've been working my way into favour with this suspect party, getting him a few useful things that are difficult to acquire down there, dropping him a bit of information that sounds more useful than it is, you know the kind of thing. And I'm on my way to deliver him an item, I'm nearly at his gaff and I hear voices. I wedge myself into this sort of scoop out of the wall, so I'm stuck there, in this soggy little corner of nowhere. And I realise I'm hearing something I very definitely should not be hearing if I want to keep all my component parts, which—I know they ain't much, but they're mine, and I'd rather they stay attached.

"And I thought, why am I doing this, anyway? Just so I can scratch my way a bit further up the greasy pole? What am I going to get out of this, in the end? Because you move up and all that really means is there's more people further down the pole who want to pull you down and send you back to the mud. And all the time I was thinking about how much I really, really fancied a biscuit. Not even a posh one, you know? Nothing fancy, just a nice biscuit."

"That is a very interesting story, Roland, but I do not see—"

"So I sneak off as soon as I think it's safe, and I had to do a bit of thinking. And I realised that I was only getting involved in this stuff in the first place because it's what everyone does. But what's it all *for*? I don't want to be a Lord of Hell, or even a, you know, part time Administrative Assistant of Hell. But before I could come to any conclusions, I got snatched up into a binding by that old... *creature* Hilda von Riesentor, then by Smarmy Charmy. And now I'm free, well, I don't want to go back to the Infernal. I want to stay here."

"I see."

"So you might be able to help with that."

"Might I, indeed?"

"And in return, *I* might have some useful information for you."

Doctor Rapunzel laced her fingers together and looked at him. "I cannot help feeling we have gone a long way around to get to the point," she said, "and since I do, in fact, have work to do, I would rather not wander any further. What information would I get?"

"A name."

"A true name?"

Roland shook his head. "Hah. If I knew *that*… no. Just a name, but one I think you might want to know."

"And what do you want from me?" Doctor Rapunzel was already suspicious, as it was unlike Roland to be quite so circumspect. Cautious, yes. But this amount of beating around the bush was unusual even for him. He looked positively *uncomfortable,* which was disconcerting in someone she had previously considered entirely lacking a sense of embarrassment.

He was probably going to ask of her something truly dreadful, or extremely dangerous. Or both.

"Roland?"

He muttered something, staring at the floor.

"What was that?"

He muttered again. The tips of his large and (if you looked closely enough) very slightly pointed ears had gone scarlet.

"Roland, if you cannot even *admit* to what you want, I doubt I can help you, however useful your information."

"An eating-house."

"I beg your pardon?"

"I want an eating-house."

"A whole one?"

"Well, yes."

"I know you're always hungry, but I think…"

"I want to *run* one," Roland blurted. He shot her a look in which wariness, hope and embarrassment warred for supremacy, then dropped his gaze. "'S stupid, forget it."

"Wait," Doctor Rapunzel said. "You want to run an eating-house for *people*."

"For anyone who wants to eat. And can pay. I'm not prejudiced." He considered for a moment. "Well, maybe against people with no money."

Doctor Rapunzel regarded him. He was odd, grubby, odoriferous, and a literal imp of Hell, but she had met less appealing people running inns.

"It seems to me a perfectly respectable ambition," she said. "More so than politics, here *or* in the Infernal."

"Not where I come from, it isn't."

"Since you do not wish to return there, why would that matter?"

He made strange shapes with his mouth, as he tended to do when he was thinking. "Hmm."

"How long have you been thinking about this?"

"Well, a while, as a, like—you know. Daydream. See, first time I came to this world, on an errand, I sort of happened to steal a pie. I mean, it was just sitting there, in the window, and I'd never smelled anything that good, *ever*. Meat pie, it was. Nothing fancy. Pork, onions, chicken, apples. I can taste it now. Nearly broke a tooth, mind, didn't realise the pastry's mostly just there to hold the filling. With a good oven, though, I could *do* things with pastry." His face had completely changed. He was staring at a corner of the ceiling as though the spiderweb hanging there was a dream of delight. "I went back and asked the woman that lived there what sort of magic she'd used to make something so wonderful, and gave her a handful of gold to teach me. Poor old stick didn't know if I was a fool or a demon or what, but she showed me. Only I never had anywhere to cook when I was here and if I was back home, well… people'd have thought I was weird.

"See, food in the Infernal is generally terrible, but no one seems to *care*. Well, there's a few things that aren't so bad, but here… And you people will eat almost *anything*. I couldn't believe it when I first arrived. Things that come out a bird's backside. Bark. Leaves. Snails. Squishy inside bits wrapped in other squishy inside bits. That's what sausage is, basically. And haggis. Ever had haggis? It's arsing *brilliant*. You lot can make almost anything taste brilliant. And I want to do it too."

"I see. But, Roland, I am a Doctor of the Arcane. Eating-houses are not Arcane."

"You haven't been eating at the right ones. But that's not the point. Thing is, I smell. I mean, I smell fine, for an imp. But humans don't like it. Charming said it put him off his food. He kind of got used to it, but…"

"Ah."

"It's the sulphur. Mostly. Only it doesn't go away."

"Washing might help."

"I wash!" he said indignantly.

"Do you wash your clothes?"

Roland squinted. "Um…"

"I think I begin to see the problem."

"Can't you just *do* something? Make me smell nice? Then I'll give you that name and…"

"I have never attempted an olfactory glamour. I am not certain such a thing even exists. The nose is rather harder to fool than the eye. I suggest you at least try laundry. If that fails to rid you of your scent, we can discuss the matter further."

"Fine," Roland said, rolling his eyes. "Scrub-a-dub-dub, imp socks in a tub."

"And as to the rest of it, you will need an appropriate building, with the right placement, in a city wealthy enough to support it. And enough money to get started. And, depending on the size of your establishment, you will need servers, and under-cooks, and potboys, and you will need to build relationships with traders... What?"

"See?" Roland pointed a gleeful finger at her. "You *know* stuff, you. How'd you *know* so much stuff?"

"I suppose," she said, "that once I was back in the ordinary world, with a little more money and power to my name, I became interested in how it all worked. And like you, I enjoyed eating my fill of good food, after so long without."

"Huh. See, I hadn't even thought about all that."

"You should talk to Her Grace. She has a great deal of experience of how kitchens work. And both Lady dei' Sogni and Princess Marie Blanche are practised at trade negotiations, they can probably guide you in that respect."

Roland nodded. "All right." He slid off the sill.

"I'm sorry I cannot help you with your other problem."

"You have helped."

"I suppose I have. Roland, in return, perhaps you could help us find Charming?"

"You don't want the name?"

"My priority is finding Charming. Knowledge of Infernal politics is of less immediate use to me."

"You don't know that. Tell you what. I'll help you with Smarmy, *and* I'll give you the name."

"In return for what, exactly? Roland?"

"Suspicious, ain't you?"

"Yes, Roland, I am."

"Fair enough, it's probably why you're still in one piece. Deal is, you act as my... whatsit... advisor. Help me set up my eating-house. You get a share of the profits, and you eat free. Oh, and you don't mention either of my names in connection with what I'm going to tell you. How's that?"

"Really?"

"Really. And I won't even make you sign in blood."

Doctor Rapunzel considered for some time. Knowledge was almost always useful. Sometimes dangerous, yes, but almost always useful.

"Very well," she said. "But on condition that I have most of my time for my own work. It is not *my* ambition to run an eating-house."

"Sorted!" Roland's grin was positively sunny. "Right. Okay. So. Look, the Thousand-Eyed was right. Righter than usual. Someone wasn't just planning on annexing a bit of territory or gaining a bit of influence, they were planning on *overthrowing* the Thousand-Eyed himself. Total takeover." Roland took a deep breath. "It's Mephistopheles."

"What?"

"The name. The conspirator. Mephistopheles."

"*Mephistopheles* is conspiring against the ruler of Hell?"

"Yeah. I kept it to myself, because he's damn near as powerful as His Lordship anyway, and if he realised who had spilled the beans my life wouldn't be worth a fart in a volcano. And he hasn't been caught yet, cos if he had been, *that* ruckus would have had echoes even up here."

Doctor Rapunzel rubbed the bridge of her nose. "I cannot see how a conspiracy against the Lord of Hell can possibly be connected to our current situation."

"Maybe not," Roland said. "In fact, let's hope not, eh? But the more you know, the better. You of all people should understand that."

The Prince and the Thorns

 HARMING GRIPPED THE windowsill with one hand and dug the knife he had kept back from his (extremely good) dinner into the mortar with the other. He felt a brief and unexpected pang of guilt as he jabbed, since the house had looked after him so well. Unfortunately, it had not been able or willing to open any doors to let him out.

"This would be so much easier if I had my boots," he muttered. Wearing those he could have sprung to the ground from his third-storey window without any risk of a broken bone, though he had at least once ended up in a midden. The boots had been enchanted to carry him away from *danger*, not from humiliation.

He looked down.

The moon was still full, and shone brightly enough to show him that at the base of the wall there was a thick tangle of rosebushes. The scent rose up, sweet as a promise. A midden might smell a lot worse, but at least it would have been a fairly soft landing. Still, a few thorns in the royal flesh were probably not as bad as whatever fate the large, hairy occupant of the house—a bear? a large wolf?—had in mind for him.

Roland would also have been quite useful at this point. He'd have found them a way out. Probably by means of trickery, treachery, lockpicking or all three.

Roland was either back in the demonic realms or stuffing his face somewhere. Greedy little imp that he was.

A shower of mortar landed on the roses. Charming wedged the knife deeper into the wall, gripped the handle, shut his eyes briefly, and let go of the sill to grab at a thick ivy trunk that squirmed up the wall. Bitter dust drifted around him, and something chittered furiously. *Go to sleep, whatever you are.* Having some angry bat— or squirrel, or whatever—flying at his head was exactly *not* what he needed right now.

Hold onto the ivy; wriggle the knife out of the wall; jam the knife into the wall a bit lower; let go of the ivy; grab the ivy a bit lower; blink dust out of eyes; try to sneeze quietly. Repeat.

The ground edged closer. The knife was a lovely piece of silver, its handle wreathed and scrolled and bearing a coat of arms he hadn't had the time or inclination to examine closely. Unfortunately that did not make it either practical or comfortable to use as a piton. The blade was already scratched and beginning to bend.

A roar, thick and dark and rough, rose from the forest. Charming froze, desperately hoping neither of his precarious handholds would give out. The roar was followed, or answered, by a rising howl. He leaned his forehead briefly against the brickwork. But one bear (or wolf, or whatever it might be) in the house was probably worse than several in the wood. Probably.

He scrambled down another few inches, and was stretching his foot towards the sill of a window when the knife blade snapped off.

Charming's hand, still clutching the hilt, waved wildly while his other hand still gripped the ivy stem. Then the stem began to peel away from the wall with a sound like ripping cloth, showering Charming with leaves, bark, and dust, and finally dumping him with a crackling thump into the rosebushes.

He stifled a yell as what felt like a thousand thorns jabbed into his flesh through his fine, but unfortunately not very robust, new garments.

Then the rosebushes heaved, and dumped him onto the ground.

"Wh…"

He scrambled to his feet, snatching his sword out of its back scabbard, vaguely aware of driving a thorn deep into his thumb.

The roses lashed about as though in a high wind, but there was no wind. Petals spun away. Charming backed away and yelped as thorns jabbed his backside. There were now roses behind him, in front, everywhere.

Petals flew about his head, clung to his clothes, his face. He stumbled for the only gap he could see in the writhing mass of stems and leaves and the pale blotches of flowers, slashing ahead with his blade.

The roses drew back, their roots writhing through the earth like the legs of half-submerged spiders, spilling soil. He gasped with triumph and ran…

…only to find himself heading straight for the steps leading to the main door of the house.

He turned.

Impenetrable thickets of roses surrounded him

everywhere, except in the single direction he least wished to go. They moved forward, driving him back. He cut about with his sword, but though leaves and blossoms fell in showers, a sword is a lot less effective against roses than a good pair of secateurs. He backed away until his heels hit the lowest step and he stumbled.

The rosebushes stopped moving.

Charming's sword arm was exhausted, his blade was blunted, he was bruised, cut, and so full of thorns he felt like a hedgehog with its skin on inside out.

The roses were too thick and tall to see past. He raised his sword one more time, and the bushes rustled at him.

He made a rude gesture, turned around and limped up the steps.

The door swung open with a creak that sounded almost apologetic.

"Traitor," Charming muttered, and moped into the hallway.

Fine wrought-iron sconces bloomed with light as he entered. A tray, bearing a generous glass of brandy, floated towards him.

"It's all very well," he said, "but I need another bath." He grabbed the brandy and downed it. "And some tweezers. And some new clothes. I'd like to face whatever appalling fate awaits me with at least a little dignity, if it's all the same to you."

Fate did not seem to require him that night. He wedged a chair under the door handle, for all the good it would do, put his sword close to hand and slept uneasily, one eye open and one ear cocked.

The next morning he woke from dreams of thrashing

thorns to the sound of something—it sounded like metal—tapping at the door. He grabbed his sword (wincing at the condition of the blade) wrapped a sheet around himself, shuffled to the door and peered around it.

A silver tray lay on the floor, containing another substantial bacon sandwich, an elegant cup and saucer decorated with roses, a jug of cream, and a heavy chased silver pot from which the aroma of coffee tempted Charming's nose almost as much as the bacon.

"Fattening me up, are we?" he said. Then he picked up the tray. "Fine. The condemned man ate a hearty meal, and so forth."

His sheet fell off as struggled to balance the tray, and he paused at the sound of something like a yelp from further down the corridor. He looked around, but couldn't see anything except a slightly open door. He shrugged and went back into the room, leaving the sheet where it was.

Once he had eaten, he dressed in the new set of clothes that had appeared on the bed. These were almost as fancy as the last ones: red velvet jacket, black breeches of fine wool, silk hose, another lace-bedecked shirt.

He fingered the lace thoughtfully. Fine work, but very slightly yellowed with age. The cut of the jacket, now he looked at it, was at least ten years behind the fashion. And all of it just a little too big, except across the shoulders, where the jacket was fractionally tight. "A previous victim? How morbid. Still, at least they don't have blood on them. I suppose I should be grateful for small mercies."

He paused, but of course there was no answer. The house, while a very good servant (except when one was trying to escape), was not the best conversationalist. Yet again, to his annoyance, he found himself missing Roland's snarky commentary.

He glared into the mirror. "My *hair*," he moaned. "Not that it matters, if I'm going to be eaten, I suppose, but a man does have some pride. Is there any hair oil in this place?"

A small bottle of rosemary-scented oil soon drifted into sight. Charming sniffed at it, then combed it through his blond leonine locks until he was satisfied that he looked as good as was possible after so little sleep and wrestling unnaturally lively rosebushes.

Then he strapped his much-abused sword back on, without a great deal of confidence, and went to explore.

SOME DOORS REMAINED firmly locked, even when he shook the handles. Others opened easily, showing rooms that were kept in beautiful condition but had the still air of little use. One door opened on a magnificent library. Charming glanced around it—books could be valuable, and might contain some useful information about his situation—but there were literally hundreds of them, and he had no idea where to look first. He noticed a large cabinet, beautifully carved, with a large keyhole. He tugged the handle. Locked. Hmm. What might be in there? But he suspected the house might object if he tried to break it open. He wondered how one went about persuading an enchanted manor house to do something.

One set of doors opened on a ballroom, vast enough for a royal palace. The floor was an elaborate geometric design of blue, black and gold tiles. Three walls were painted pale gold, divided by columns of black marble veined with blue. Each section was decorated with a round plaster plaque embossed with bears or wolves. The fourth wall was all high windows, interspersed with those same black marble columns. Painted cherubs fluttered about the coffered ceiling, leading winged horses and wyverns across the sky-blue panels; a gallery, its front of golden oak carved fine as lace, ran across one wall; and against the opposite wall was a huge grandfather clock of gilded brass, with gold numbers on a deep blue face. Its hour hand was as long as a javelin, its minute hand a spear. It ticked loudly, the sound not so much a *tick* as a *clunk*. In the centre, looking oddly plain and out of place among all that splendour, was a small stand of plain white marble, about the height of Charming's waist. Whatever it was meant to display was nowhere to be seen.

Charming wondered if it had once held treasure, and if so, what, and where it had gone.

The ballroom was chilly and had the uneasy resonance of a room which is meant to be full of people but hasn't been, for too long. He closed the door and moved on.

He eventually found a cellar, even more magnificent than the other rooms. He paid much more attention here. "Ohh, Roland," he muttered, examining the dusty bottles. "You'd be in your absolute element. Look at what you're missing out on, you disloyal little wretch." Charming kicked moodily at a wine rack, sighed, and went back upstairs.

He glanced at the portraits adorning the walls. The family, judging by the pictures, were a lanky lot, towering over their wives and servants and occasionally even their husbands. They tended to either curly black or straight red hair, and square jawlines. They appeared to be handsome, but Charming knew that meant little. Portrait painters were well aware that their patrons wanted the best possible version of My Lord Duke, not what My Lord Duke saw in his mirror after a hard night on the brandy.

Partway along was a lighter patch and a gouge in the plaster, as though a picture had been knocked violently off the wall—perhaps a passing servant had been more than usually clumsy. Perhaps, Charming thought, examining the ugly scrape, a servant who was carrying some sort of polearm at the time.

He remembered looking at the portraits of Bella dei' Sogni on his way to be handily close by when she woke from her charmed sleep. *Her* portraits had been totally incapable of doing her justice—but then, he thought (with an unfamiliar and unpleasant jab of conscience), so had he.

That thought put a scowl on his handsome features and he strode on down the corridor towards a heavy oak door, carved with birds and vines. Just as he reached it, all the other doors behind him snapped shut in quick succession, making him jump.

The oak door creaked open, either welcomingly or menacingly, depending on one's point of view.

Charming straightened his shoulders, fluffed his hair, and went to meet his fate.

The Riddle of the Manor

HARMING'S FATE APPEARED to involve two handsome young men. Charming eyed them warily. One was a dark, muscular, broad-shouldered fellow, with thick curly hair, who stood at the window, and turned to look at Charming with wide brown eyes, and a hesitant smile, then tugged at his collar as though it were too tight. He was dressed in dark green satin, which might have been chosen to compliment his colouring.

The other, seated in one of the chairs, was lean, with pale blue eyes, currently blinking at Charming from behind a pair of small round spectacles, and hair so blond it was almost white, falling straight as heavy silk over his shoulders. A book rested open on his lap. He wore soft brown velvet.

The room was also handsome, if a little fussy for Charming's taste, with a fine moulded ceiling with painted panels of dancing figures and a floor of creamy marble veined with soft russet. The central table was of golden oak, its top glossy smooth and its sides and legs a mass of elaborate carving.

On a rather charming marquetry table between the chairs lay three perfect red roses, just opening from their buds. Charming noted that their thorns had been removed.

"Well, good morning," said the blond, removing his spectacles. "I see you encountered the rosebushes." He raised a hand, revealing a long, healing scratch. "Join the—Ah. *Club* seems inapt. One normally *wishes* to belong to a club, I believe." He stared off into space for a moment, scratching his cheek. "Hmm. And one would rather hope *herd* is inaccurate. Perhaps *band*? That seems apropos. We are, after all, bound, it seems." He returned to earth with a vague smile. "Forgive my manners. I'm Johannes; you can call me Hans. That's Wilhelm." He waited.

Charming ran through his mental catalogue of personalities and identities, and decided that he really couldn't quite be bothered. These two seemed harmless enough. "Charming," he said. "For my sins. Blame my dear Mama. Jean-Marc Charming Arundel."

"Arundel," Hans said. "Arundel. Floriens? I associate that name with Floriens."

Perhaps not *entirely* harmless. Charming forbore to answer that. "You?"

"Oh, a mere local, as is Will. You *have* been unlucky. It's usually locals. At least, we're assuming so, but perhaps there have been more passing travellers we don't know about."

"What, exactly, is *it*? Why have we been trapped here?"

"We don't know," Will said. He had a soft, slightly gruff voice, as though he'd spent a great deal of time out in the weather, and his accent was that of the local area. "But we think it's what's happened to the others. People usually come out, though. Anything from a few days to a moon's span later. So..." He shrugged. "We probably won't die."

"People *usually* come out?" Charming said. "You mean this happens a lot? And what do you mean *usually?*"

"There have been one or two from the nearest town who disappeared and didn't reappear," Hans said. "But they may simply have fallen victim to ordinary misfortune. Or just left; Felendstadt provides few opportunities for anyone with ambition."

Charming had a feeling there was something else, something vital, that he had missed. Then it hit him with an internal sensation like a bag of cold custard being emptied into his stomach. "But... wait... you said a moon's span? A *month?*"

He did his best to conceal the sudden panic. It was almost exactly a month—now slightly less, in fact—until he was due to meet a demon atop a mountain, accompanied by his height in gold. And even if the women kept faith in order to save his father's life (he had doubts about how much they'd value his own), the demon Mephistopheles had insisted Charming be there. In person.

Also, a lot of bad things—worse things than falling into some unnecessarily lively rosebushes—could happen to a person in a month.

"What do you mean you don't know?" he said, striving to keep his voice even. "Did the... escapees... say nothing?"

"We've both encountered a few. They don't remember," Hans said. "Not a thing. Sometimes they talk about dreams of feasting and comfort, which..." He waved a hand at the luxuriously furnished room, the bowls of fruit and sweetmeats, the gleaming decanters. "Odd, don't you think? Some trace remains, but only unimportant details."

"Not that unimportant," Will said, a little abruptly. "Not if you've spent your life sleeping on straw and eating whatever you can get." He tugged at his lacey cuffs. "Though why anyone would want to wear all this... It *itches*."

Hans blinked and tilted his head. "You know, you're quite right. I wonder what I'll dream of, after."

"You're assuming there will *be* an after," Charming said.

"True," Hans said. "But I have been in worse situations. And if we are to be horribly slaughtered, or turned into frogs, why provide us with fine clothes? It seems wasteful."

"You don't seem dreadfully bothered," Charming said.

"Well, it's all rather intriguing, don't you think? And as Will says, it generally seems people don't die. Oh, and there's a *magnificent* library." His gentle, dreamy face lit up with something almost like greed. "*Magnificent*. A month will not be long enough to explore it. A *year* would not. I wonder if one can petition to stay."

"You don't have people waiting for you?"

"Oh, well, my sister. But I'm sure she's keeping herself occupied," Hans said airily. "And she's used to me travelling."

"She won't worry about you?" Charming said.

"She might, I suppose." Hans frowned. "If she does... Oh. Oh, dear."

"My whole family will be looking for me," Will said. "I hope..." He turned back to the window, gripping the sill. "I hope no one does anything stupid. I don't want anyone *hurt*."

Charming raised an eyebrow at Hans, who shrugged.

"I'm sure they are looking for you," Charming said. "But why would they hurt anyone?"

"They might blame someone, for me going missing," Will said. "The *wrong* someone. I want to go *home*." He suddenly sounded very young, and Charming realised that for all his bulk, he was only a young man completely out of his depth, and frightened—more, it seemed, for others than himself.

That reminded him of a women he had met in his travels: the Lady Ysoude, whom he had come as close as seemed possible for him to actually falling for. Well, her and Bella dei' Sogni. He had a soft spot, it seemed, for people very unlike himself, who lacked his own selfishness—or, as he preferred to think of it, his sense of self-preservation.

Though in Ysoude's case, she had been playing a part to trap him. And had apparently thoroughly enjoyed doing so.

Not *entirely* unlike himself, then.

Really, this sudden tendency to brood over past encounters was becoming irritating.

"Maybe you'll be out in a few days," Charming said. "Surely nothing too bad can happen in a few days, hmm?"

"I hope you're right," Will said, not sounding remotely hopeful.

Charming wondered whether to mention the large furry creature that had stood outside his chamber the previous night, and decided perhaps it would not be wise. It hadn't, after all, killed him—and there was no point terrifying Will. Scared people did foolish things.

"Did someone take their revenge on those wretched bushes?" Charming nodded at the roses on the table.

"Oh, those were here when we came down," Hans said. "They don't seem as... excitable, as the ones outside."

"Well, they are dying," Charming said. "Cut flowers do that."

"That would undoubtedly explain it."

Charming glared at the flowers. To him, their presence seemed almost mocking. "I intend to get out of here," he said.

"So did we," Hans said, unhelpfully.

THE THREE MEN spun to look at the door as it opened with an unnecessarily ominous creak.

The figure that entered the room was huge. Huge, hairy, toothy, clawed and... frilly.

It was at least seven feet tall, and looked like a cross between a large bear, a dire wolf, and a long-suffering dog that had encountered a small child with access to a dressing-up box.

There was something almost defiant about the frilliness, as though someone was convinced that given enough embroidery, enough pearls, enough rich fabric and puffy sleeves and layered necklaces, the clothes would overcome their contents and render the wearer not only human, but fashionable.

The perfume might have been pleasant had there been less of it. The sickly fog of mashed tuberose and bruised jasmine was so intense it seemed it should surround its wearer in a lurid pink cloud.

The creature held its head high, but its paws were clenched into fists and its ears lay back against its skull.

Will yelped and knocked a small ornament off the windowsill.

Hans stared with his mouth open, then closed it.

Charming, after giving his agile mind a moment to do a couple of fast circuits around the available possibilities, bowed. He chose the bow carefully; it was one appropriate to being introduced to a new acquaintance of one's own social standing, in a semi-formal situation. Not so over-elaborate it might be taken as mockery, not so casual that it might be seen as perfunctory.

"Gentlemen," the creature said. "Please do not be alarmed. You will come to no harm here, unless you try to leave before your time is up." Her accent would pass muster at any court, and though there was a huskiness to her voice, it was no more than the aftermath of a heavy cold.

She flicked her gaze towards Charming and quickly away. Her eyes were a deep amber, and, given their setting, remarkably attractive. He gave his best reassuring smile, but was not sure if she had actually looked at him long enough to see it.

The excessive perfume reminded him of his time in Eingeten, where many people had been drenched in scent. He had thought it was merely an unfortunate local custom, and only later realised it was intended to fool Roland's exceptionally accurate nose. *Perhaps she's trying to conceal her scent, too.*

"May we know why we have been brought here?" Charming said.

The creature's posture stiffened even further, and in the strained chant of a child reciting a lesson they have been beaten into learning, she said: "I cannot tell you more than this. When the moon has run its course, some of you, or all of you, will be going free, and one of you, or none of you, will be bound, but willingly."

"Willingly bound?" Charming had a brief but incredibly clear vision of Roland's smirk, to be followed, next time they were alone, by a number of thoroughly inappropriate remarks. And possibly—he stifled a shudder—personal reminiscences. "But how intriguing."

"A riddle!" Hans said. "I do love a riddle." He got to his feet. "Forgive my poor manners," he said. "I am somewhat out of the habit of polite company." He bowed. "Johannes von Behr."

Will, too, had recovered himself, though he was still staring openly at the Beast. He also bowed, a sort of awkward bob, with no grace. "I never had the chance to get *into* the habit, really—'cause I don't know any polite company, I mean... but anyway, my name's Will. Wilhelm. And I'm pleased to make your acquaintance, Miss... er..."

The creature smiled, or at least, it seemed that was what she was trying to do, though there were an uncomfortable number of teeth in it. "Call me Beast," she said.

Charming stepped forward, took the great hairy paw, and bowed over it. He wasn't so much *holding* the paw as balancing it on his hand, like a servitor holding a large plate. She had claws in proportion to the rest of her. *Great Goose, she could take my head off with a swipe.*

"Jean-Marc Charming Arundel," he said. "Charming to my friends. I know, it's a ridiculous name." He straightened, and smiled at her, open, honest, and sunny. "Charming *and* charmed."

His smile was wasted; the Beast was looking down at her paw. She withdrew it. *Dammit,* he thought. *Think I might have overdone it there.*

"So if we solve the riddle, we will be free?" Hans said.

"The one who solves the riddle will be the one who is bound. I'm sorry, that's all I can say."

"Sounds like I'm going home then," Will said. "I was never the least good at riddles, or anything like that."

"You have as good a chance as any," the Beast said. "As do I."

Of leaving, or of staying? Charming regarded her carefully. He was generally very good at assessing people, a necessity for any skilled conman. It was a great deal harder when someone didn't have human features. He wasn't familiar enough with bears to tell much from that aspect. Wolves were basically dogs with less reason to be polite; and a dog that, like her, would not meet your eyes, and had its ears low to its head, was not a happy dog.

Her voice was human enough, if, like Will's, a little gruff. It sounded deeply weary, as though she had given the same speech too many times to count, and no longer expected anything good to result.

"I will see you again soon," she said. "Please make yourselves at home in the manor, and if you need anything, it will be provided if you ask."

Her gaze flickered over each of them again, then she lowered her head, and turned away. The door closed behind her.

"Well," Hans said. "How very... unusual."

"That's one word for it," Charming said.

Will collapsed into a chair with a huff of relief. "So now what?"

"Now, I suppose, we attempt to work out the riddle." Hans took his spectacles off, and rubbed the bridge of his nose.

"So we can't go before the month's up unless we solve the riddle, but whoever solves the riddle doesn't get to leave?" Charming said. "That has the Good Folk—or the Infernal—written all over it. Gah, I wish Roland was here. Cunning little bastard."

"It is a problem, isn't it?" Hans said. "I wonder if there's anything in the library."

"I had that thought," Charming said. "But it seems unlikely that a clue would be just lying about. That's not *complicated* enough for this sort of thing, is it?"

"I wouldn't know," Hans said. "I have kept my dealings with either the Good Folk or the Infernal as limited as a man of education can. But I suspect you're right."

They both turned to look at Will, who was staring morosely at his hands. "Well it's no good asking *me,*" he said. "I don't know anything. If she wanted someone clever, why am I here? I'm not important. Well, except to my family."

"Clever isn't a matter of rank," Charming said. "Trust me, I've met some *incredibly* stupid people of *incredibly* high rank. I've *been* one of them, on occasion." He sighed. "Like when I tried to take a shortcut through these wretched woods." Although he hadn't *intended* to, originally. He had been quite happily sticking to the road when a broad, open path, clearly in the direction he wanted to go, and with a warm, beckoning light not far along it, had happened to appear just as he was getting bored and wondering if there was any chance of a decent inn for the night. But the light had gone out the moment he was out of sight of the road, and then…

"She said 'As do I,'" Hans said. "Which would suggest, would it not, that she is as trapped as we are, or at least considers herself to be so? I am assuming *she*…" He shrugged. "Clothes maketh man, as they say. Or woman in this case."

"She certainly isn't *happy*," Will said. "Last time I saw that look was someone who'd been backed into a corner, ready to take a bite."

Someone? Charming thought. "You seem to have a good sense for her mood," he said. "That will certainly be useful. Now I don't know about anyone else, but personally, I'm going to investigate the cellar."

"You think there might be a clue?" Hans said.

"I think there might be a very good Riesling."

"Why not just ask?" Will said. "She said to ask."

"Hmm. This is an excellent house and its amenities are beyond compare, with the exception of those unnecessarily vigorous roses. But I have my doubts that even a magical house will have the skills to choose the best wine."

He had barely made it to the door when a tray floated into view, with three glasses and a jug of wine. It was placed on the table with a certain emphasis. Charming raised an eyebrow, sniffed the contents of the jug, raised the other eyebrow, poured a small measure, and sipped.

"I fear I may have hurt its feelings," he said. "This is an *excellent* Riesling." He filled his glass and raised it in the general direction of the walls. "My apologies, House," he said. "Or should I say Manor? How does one properly address a sentient house?"

"Politely, I imagine," Hans said, filling another glass. "Will?"

Will accepted the glass in the manner of someone who does not usually handle fragile objects, for fear of breaking them. He sniffed the wine, tasted it, and looked surprised. "That's actually nice."

"What were you expecting?" Charming said.

"I've only ever had what we brew, and the beer's all right, but the wine..." He screwed up his face. "My aunt says it's more trouble than it's worth, and she's been right so far. But this tastes like ripe apples, and... I dunno, other stuff. Anyway, I like it."

Charming settled himself back in his chair and turned his glass in his fingers. It was a *very* good Riesling, and he was currently quite comfortable, apart from the remaining stings and scratches the roses had left him with. But he could not afford to ignore the deadline. If the riddle was not solved, his father was dead, and so, very soon, was he. And if the riddle was solved, and he was bound here...

You might not be the one to solve the riddle, he told himself. Hans seemed a clever fellow, if a bit head-in-the-clouds; probably he would be the one. And he seemed to like the place anyway. Perhaps Charming could help *Hans* solve the riddle, as fast as possible, and Will would be off back to his family, and Charming would be off to meet Mephistopheles... and deal with whatever happened next.

He wondered what the women were doing. Doctor Rapunzel was sharp as a good sword, and had a deal of magic at her occasionally glowing fingertips. Nell had a godmother who was at least partly of the Good Folk (however often that godmother might deny her heritage) and a wit like a needle. Bella dei' Sogni had all the gifts that the Fey had bestowed on her, and was a great deal more capable and dangerous than she herself knew.

And then there was Marie Blanche. Of them all, she might despise Charming the most, but she was an expert hunter, with an extraordinary affinity for beasts—

probably the only person he could think of who could negotiate a wood overrun with wolves and bears and who-knew-what other ferocious creatures, and come out on top.

The Princess and the Wolf

ARIE BLANCHE, AT that particular moment, was on her back, holding up her hands defensively, blinking blood out of her eyes and watching the wound she'd made in her opponent's grey-furred hide close over.

Dammit.

She rolled just in time as a heavy body slammed into the ground, great claws raking grooves in the leaf mould. Teeth snapped at her ankle and she whipped her legs out of the way, jumped to her feet, jabbed.

The knife scored the wolf's shoulder, it yelped, turned with appalling speed, slamming its shoulders into her legs, sending her flying over its back. This time she managed to get her feet under her—just—before it came in again, and she jabbed, again.

The air rang with the yipping and howling of the pack and the deep-throated roars of the dwarves she'd brought with her. Closer, the sounds of her and the wolf both panting hard.

She was tiring.

And this was stupid. None of this was necessary.

The wolf hunched, great haunches shifting, rear feet digging into the leaf mould for purchase. Its hide was stained with blood, its chest heaving.

You're tiring too.

Marie Blanche braced herself. As the wolf launched at her, leaf mould spraying, she ducked aside at the last possible moment, and when it landed, she leapt on its back. Its muscles bunched and writhed under her.

She felt in her pocket. Her fingers were wet with sweat or blood or mud, or all three; she couldn't get hold of the chain. As she finally got a grip on it, the wolf heaved and flung her off.

Marie Blanche felt the chain go flying from her hand. She rolled. Where was it? A glint among the brown clutter of the forest floor. She reached, grabbed, caught it just as a hundred and twenty pounds of wolf landed on her back, pressing her face down into the mulch.

Hot breath in her ear, so *loud* she couldn't hear anything else, claws digging into her shoulders, stupid, *stupid,* she wriggled furiously, the panting changed, almost like laughter.

The weight shifted, just a little.

Marie Blanche got an arm up behind her head and threw the looped chain over the wolf's head, unable to see what she was doing, praying it would fall right, holding the free end in a death grip.

There was a pause, a snort, then the weight was gone, and the wolf was rolling on the ground, shaking its head furiously, howling, clawing at its neck.

Marie wrapped the end of the chain around her hand, knelt next to the wolf as its muzzle shortened, its legs warped, the fur began to shed in great soft piles.

Dropping her knife, switching the chain from hand to hand, Marie Blanche shucked her ripped surcoat and threw it over the naked woman lying in a pile of shed wolf fur.

"Never mind your bloody modesty, get this cursed *thing* off me," Red Cap hissed, sitting up. She glared, tried to touch the chain and swore. There was a red mark on her neck, like a burn.

"Will you negotiate?"

"Yes! Yes! Get it off!"

Marie Blanche leaned over and lifted the chain. A small silver key dangled from it. She slipped it over her own head.

"You'd better come inside," Red Cap said. She stood up, flung the surcoat over her shoulders, and strode across the clearing. Marie Blanche followed. The four dwarf warriors walked with her, glaring at the wolves, who glared back.

They reached a cluster of wooden buildings, so well hidden among the trees that if you did not know they were there you would be hard put to find them. A large mead hall stood surrounded by smaller huts, like a hen with its chicks. Red Cap opened the door of one hut, and gestured Marie Blanche inside with a slightly mocking bow. "Your escort may come in if they wish, but they may find themselves somewhat cramped."

"Wait outside," Marie Blanche said.

They glanced at each other, but said, "Yes, your Highness."

"No one is to cause any trouble," Red Cap said to the wolves. "That means you, Claus." She glared at the tall young man with the cap of white-blond curls. "*And* your brother."

To the dwarves, she said, "There's ale, bread, meat, inside the hall, help yourselves. Oh, and the meat's venison. Just in case you were wondering."

The dwarves' faces went rigid.

Marie Blanche bit her lip, trying not to smile. "You are guests," she said. "Please act accordingly."

"Yes, your Highness."

Inside the hut was indeed small, but solidly made. Green-tinged light fell through the small window. The furnishings consisted of a bed with a shirt and a pair of breeches lying on it, a table, a stool, a cupboard, and a chair. It smelled of smoke and cooked meat. Red Cap tested the weight of the kettle hanging over the smouldering fire, added wood and blew on it until the flames leapt up. She turned back.

"You're bleeding," she said. "Your Highness."

Marie Blanche realised she was; the wretched scratch on her forehead had finally stopped seeping blood into her eyes, but there was another on her shoulder, deeper, that was still oozing. And she was bruised all over.

"And you are burned," she said. "My apologies."

"Ach, I've had worse. But it wasn't necessary. All you had to do was submit."

Red Cap turned her back and pulled on the clothes that lay on the bed, and tossed Marie Blanche her surcoat. She poured hot water into a bowl, and got a cloth and a small bottle from the cupboard.

"I'm not convinced the entire *charade* was necessary," Marie Blanche said. "Wolf *packs* fight, yes, if they must; but this?"

Red Cap sighed. "We are not wolves," she said. "We are, most of the time, people. And when you're in charge of people, you have to act how they expect a leader to act. Stupidly, quite often. Like challenging everyone who might be a threat to a fight."

"That must be tiring."

"Oh, it is. I'm trying to teach them better, and I thought I was getting somewhere, but these last few years…"

"So I understand. What changed?"

Red Cap added a shot from the bottle to the hot water. The smell of raw alcohol made Marie Blanche sneeze. Red Cap dipped the cloth in the hot water and passed it over. "Use this, it will help. Don't get it in your eyes."

The werewolf frowned. "As to what changed, I don't know. *No one* knows. I came here—what? Ten, twelve years back. I remember it being calm enough. I mean, this lot were a mess, half pack, half gang, living like stray dogs and with every village for miles around out for their blood, but the *bears* weren't a problem."

She took two crude clay mugs from the tiny cupboard, a small bunch of herbs.

"But the last five years it's been one dispute after another. And I think the Witch may have something to do with my nephew going missing."

Marie Blanche watched her, at first wary. Red Cap moved with utter ease, as at home in clothes as she had been naked. She was wiry, spare but corded with muscle. Her short-cropped hair was bright copper—hence, presumably, the name. She was shorter than Marie Blanche, but held herself as though she were tall.

"Your nephew?" Marie Blanche asked.

"He hasn't been seen for a couple of days. We know he wandered into their territory, though not by much. Then we lost the scent. If she's hurt him, I'll have her throat out."

"The Bear Witch?"

"The townsfolk call her that. I'm not sure *what* she is, but she rules the bears. She won't talk to me, though. She doesn't talk to anyone. The townsfolk are terrified of her. She'll make spells for them if she's inclined, but they have to be desperate to ask, and even then they do it by getting someone who can write to leave her a message in a hollow tree. Hardly anyone's ever even seen her."

Red Cap set down the mugs. "This is tea, of a sort." Herby steam rose, pleasant enough. "I'd kill for real tea. Not really," she added. "Almost, though." She sighed, and sat down. "And why is a princess wandering my woods, looking for a fight?"

"I'm looking for a man."

"Come to the wrong place for that," Red Cap said.

Marie Blanche blinked, and decided to put that remark aside for later consideration. "His name—one of the names he goes by—is Charming."

"Oh, dear."

"He lives up to it. He is blond, extremely handsome, and has a habit of promising marriage and then running away, with all the most choice items in the treasury."

Red Cap snorted, and gestured at the hut. "Obviously he came here planning to rob me of my immense wealth."

"We don't know *why* he came here, but he disappeared in the forest. We need to find him."

"He ran off with your treasury?"

"Yes, but that was some time ago, and much of it has been retrieved. We need to find him before the end of the month, because he has an appointment that cannot be missed, or people will die. Have you, or any of your people, heard anything?"

"Well, it wasn't us." Red Cap frowned. "And my nephew isn't the first young man to go missing."

"If the Bear Witch has taken Charming, she may have bitten off more than even a bear can chew." Marie Blanche watched as Red Cap scratched at the fading burn mark. "I *am* sorry," she said.

"Ach, it's no matter. It's going. What was the key for? Your dowry chest?"

"Oh. No. It belongs to a friend. It opened a box that no longer exists. But it means something to her. The chain was the only silver thing we had on us. I'm glad I didn't lose it in the fight."

"Tell your friend she's welcome," Red Cap said coolly. "I suppose we'd better go see if our followers have killed each other yet."

The Poor Boy and the Books

ILL SWALLOWED AND fidgeted with his cuffs. He didn't know where the other men were, or what was expected of him. He had fallen asleep, and been woken by the door of his room opening. A candle in a holder bobbed at him until he got up and followed it.

Now he stood before a set of doors beautifully carved with owls and ravens. He ran a finger over the finely detailed ruff of a raven, wondering at the delicacy of the work, then hastily polished it with his cuff in case he had left a mark.

The door groaned open, and he walked into a room to see the Beast sitting by the fire. The room was full of books, and fragile chairs, and spindly tables. Little pastries and sweetmeats were laid out on porcelain so fine it glowed translucent in the firelight. A finely moulded, beautifully painted glass jug of wine, a fragile glass and a large pewter tankard stood on the table; all but the tankard looked as though they would break at a harsh word.

He wasn't sure if the room or the Beast were more frightening.

She—the Beast, he must remember to call her by the name she had asked for, anything else would be rude—was dressed, this time, in green satin. He himself was wearing an outer coat of red velvet, massively padded and boned, and slashed with gold satin. There were also an undercoat, and a shirt, and puffed red trousers, all of it put together with an inordinate number of hooks, and eyes, and laces.

The only thing he had been able to put on by himself, apart from his hose, were the boots. The rest the house had got him into in a whirl of fabric, confusion and embarrassment. He felt as though he were wearing an entire other person, and it was all far too hot, and he had no idea how to take any of it off again.

"Good evening," said the Beast. Her ears were still a little back, her claws flexing—though as soon as she caught him looking, she hid her paws under the table. Not happy, but not, so far as he could tell, about to take his face off.

"Good evening," Will said, and bowed, then wondered if he should have. Should he do that every time, or was it something you only did the first time you met someone? Things were so much easier with his family.

"Please," the Beast said, and gestured to the chair opposite her.

Will lowered himself carefully into the chair, which creaked but didn't break, and put his hands on his knees. Then he crossed his arms, then tried to shove his hands in pockets that, if they existed, were impossible to find among the folds of his coat. He put his hands back on his knees again.

There was a book lying on the table. He stared at it. It

had a heavy cover of tooled leather, very nice work, with birds and beasts all over.

"Do you like books?" the Beast said.

"Um... That one's very pretty."

"Pretty?"

"I can't read," he blurted. "I'm sorry. My aunt tried to teach me, but I'm no good at it."

"Oh. Well, we must make the best of it."

Her perfume was even stronger, this close, with the warmth of the fire bringing it out. Will felt a sneeze building, and began a panicked search for a handkerchief.

"Is something wrong?" the Beast said.

"Gonna sneeze..."

"Oh! Here." She thrust a square of fine linen at him, in which he buried his face gratefully, just in time. He sneezed, and sneezed again, and finally emerged, eyes watering. "Sorry."

"It's quite all right."

Now he didn't know what to do with the handkerchief. He eventually tucked it under his thigh. He got the sense that she was waiting for him to say something, and stared at the table. Finally it occurred to him to say, "Would you like some wine?"

"Thank you."

With agonising care, his hands shaking, he lifted the jug and poured, cringing when the jug clinked against the glass, convinced one, or both, would shatter.

He put the jug down again, having, to his own amazement, not spilled any, and offered the glass to her, his hand still trembling. "The glass is for you," she said. "I cannot hold it."

"Oh! Oh, right." He poured more wine into the pewter mug, and offered it to her.

"You needn't be so scared of me," she said, looking at his trembling hand.

"It's not you, Miss... ma'am. I mean, Beast." He realised he meant it—he'd been so focussed on trying not to make a mess, he'd actually forgotten he was sitting in the room with something that could tear him apart. "It's just I'm clumsy, and I don't want to break your things."

"Oh, don't worry," she said. "I'm amazed there's a glass left in the place, I've broken so many." She sighed. "It took me some time to realise I wasn't going to be able to use them with these great paws"—she held them up—"however careful I was."

"So you haven't always..." Will blushed and closed his mouth. "That must be annoying."

"No, no. I have not always been what you see. And yes, it is very annoying. Well, even if you don't read, perhaps you like stories?"

"Oh, yes. My aunt reads to me, and the family are always telling stories." Though somehow he had a feeling they might not be the sort of stories the Beast meant.

"Then I shall read to you. But you will have to hold the books for me, and turn the pages," she said. "I can't even do *that*."

"Well, I can." He looked at his own broad hands. "I mean, probably." He wiped his hands on the puffy red trousers, just in case they had somehow magically acquired dirt since he'd scrubbed them a few minutes ago.

"Just turn the book around—yes, that's right. Now open the cover, gently, please. Let's start with one by a man called Skelly. Well, probably by him, but scholars say... Never mind."

The story was called, 'The Dog and His Reflection.' Will found the idea of the stupid dog highly amusing.

"I mean, I know I'm not smart, but I hope I know better than to try and fight my own reflection over a bone! And he ended up all wet, too."

"Ah, but you know what a reflection is," the Beast said. "Most animals don't. Have you ever seen a kitten puff itself up and hiss at a mirror?"

"Not really; do they do that? I mean, we don't have any mirrors back home, so…"

"Well, yes, kittens do that. When they grow up, they just ignore the mirror. They've worked out it isn't another cat, but they haven't worked out what it is. It doesn't hurt them or help them, so they ignore it."

"Huh. Well," Will said, "a lot of people are like that, too."

The Beast gave him a look he thought was slightly surprised. "Yes," she said. "Yes, I suppose they are."

She read more stories, and Will, intrigued, almost forgot who was doing the reading. He laughed aloud at the antics of cunning foxes and wise fools, then felt awkward and covered his mouth, though the Beast didn't seem to mind.

He scowled at the story of Patient Myrtle, proving her worth by enduring insult after insult. "I don't see why she put up with all that," he said. "Try that malarkey on my aunt and she'd have your guts."

"Your aunt sounds like an interesting woman. Many men think the only virtue of a woman is to put up with everything they ask of her."

"But why would she?"

"I suppose she loved him," the Beast said. "And she wanted to be a good person."

"You can be a good person without letting people walk all over you, can't you? And someone who'd do that, I don't think they're worth loving."

"We can't always decide who we love."

"No, I suppose not. But why not?"

"Ah, well, there is a question for the ages," the Beast said. "Life would be so very much easier."

She looked suddenly very sad, and Will suffered what he realised was an extremely unwise impulse to rub her ears and tell her she was a good girl.

The next moment the sad look was gone. She stood up and smoothed her skirt. "Come, let me show you some of my treasures."

Will followed meekly as she strode towards a great locked cabinet in the corner of the library, her silk skirts hushing about her legs like wind in the trees back home.

The cabinet was twice as tall as Will, and twice as broad, made of dark glossy wood and carved all over with spiky leaves, and poisonous looking flowers, and writhing, snarling beasts.

The Beast showed him a strange structure of wood and wire.

"Is that…?" He could not work out what it was for. "Nice bit of wood," he said, helplessly.

"It's a harp," she said. "A musical instrument. Have you never seen one before?"

"No, ma'am." But it had strings, and a frame… "Is it like a fiddle, then? My cousin Ludek plays the fiddle." He tried to imagine cousin Ludek tucking this great thing under his chin.

"Maybe a little," she said. "But this one is special." She brushed the pads of her paw across the wires.

The voice of a man, deep and sweet, sang out, "What would you hear?"

Will leapt backwards, knocking over a small table. He scrambled to right it, keeping a wary eye on the harp.

"It can't hurt you. If you ask it a question, it will tell only the truth," she said. "But don't ask it for the answer to the riddle, please. It can't answer any more than I can." When she said that, she glanced away, and down.

Will thought, *She's ashamed. I wonder why.*

"Can I ask it something else?" he said.

"Of course."

"Harp, is my family safe?"

The harp's wires shivered. "None are safe," it sang, "this world is sorrow. But they will live until tomorrow."

"Oh, he's in one of his moods," the Beast said. "He does get so very *glum*." She put one of her huge paws on Will's arm. "Try not to worry," she said. "You care about your family a great deal, don't you?"

"Well, they care about me," Will said. "Even though I'm not the same as them."

"Oh? And how are you different?"

"It's sort of complicated."

"Families often are," she said.

Next she showed him a ring, a great heavy thing in some dark metal that had an uneasy, oily shimmer. "This ring, if you put it on your finger and turn it three times, will take you any place you wish to go. Or it did. I can't get it on now, of course." She sighed, and put it back on the shelf.

"I don't think it would fit me, either," Will said, looking at his broad, work-worn hands.

"It's not as though it's even pretty," the Beast said. "Not something one would wish to wear."

"Well, *I* wouldn't," Will said. "It doesn't look wholesome. But then, I've never worn a ring. Don't they get in the way when you have to do things?"

The Beast said, "I suppose it depends on the ring."

Finally she showed him a rather shabby green coat, with several of its buttons missing. Will looked at it with envy. It was probably a great deal more comfortable than what he was wearing. The Beast put her hand in the pocket and drew out a pile of gold coins that clinked and sparkled, and put them carelessly down on one of the shelves. "Now you try," she said.

Will, a little cautiously, dipped his hand in the pocket, only to find more coins.

"Try again," she said.

And more. And yet more. He stood there with both hands full, bemused. "How...?"

"Its pockets are always full of gold," she said.

He tried to put the coins back in the pocket, but it had filled again and they spilled onto the floor. He bent to pick them up. "But where do they all come from?"

The Beast shrugged. "The Infernal, or the fey realm, who's to say?"

"And it never runs out?"

"No. But if you take too many, it will sulk for a few days."

Will eyed her, not sure if she was joking with him. "It's true," she said. "I was bored one day, and must have taken enough to fill three chests with gold, but then the pockets closed up and I swear it *glowered* at me. I almost apologised to it."

"What did you do with all the gold?"

"Dresses, perhaps, a good horse... Oh, yes, I put some in the poor box. I don't know how much good it did the poor, but I remember the priest's house getting a lot bigger. Father was annoyed with me, but then he often was. What would you do with it?"

Will looked at the coins in his hands, then put them

down on the table. "I don't know. Perhaps I'd buy some bricks, and I could build my aunt a better house, with a proper fireplace. Would there be enough here?"

The Beast smiled. "With that, I think you could pay for the bricks and someone else to build it, too," she said. "And for yourself?"

"Well, I should like to build a cosy little house, too, and…" He looked at his feet. "But really, I should like to do something for all my family. Only I don't know how much money would help." He sighed. "Can money make people treat each other better?"

"In my experience," she said, "it often has the opposite effect." Her voice was like the sound of the winter wind outside his hut, when inside was cosy and warm and only the poor cold wind moaned lonely in the eaves.

He was suddenly, desperately homesick, and full of a strange heavy sadness for himself, and the Beast, and the other men trapped here, and his family, who might be safe *now* but would be worried and perhaps angry and maybe getting ready to do something foolish and dangerous. Who had *done* this to them all, and *why?*

Four Players and a Cat

EANWHILE, IN ANOTHER part of the forest, a lanky figure with a pointed beard and a half-mask of black satin flourishes his sword. "Unhand that maiden!" he cries.

A large and muscular troll looms over the maiden in question, and waves a threatening club. "Who are you, that...?" The troll pauses, and an expression of panic spreads over its green features. "Who are you, that...?"

"...*dares to challenge the great Trevor*..." comes a whisper.

"...dares to challenge the great Trevor!" the troll cries triumphantly. "I'll eat your head, and make necklaces of your insides!"

"Oh will you indeed?" says the masked figure. "I am none other than Prince Charming, and better trolls than you have tried to turn me into jewellery! Have at thee, villain!"

The troll lumbers towards the dashing hero, and aims a furious swipe with its club. The hero leaps nimbly over the club, to gasps from the watching crowd.

Well, one gasp. The crowd consists of three old men (one of whom is asleep), two small muddy children, a goat, and a cat that has curled up at the side of the stage, watching the proceedings with bright green eyes.

THE TROLL MADE another swipe, overbalanced, and put its foot in a bucket. It tried to shake the bucket off, hopping on one leg, as 'Prince Charming' chased it around the stage, whacking it across the shoulders and backside with his sword.

The 'maiden' clasped her hands, rolled her eyes skywards and proclaimed, "My hero!" and, "Behind you!"

The troll fell over, with its head conveniently hidden behind the strip of cloth hanging from the side of the stage.

'Prince Charming' flourished his sword, and cut downwards. Then he stood up again, holding a severed and bloody troll's head.

This proved too much for the smallest child, who looked open-mouthed from the prone body to the head, and promptly began to wail.

'Prince Charming' took the 'maiden' by the hand and gave her knuckles a smacking kiss, to the enthusiastic approval of one old man accompanied by remarks about giving him a run for his money thirty years ago, and the tooth-sucking disapproval of another. The third snored.

"And they all lived happily ever after!" 'Prince Charming' said. "Even Trevor the troll, who got better."

The 'troll' leapt up and grinned at the wailing child. His very large and warty nose fell off, and the wailing grew louder.

The actors looked at each other and shrugged. "You tried," the 'maiden' said.

As they took their bows, a harassed woman appeared with a basket of plums in one hand and a dead chicken swinging by its neck from the other. "Rudrich, there you are! Why's your brother crying, what have you done?"

"I din't do nothing. It was them," Rudrich said, pointing at the stage.

The woman looked at the actors with a stern glare. "Shameful," she said. "Nothing but troublemakers. Boys, come with me. Where's the goat?"

The goat, it turned out, was trying to eat the stage curtain. It was persuaded, with some effort, to let go, and dragged off, still chewing. "If she gets sick, I'll have you," the woman said. "Go do your nasty tricks somewhere else."

The two old men woke up the third. Each threw something onto the stage, and wandered off.

'Prince Charming' sat on the edge of the stage, pulling off his mask, and scraped together the takings.

"What'd we get?" said the 'maiden,' sitting down next to him. Her name was Mouse and the glint of one of several knives could be seen through the gauze of her costume. The cat wandered over and she rubbed its ears. "Hello, pusscat. Who's a good pusscat? Yes, that's right, you are. Ooh, someone made you tiny boots! Look at that, everyone, isn't that just the most adorable thing? Look at you in your little boots!".

"We got a plug of tobacco, three hazelnuts and I don't even *want* to know what that is," the erstwhile 'prince' said.

The 'troll' sat down next to him. "Cheer up, Dance. Coulda bin worse."

"Not much," Dance said, tugging dejectedly on his natty little beard. "Sorry. I don't know why I took that stupid track, it just looked like it was going where we wanted. If I'd stuck to the road we'd be most of the way to Wohlhabendberg and a nice cosy inn by now."

"And an audience of two off-duty barmaids and a dog," the 'troll' said, wiping green paint off her face. Her name was Gilda, and the troll's muscles were her own.

"Oh, come on, it's not that bad," Mouse said. "Few days back we had loads of people at that place—what was it called—inn sign had a bird on it?"

"Schlaudorf," Gilda said. "That was the first night. By the last night we had, what, two?"

"Yeah, well, not everyone appreciates talent," Mouse said.

They all stared gloomily at the place where their audience had been.

"Hope Curly gets back soon with supper, I'm famished," Mouse said.

"Wait, Curly's not back?" Gilda said.

"Not yet."

"Who gave me my prompt, then?"

"That would be me," said a voice.

The actors looked round. There was no one in sight. "Down here."

Everyone looked at the cat. "Yes, dear," the cat said. "I think you're cute too."

Mouse shrieked and clapped her hands to her face. "You're a… but I… aaaagh!"

"Don't worry about it," the cat said, and stretched. "I can take a compliment."

"You can *talk*," Gilda said.

"Yes. I shall refrain from suggesting you were typecast as a troll. Why *Trevor*?" The cat turned to Dance, who was stroking his beard and watching it carefully.

"Oh, here we go," Gilda said.

"Trevor is an old and well-established troll name," Dance said. "It's in the original story about the goats."

"But it's hardly terrifying," the cat said. "Surely something like Bloody Bones. Eater of Lungs. Oglag the Great and Terrible. Not *Trevor*. Trevor sounds like someone whose mama tucks his scarf around his neck before he leaves the house."

"We told him," Gilda said.

"We did," said Mouse.

"Well forgive me for trying to pay homage to the classics," Dance said. "Who are you, what are you doing here, and why did you give Gilda her prompt?"

"What a suspicious chap you are."

"Yes."

The cat flicked its tail. "An excellent characteristic."

"So?"

"Suspicious *and* persistent. I think we'll get along, Mr Dance."

"It's just Dance. And you haven't answered any of my questions, Cat."

"Puss. Professionally speaking, Puss. My actual name is Cassia."

"And what would your profession be, exactly?"

"Whatever comes to hand, or paw. And I think I can be of use to you and your charming troupe."

"Why would we need your help?" said Dance.

Cassia looked out at the patch of mud where the audience had been, at the bit of tobacco and the unidentified lump, and the chewed curtain, and back at Dance. "My mistake. I can see you are in fact doing brilliantly well and need no help from me whatsoever."

Dance shrugged. "So we got off track."

"We've got..." Mouse began, then caught a look from Dance and coughed. "Resources. If we need 'em. So we're not as bad off as it might look." She sighed. "It'd be nice to play to more than five people, though."

"And a goat," Gilda said.

"And a goat," Mouse said. "Not known for their appreciation of the finer points of theatre, goats."

"So what do *you* want?" Dance said.

"A bed out of the rain, to start with," Cassia said. "And a mouthful of that chicken your friend's carrying wouldn't go amiss."

"Wha...? Oh, there he is." The final member of the troupe, a young man with a cheerful face and a tightly curled mop of black hair, appeared through the dripping trees, holding up a brace of chickens triumphantly.

"See you've made a friend," Curly said. "I suppose it wants some chicken."

"See? I knew *one* of you had to be clever," said Cassia.

"Any more of that and you can say goodbye to any chicken," Dance said.

"Terribly sorry," said Cassia, not looking it.

Curly looked from one to the other, then closed his mouth. "Either Mouse's ventriloquy has *really* improved, or we have a talking cat."

"Darling, no one *has* a cat," Cassia said, "We *choose* to be with people. Or not." She then looked slightly bemused, as though her own words had been unexpected, and discovered a bit of fur that required sudden vigorous attention.

"Fine, fine, whatever," Curly said. "I'm going to put these

in the pot before they get any older. The only other thing I could get was a very limp carrot and a couple of turnips that have definitely seen better days. Possibly better *years*. I don't suppose the audience threw any usable vegetables?"

"Not unless you want *chicken a la tabac*," Dance said. "And *no*, Curly, that was *not* a serious suggestion, please do not put tobacco in the stew, dearest."

"As if I would."

"I've *seen* you make stew," Mouse said. "In fact, I'm going to come watch you. In case."

"Fine," Curly said. "You can peel turnips. Are we moving on tomorrow? Because I think we should. That town had a funny feel about it. A waving-pitchforks sort of feel. I don't think the people round here are very fond of strangers."

"What makes you say that?"

"I noticed that, yesterday. I mean, lots of people don't trust travelling folk, but this was worse'n usual. Glaring," Mouse said. "And muttering. And hurrying their children out of the way. Why do they think we'd want their children, anyway? Never work with children or..." She glanced at Cassia and shut her mouth abruptly.

"At least we haven't had to deal with any bothersome men," Gilda said.

"Yeah, that's odd, too," Mouse said. "I've noticed a couple of 'em actually ducking out of sight. And that woman in the tavern—well, I say *tavern*, more a bench with a barrel on it—hurried her son away the instant I walked up. I'm not *that* irresistible. Not that I'm complaining, but it's weird."

"Before we go any further," Dance said, "what exactly is your plan, cat? A lift to the next town? A part? Post as Troupe Mouser? What?"

"I want you to help me get something," Cassia said.

"What and from who?"

"A spell. From a witch."

"Hang on," Mouse said. "If she's a witch and she has a spell why don't you just ask her for it? Isn't that sort of what they do? Give people spells if they ask for them?"

"Ah, well, they do tend to want paying, and I am rather lacking in resources just at the moment."

"You want us to *steal* a spell from a *witch*?" Dance said. "No. Sorry, but absolutely not. I like the shape I am, thank you."

"Yes, well, so did I," Cassia said. "That's why I want it back."

"Ah. So you weren't always a cat."

"No. I wasn't always a cat. But now I am, and I'd like to do something about it."

"Look," Dance said. "I'm sorry. But I'm not going up against a witch. No chance."

"You wouldn't be going up *against* her," Cassia said. "You'd just be getting her something she wants, in return for that spell."

"What have we got that a witch could possibly want? Unless she's hiding a hankering for the stage," Dance said. "Which, much as I love it myself, strikes me as unlikely."

"She's lost something. She wants it back. We'd promise to get it for her."

"Why can't she get it herself?" Dance said.

"She doesn't know where it is; I do. And she couldn't get in, and I can."

Dance stroked his beard. "So what's *our* part?"

"Distraction. Misdirection. *Acting*," Cassia said.

"A con, in other words," Dance said.

"Worked out all right the last time," said Gilda.

"Unless we ever cross paths with His Charmingness again," said Curly, "and he guesses we were involved. He wasn't stupid. Selfish, slimy, and slick as a greased herring, but not stupid."

"Why would someone grease a herring?" Mouse complained.

"They wouldn't. It's a *metaphor.* You aren't supposed to *do* metaphors, you just, you know, *say* them," Gilda said.

"You'd grease a herring if you were cooking it," Curly said. "Or you'd put a bit in the pan, at least."

"Depends," Mouse said. "If it was dried, you'd want more than a bit of grease, wouldn't you?"

"Nah, if it was dried you'd soak the salt out, then poach it, make it plump up all juicy," Curly said.

Cassia gave Dance a pointed look. "They do rather wander off, don't they?"

Dance shrugged. "It's easier to let it run its course," he said. "I'm only the director when they're on stage."

"Rubbish, sweetie," Cassia said. "You're plainly in charge."

"Doesn't feel like it."

"Oh, please." She grinned, a grin that was surprisingly human, while still showing a disconcerting number of very sharp teeth. "You're the most catlike of the lot of them."

Dance stiffened. "What do you mean by that?"

"Don't bristle up like a terrier, dear. I just mean you're in charge, in a way that's totally obvious to anyone who lets themselves see it. You'd just rather let people think that what you want them to do was their own idea, most of the time."

There was a moment of silence as the troupe considered this. Then Gilda shrugged. "Who wants to be in charge of this lot anyway?" she said. "You couldn't pay me enough, and I *like* you all."

"Thanks, I think," said Mouse.

"It's not a *con*," Cassia said. "More of a rescue."

"And what do *we* get out of it?" Dance said.

Cassia tilted her head. "The audience you deserve."

"That could be taken in more than one way."

"*Someone* paid you enough to afford a very nice travelling set-up. Apart from the chewed curtain. The wagons are sturdy and watertight, the horses are good quality, and you can afford a couple of chickens for supper even when the audience is five people and a goat. But that wasn't exactly a standard acting job, was it, though?"

"If you knew about Eingeten," Dance said, "why didn't you say?"

"Never show all your cards at the beginning of the game," Cassia said. "The Grand Duke was very pleased with you, and you were, by all accounts, extremely convincing in your several roles. You conned a con man. That takes *talent*. Talent that deserves a wider audience."

"You think we want people bespelled to watch us?" Dance said. "Because no."

"Ugh, no," Curly said. "I'll not have anything to do with that sort of thing, thank you very much."

"Not in the least," Cassia said. "But you need better material, and I know where you can get it."

"Our material is fine," Dance said. "Isn't it?" He looked at his troupe. "Well?"

"Um," Mouse said.

"Er," Gilda said.

"Curly?"

"Dear heart," Curly said. "You know I love you. I admire you immensely. You have kept us together, alive, fed, and paid. But… your plays… could use a little help. Here and there. Sometimes."

Dance stared at the mud for a while. Then he straightened his shoulders and looked at Cassia. "So, what's the witch lost, and where is it?"

"Her brother. He's in a place that isn't exactly there."

"Oh, that's helpful. And how did you come by this knowledge?"

"I'm lucky," Cassia said. "And I pay attention."

Hans and the Library

ANS CLOSED HIS book, took off his spectacles and rubbed the bridge of his nose where they tended to rub. He had visited the library the day before and grabbed a handful of books: a collection of poems by an obscure but interesting person going under the name Felix Steward; a herbal; and something that looked interesting, but proved to be a tedious philosophical treatise which suggested that true intellect could only be exercised on a diet of cold water and gruel.

Hans had taken a certain sardonic pleasure in reading the latter and making a great many snarky notes destroying the author's arguments while consuming the substantial breakfast that had been brought to his room. He had also taken the opportunity to work on his latest play, but the words refused to come.

He wanted to go back to the library. He always found libraries helped his writing. Something about being surrounded by the work of others pushed him to get on with his own. And work distracted him from worrying about his sister. Work had always been what he turned to. Work and travelling, seeing what was around the next corner, moving ever further away from the tall, gloomy old house of his childhood with its rooms that stank of damp and fear.

His sister was always afraid. He had half-known it, but hadn't *really* known it until the old woman they called Grandmother had sat him down one day when his sister was out in the woods, gathering herbs. She already had one bear familiar, then, which went everywhere with her, like a great dog. He had paid it little mind; it left him alone, and he was happy enough to leave it alone.

"Hans, I'm nearing my time," she said.

"Grandmother…"

"Now, don't give me platitudes or wailings, I'm an old, old woman and we all have our time. Just listen. I made mistakes with your sister. I knew how to teach her power, but I didn't know how to teach her *courage*. If I'd known how bad it was, perhaps I'd have done different. But she needs careful handling. The bear won't be enough, she already means to put the 'fluence on more."

"Why?"

"Because she thinks they'll make her safe. But she doesn't feel safe on the inside, and I don't know how to change that. And scared people can do bad things, and get people hurt."

"Margarethe would never hurt someone!"

"Yes, she would, if she got scared badly enough. She might not even mean to, and I'm sure she'd be sorry after, but she would." The old woman sighed, and stretched her aching back, and Hans looked at her and realised that she was, indeed, very old, and very tired, and that soon he and Margarethe would be alone again. He felt once again like a small boy, scared and miserable and full of resentment and fury and a deep cold sadness that only disappeared when he could lose himself in a book. "I don't want you to die," he said, knowing how pitiful and useless it sounded.

"Better now while I've still my feet under me and my wits about me," she said. "It happens to us all. It's as natural as the leaves falling." She laid one hand on his hair. "My bright children. I have been so blessed, that you came to my door, and I'll do what I can, while I can. And so must you. She's got great power for good, your sister. It's not fair to ask you to be all the family she should have had, and I don't. You need a life of your own, too. But we must find ways to help her."

They had tried, and once Grandmother had gone, Hans had kept trying, though he knew he didn't really know how. Margarethe had gathered more bears under her influence. She begged Hans to change his name so they could never be found, which he had done willingly enough. She had taken over Grandmother's dealings with the townsfolk, though no one came to their door any more, instead leaving messages in the hollow tree, which only those unable to walk to the cottage had done in Grandmother's time. Then there were the keep-aways, and the wards.

He had begun to hear the rumours in the town, and when he told Margarethe that people spoke of her in whispers, and hurried their children away when they saw him, she only shrugged and turned away, with a small cold smile.

He had thought she was doing better, in recent years; or at least, he had told himself she was. That was why he had started travelling. And because he itched to see the world.

And now here he was, no more than a few miles from home, and she no doubt going frantic, and perhaps getting ready to do something bad…

He wanted to go to the library and work, and stop thinking about anything except putting one word after another.

But when he tried to leave the room, the handle would not turn.

He banged on it a few times, said, "I should like to get out, I only want to go to the library," but nothing happened. So he tried to engage with the poems, but quickly decided that eighty-eight sonnets in a row about courtship were overdoing it.

"Can I at least have another book?" he said. "*Not* about courtship. Or gruel. Or the fifteen different uses of borage, at least seven of which are nonsense. Please?"

The next time food appeared, a random selection of books came too. They seemed to have been chosen by grabbing whatever came to hand, and included a set of household accounts, a book about fishing so dull it made his brain feel as though it were being slowly filled with cold porridge, and a set of extremely graphic medical illustrations.

The next evening, a new set of clothes floated into the room, and hung pointedly in front of him.

"Really?" Hans said. The sea-green doublet embroidered with gold and matching sea-green hose wiggled at him. There was also a huge padded coat, its sleeves slashed to show gold satin beneath. "Fine, but I'm dressing myself. I'm perfectly capable." He wasn't sure how it was possible for clothes to look doubtful, but somehow they managed it.

* * *

HAVING SUCCEEDED IN getting himself into the clothes with minimal interference, and having followed, as before, a floating candlestick, Hans was delighted to find himself back in the library, though he had a moment of anxiety when he saw the Beast. Would she be angry about the books? It was a magnificent collection, and she had no reason to believe he wasn't the sort of person who borrowed books and failed to return them, or—he shuddered—*turned down the pages*.

He bowed, saying, "Good evening. I borrowed several books. I promise I have taken good care of them. I hope you don't object?"

"Not at all." She gestured towards the chair opposite her. "Please, keep them as long as you wish."

He sat himself down. "Oh, I've finished them."

"Already?"

"Well, I didn't read all of the Steward," Hans said. "He's a little obsessed with the subject of courtship. All very well in its place, but not for eighty sonnets."

"I can see how that would become tedious," she said. Her tone was dry enough to desiccate an ocean.

Hans blinked at her. Though he knew he was not always the best at reading people—even when they looked like, well, people—he had a feeling he had put his foot in it. *If she snaps my head off, it… probably won't be a metaphor.*

From previous experience, he thought that trying to apologise would almost certainly make things worse, so he leaned forward and poured them each some wine. Her perfume really was a little much, but he contented himself with analysing it to the best of his ability.

Polianthes tuberosa, and *jasminum sambac,* and, crushed under them, *citrus aurantium,* orange flower, too light and delicate for its companions. Undoubtedly something else as a base, but his nose took him no further.

"I assume yours is the tankard?" he said.

"Indeed."

He glanced at her paws. "You must find reading difficult."

"I can make shift of it if someone turns the pages for me."

"Isn't that rather tedious? What if they do it too fast, or too slowly?"

"Oh, they're *always* the wrong speed," she said. "I am trying to school myself in patience."

"Well, I should imagine you have had to practise a great deal of it, one way and another," Hans said.

She glanced at him, with a look he thought was surprise. "Yes," she said. "I have."

"What would you like to read?"

She looked at the shelves, and tapped her chin with what he could not help noticing was a very long, if clean and neatly filed, claw. "Oh, you choose," she said.

He put on his spectacles and let his gaze drift over the shelves. Suddenly every choice seemed bad: if he chose a book of fables intended for children, that would be insulting; if he chose something too obscure and intellectual, he risked boring her. And as for the memoirs of a certain notorious adventurer… He shuddered.

"You need not be afraid of me," she said, and he realised she had seen the shudder.

"It's not you I fear, but my own ignorance," he said. "I have no idea what you would like."

"I assure you even if you choose poorly, I shan't tear you to pieces," she said.

He heard the resignation in her voice.

"I am delighted to hear it," he said, "but I may instead bore *you* to death."

She made a whuffing sound he hoped was amusement. "I'll take the risk."

"Oh!" Hans leapt for the shelf. "*Travels in the Barbary Coast and Environs*. Have you read it?"

"I was a little daunted by the size," she said. "It *is* nearly a thousand pages."

Hans, staggering under the weight of the volume, slightly regretted his enthusiasm. "Yes, but the section on the ancient cities is fascinating."

"I confess I hadn't got that far. Shall we begin with that?"

Hans read the lyrical descriptions of ancient ruins, which were interspersed with droll observations about the writer's sore feet, sunburned bald patch, and his attempts to evade a large and irritable goat by climbing onto a crumbling altar and losing one of his shoes, which the goat promptly ate.

The Beast made that whuffing noise at least twice. Once, when she had been silent for a long time, Hans looked up to see her leaning her chin on her paw and watching him intently. She immediately looked away. Hans felt slightly uneasy, but went back to reading, until he paused because the light was too bad. The candles had burned down and were guttering in their holders.

"That was delightful," the Beast said. "But I hope you haven't given yourself a sore throat."

"Not at all. Perhaps another time I could read you a section on some of the different peoples he encountered." He sipped his wine. "Although I'm not sure I believe in the Blemmyae, with faces in their chests."

The Beast gave what probably should have been a restrained and ladylike snort, but emerged as more of a cross between a growl and a bark. "I find myself more willing to believe in monsters, these days."

"Looks do not necessarily make one a monster," Hans said.

A smile that looked almost human touched her mouth, before she looked away again. "Now," she said. "I have something to show you."

Hans examined the cabinet with interest. "Fine work," he said. "From Myrkvior, or thereabouts, yes?"

"I'm afraid I don't know." She opened the cabinet and took out a harp. It thrummed as she set it down.

Hans polished his spectacles. Something about the harp disconcerted him. "Is it…?"

"What would you hear?" the harp sang.

"Oh! Oh, dear."

"You may ask him a question, if you wish. He can only speak the truth," the Beast said. "Please don't ask him to answer the riddle, though. He's not allowed."

"Hmm."

"You don't have anything you wish to ask?"

"Not without some further consideration, I don't think. There are so many questions to which I would like answers, but every one I think of only sparks a dozen more."

"Perhaps this will be more to your taste." She took out a shabby green velvet coat, and demonstrated its ever-flowing pockets.

Hans blinked at the gold. "Well, that is certainly more convenient than drawing money from a bank. They always seem to be closed whenever one has just found a book one wants."

"Is that what you spend your money on? Books?"

"As a rule." He peered more closely. "Why, they're all different coinage! Caraggian carres..." he picked up a handful and sifted through them. "Some from Macqreux, these are Trollmansted gold dalers, and—look!" He held up a many-sided coin with a square hole in the centre. "That, I believe, is from Chitan. How intriguing!"

"Many people would be more interested in the value than the origin of the coins."

"But how do they get there? Where do they come from?" He shrugged. "That to me is far more interesting." He laid the coat aside.

"And there is this." She held out the ring. "If you put it on, and turn it three times, it will take you wherever you wish."

Hans looked at it warily. "Really? Are you sure?"

"Yes." She looked at his slender hands, and shrugged. "But you won't be permitted to use it. The house will stop you."

"Ah. Well, given how... tricksy... magical objects tend to be, I'm not sure I'd take the risk in any case. How do I know that where I think I wish to be is where I actually, truly wish to be? Or need to be?"

"Anywhere but here?"

"That leaves far too much open for mischief. Magic is one thing—I have some experience of it—but magical objects tend to have their own agenda." He looked at the harp, and said, "No offence intended."

The harp did not reply.

"Well," the Beast said, "this has been very pleasant."

Hans realised he was being dismissed, bowed over her paw, and went thoughtfully to bed.

An Interlude

HE BEAST ALLOWED herself to be dressed, standing passively, lifting an arm or a leg as required. She had, at first, fought against this— tearing at the clothes, breaking the necklaces. Nothing, no clothing made by human hands, could make her look like anything other than a beast. And the more fine and frilly the clothing, and the more elaborate the jewellery, the more ridiculous she felt. Eventually she realised that it was well intentioned, and so she had stopped fighting. But she had had all the mirrors put away.

In the early days, sometimes, when the visitors had left, she had raged and wept and roared and broken things, and paced the gardens and howled at the moon, because if she was doomed to be a beast, a beast she would be. The wolves in the forest had howled back at her, and she thought, *I'd rather be one of you. At least you have a pack.*

It had made her so lonely, but still, she had done it again, every now and then, just to be part of something if only for the length of a few howls.

But she started to lose herself, in those moments. Started to come to, blinking and fuddled, uncertain how much time had passed. And she realised that, in fact, she did fear becoming a beast altogether. She stopped listening to the howls, stopped going into the gardens at night, and instead plunged herself into the library and the books. If there was anything that could hold back the beast, surely, it was books. The wisdom and kindness and wit of those distant voices, sometimes more real to her than the men who stumbled into her life and out again.

She had been trained from an early age to make herself pleasant to men. It stood her in good stead with her visitors, even though there were times when the effort was almost more than she could stand. Not that it ever made any difference. She had tried clues and hints and been as clever as she knew how—and she knew she was quite clever, if nothing else—as far as the curse would allow, and here she still was.

Because, of course, the nature of the riddle meant that guessing it, and *solving* it, were by no means the same thing.

And now, there were these three. All of them remarkably calm in her presence, even polite; all of them handsome, one of them *ridiculously* pretty and entirely too appealing, to the point she almost laughed at the absurdity of it. As though a man like that would have paid the slightest attention to her even before she was cursed, if she had not come with a substantial dowry. And once the fever took the rest of the family and left her the sole heir, there had been even more men, and their parents, trying to hook her into matrimony as though she were a salmon.

Sometimes, now, bitterly, she wished she'd said yes to one of them. She'd been hoping for a marriage that was something more than a business contract, but a business contract with a man who cared nothing for her would at least have left her in her own shape.

The last ruffle was tweaked into place. It was time for the next step in this charade.

Her great shoulders slumped. This one, Charming— at least he *knew* his name was ridiculous—was so stupidly handsome, and from his accent and the way he carried himself, he was nobility to boot. And he had nice manners, which wasn't by any means always true of nobility. And he was the first one of her visitors *ever* to bow over her paw. She'd been so shocked she'd just let it sit there. The other two men had followed suit, which she doubted they'd have done had he not done it first.

No doubt there were dozens of women out there waiting for him. Battalions of them, probably, legions of them. They didn't even have to be beauties, though no doubt many were. They just had to be human. Why was she even bothering?

Her claws flexed. The temptation to smash something gripped her like fever. She fought it down and gritted her teeth. *Just get through it,* she told herself. *It's not as though it will make any difference.*

The Prince Who Doesn't Read

CHARMING WAS SHUT in his room for two days and nights.

By the end of the first afternoon, he was bored. Not having taken any books from the library, he had little to do but pace the floor, practise his swordplay (which had its limits when your only opponent was the bedpost) and think.

He tried to nip out of the door when his supper was delivered, and almost made it at the cost of a torn sleeve and a bruised elbow, but the house was too quick for him. After that, his meals only appeared when he was asleep or distracted.

He spent some time considering the locked cabinet in the library. What could possibly be in there? Maybe it was just the family silver—which, right now, he was a great deal less interested in than he would usually have been. But it might contain a clue, or something magical, which would help him get *out* of this wretched place.

Without Roland and his lockpicking skills, though,

Charming's only hope of getting into the damn thing was probably with an axe. And even then, only if the house didn't try and stop him.

And he didn't have an axe. Next time he was allowed out—*if* he was allowed out—he'd have to see if there were any hanging about, mounted over the fireplace or some such. In the meantime he paced, and brooded, and paced some more.

There was a large clock on the mantel, a fantastic concoction of gilt and blue enamel, which he had at first rather admired. But when he examined it more closely, he realised that the figures he had thought were cherubs were actually grinning imps, and the elaborate pendulum he had thought was some sort of fruit was, in fact, a small gilt skull. The clock also had a loud and persistent tick, which started to eat into him.

Finally he decided it was gaudy, tasteless, and far too loud. He reached in and stopped the pendulum, but the clock's silent presence still got on his nerves. He threw a shirt over it, but then it started to look like a shrouded corpse. It made little difference anyway as the house immediately whisked the shirt away, presumably to be laundered, and set the clock going again. He turned his back to it.

Where in the Infernal were those wretched women? Why hadn't they rescued him yet?

Maybe they've found a way to save your father without worrying about you. Maybe they've made a bargain with Mephistopheles.

They were, after all, very smart women. And Lady Bella, as a result of her gifts from the Good Folk, could wrap almost anyone around her little finger. Perhaps they'd managed to work something out with the demon, and decided to leave Charming to his fate.

Of the four of them, Bella was the only one who he thought might object to simply leaving him to rot. It wasn't that she was still fond of him—he'd made *very* sure of that. Simply that she was the sort of person who had principles, and tried to see the best in everyone.

And what if there isn't any best in you to see? Why should they work hard to save you, after what you did to them? You robbed and betrayed all of them, and how many more besides?

He didn't like these thoughts. They were nasty thoughts. It had been bad enough when Roland was being snide and making him uncomfortable, now his own mind was turning on him.

What about Roland, anyway? You basically forced him into servitude the instant he escaped from that terrifying woman Hilda von Riesentor. Whose adopted daughter you also robbed and betrayed on the pretext of freeing her from servitude. You're lucky Roland didn't do worse than simply hand you over to your pursuers and leave.

It was all the house's fault for locking him in his room.

Maybe it locked you up because there's only one real monster in this house. And maybe you deserve your fate, Jean-Marc Charming Arundel. Maybe you earned every last wretched coin of it.

WHEN THE DOOR finally opened to reveal a new set of clothes, Charming simply glared at them. He had had very little sleep the last two nights, and neither felt nor looked his best. "Really? I've a good mind to…" *To do what, precisely? Refuse to dress? March about naked? Exactly what good will that do?*

At least this meant he was going to be leaving his

room, although two nights of isolation and far too much brooding had done nothing either for his self-esteem, or to help him think of ideas for escape. He desperately hoped for something from Hans, who seemed like a clever fellow, or maybe a way to get into that damn locked cabinet in the library.

The clothes that had appeared were of forest-green velvet and peacock-blue satin, which looked better together than he might have expected. He did draw the line at the ridiculous matching shoes with excessively long toes. "No, absolutely not. My feet are a perfectly normal length. Who did these belong to, a heron? I shall wear my boots, thank you."

His mirror informed him that despite his lack of sleep the outfit showed him off to advantage, and he gave a sweeping bow. Roland, no doubt, would have made some sarcastic remark. Not that he missed him, the smelly, irritating little imp. Not one bit.

A floating candle guided him to the library, where he found the Beast, in yet another over-elaborate gown. This one was of gold brocade and white satin, with an overdress of crimson velvet, absurdly huge sleeves slashed with gold, and a ruff of starched lace. Ropes of pearls, interspersed with gold and ruby pendants, cascaded down the bodice. Out of sheer habit he mentally valued the jewellery—very nice, and easily transported, always an advantage—as she stood up to greet him. He bowed over her paw again. He realised it was shaking a little. Surely, in that gown, she could not be cold? Was she *nervous?* It seemed absurd.

That perfume was awful. He tried not to cough.

"I thought perhaps," she waved at the books, "a little reading."

"That seems to me like a great deal of reading," he said, smiling. "I fear I've never been much of a scholar."

"You don't like to read?"

He realised he'd made a false move. Dammit. This was no time for his instincts to fail him. *Whatever she currently looks like, she is a woman, in unpleasant circumstances. You spent years actually putting yourself in these situations, man, don't fall to pieces just because she could rip you in pieces.*

In fact, especially because she could rip you in pieces.

"Oh, I read now and again," he said, "but I've travelled a great deal, and books are cumbersome when one is trying to move swiftly."

"Why would you need to move swiftly?"

Because I'm running away from the people I just robbed. "Itchy feet, I suppose," he said. "Always wanting to see what's around the next corner."

No, no, no... That's not the way to make her think you're a reliable, trustworthy sort! For Goose's sake, what's wrong with me?

He almost snatched up the jug of wine. "Allow me."

"The tankard, if you please."

"Of course." He overfilled it, and she simply looked at the brimming wine, as did he. If she even lifted it, never mind tilted it to her mouth, that ridiculous gown would be drenched.

"I'm sorry," he said. "I seem to have been cursed with clumsiness this evening."

"There are worse curses."

Yes, yours, for example. Or mine. I'm going to be consumed—or enslaved, or who knows what—by a demon, if I don't get out of here very soon.

The thought that he should be honest with her about his

situation briefly crossed his mind and was immediately dismissed. Start being honest with people and who knew where he'd end up?

But perhaps that was all that was wrong with him. He was twisted up with anxiety, and small wonder.

He decided partial honesty was his best bet. "I apologise," he said. "I am a little agitated."

"Of course you are," she snapped. "What else could I possibly expect?" She spun about, and strode for the door. "Enjoy the wine."

Her voice was shaking, and sounded almost on the verge of tears. Charming opened his mouth, but before he could say anything, the door had snapped shut behind her.

He dropped his chin to his chest, then threw back his head. "Gaaaah! I put my foot right in it, didn't I? And I'm not even sure what I *did!*"

He slumped into one of the chairs, picked up the overfull tankard, and drained half of it. Wine spattered on his clothes. "Dammit," he said. "And I still don't know what's in the cabinet. Here, House, I don't suppose you'd unlock it for me?" The silence felt distinctly disapproving. There was no sign of a key floating into view.

"All right," he said, morosely. "I don't blame you, really."

A Rose for Hans

HEN CHARMING ARRIVED for dinner, he was in that unpleasant state between not quite drunk and not quite hungover, and feeling distinctly unsettled. The house seemed too quiet, and both chilly and stifling, as though all the empty rooms were filled with cold, slightly damp pillows.

He arrived at the dining hall to see that Hans and Will had got there before him. Will shifted his shoulders uneasily, sending gleaming light over the satin of his coat. Hans had taken off his spectacles and was polishing them. In the light of several heavy candelabra positively infested with cherubs, both men looked strained and shadow-eyed, their attention fixed on the table.

He realised they were staring at the place setting in front of Hans. Lying next to his knife was a perfect, crimson rose.

"It arrived as I did," Hans said.

"Neither of us has one," Will said.

"I noticed." Charming shoved a hand through his hair,

glared at the decanter of wine on the table and decided, grumpily, that it would only make him feel worse. "What do you suppose it means?"

"I don't know," Hans said. "But I can't say I like being singled out."

"It might mean you're about to be let go," Will said.

Hans tapped his long fingers on the table. "Hmm. Possibly. In that case, I shall make a good dinner."

"So," Charming said. "Did you gentlemen get locked in?"

"Yes!" Will said. "I yanked and yanked on the door, but it wouldn't open."

"Me too," Hans said.

"Why in the name of Goose were we locked in and then released? It doesn't make any sense."

"So... something could happen? Or not happen?" Hans said. "Maybe so we couldn't give each other any clues about the library? But I'd already *seen* the library, so..."

"So had I. Gah, fairy rules. They make them nonsensical and then you get in trouble if you break them. If I'm locked in again I shall start breaking more than rules. You were both invited to the library too?" Charming said.

"Oh, Goose," Will said. "Yes. I made *such* a fool of myself."

"I'm sure you didn't," Hans said.

"I did. She got..." Will looked over his shoulder, as though the Beast might be behind him.

Honestly, Charming thought. *It's not as if she could exactly sneak in. You'd hear the jewellery rattling... and smell that appalling perfume.*

"She got quite upset," Will went on. "I didn't mean to."

"You can't have upset her that badly, since you're still in one piece," Charming said.

"She wouldn't have hurt me," Will said. "She didn't *want* to. She's just… unhappy. She wasn't always like this. She used to be—well, you know, a lady, I think."

"She told you that?" Charming said.

"Well, she said she wasn't always what we see, so…"

"It makes sense," Hans said. "Nothing in this house is designed for her as she is. Apart from the clothes. I suppose they're specially made. How unpleasant for her. And I imagine she's lonely. Even books can only provide so much company."

"Your visit went rather better, then?" Charming said.

"I think so. She seemed entertained enough. Oh, dear, I just had a thought. Are you familiar with the tale of Urbanus?"

Will shook his head. Charming felt a sinking sensation. "Is that the chap who had to tell the dragon a tale every night so it wouldn't eat him? You think that one must be entertaining to… No, if that were the case I'm pretty certain I would now be partially digested."

"It didn't go well, then?" Hans said.

"No," Charming said, "it did not."

"Well, if she doesn't like you, maybe you get to leave," Will said.

"One can only hope." Charming was, nonetheless, aware of a spark of irritation. People liked him. Women, especially, liked him. It was his stock in trade. And whatever the Beast might currently look like, she was still a woman. The idea that she had taken a dislike to him after a few moments of conversation—and, what's more, been more entertained by bookish Hans—offended his soul. Part of him wanted to put himself out to be as… Charming… as possible, but that might mean he would be kept here even longer. And whatever magics surrounded this house, he doubted very much that they could withstand one of the Lords of Hell.

He wondered what would actually happen if he failed to show up for his meeting with Mephistopheles.

Being of generally buoyant nature, he had refused to dwell on this before; but now, stuck here with no apparent way out, he could not help it. His imagination presented him with a demon breaking down the door of the house, plucking him out of his chair, and swallowing him whole while his companions looked on in horror… or maybe he would be ripped apart, showering them with blood… or perhaps simply transported to the Infernal in a flash of sulphurous flame and screams, to have his entrails used as maypole ribbons by giggling imps…

"Charming?" Hans said.

"We're no closer to solving the riddle," Charming said. "At least, I'm not. Have either of you any thoughts?"

"Apart from the idea that we must entertain her, no," Hans said.

Will shook his head.

"That doesn't seem…" Charming drummed his fingers on the table. "It doesn't make sense. I don't get the impression she has a *choice* in this situation, do you?" He eyed the rose suspiciously. "Maybe it isn't her who gives the roses? Maybe it's the… spell, curse, whatever this is."

"The spell chooses who's to stay? But they have to stay willingly?" Hans leaned back in his chair and pressed his fingertips together. "Hmm. Is it a choice, or merely the illusion of a choice?"

"Now you're being philosophical," Charming said. "I'm not sure that's entirely helpful."

"I am merely trying to consider all aspects of the problem."

"I'm sorry," Will said. "I wish I was clever, but I'm not. If she was like…"

"If she was like…?" Charming said. "Like what?"

Will shook his head. "Nothing. Sorry. It doesn't matter."

That boy is hiding something. Yet he didn't seem the deceptive type. Not perhaps overburdened with brain, but straightforward.

And Charming needed all the help he could get.

"There are different types of clever," he said. "Hans has one type of mind, I have another, you another still. I expect you can do things neither of us can."

"Oh, well, I don't know," Will said. "I mean, I suppose, if you show me how something's put together, I can usually copy it. Like a table or a meal. I'm good at that sort of thing."

"You see? That sounds like an astonishingly useful talent," Charming said. "I am a lamentable cook, and if I attempted to make so much as a three-legged stool I would probably end up with something that you couldn't even sit on without falling off, and would no doubt have chopped off at least one of my fingers into the bargain."

Will laughed. "You can't be that bad."

"Oh, I can. I can be absolutely terrible." Truth rang uncomfortably loud in that sentence, and Charming found himself glancing at his companions to see if they'd noticed, but Will was smiling and Hans was contemplating the ceiling and murmuring to himself.

"Hans?"

"Hmm? Oh. I was wondering what sort of spell this actually is. There are a number of different forms, and

I have to say I think you were right that it does have the feel of the Good Folk about it."

"You have some experience in these matters?"

"Experience, yes. Skill, no."

And our clever Hans is hiding something, too. How very intriguing. Or it would be if I were simply planning on whisking away with whatever I can carry as per usual, instead of frantically hoping I get out of here on time and unchewed.

"If you know of anything that might *expedite* matters," Charming said, doing his best to keep his voice calm and pleasant, "I would *greatly* appreciate hearing it."

"No. Not yet, at least. I assure you if I think of anything I believe may be helpful, I shall share it. We are, after all, all in this together, are we not?"

"Of course," Charming said, through teeth he was trying very hard to ungrit. "Of course we are." He pulled the jug towards him. "Let's see if a little wine helps lubricate the thought process, shall we?"

The Bear Witch

OCTOR RAPUNZEL, HER hands close at her sides, a faint glimmer of magic at her fingertips, walked as though the very large bears to either side of her were her personally chosen honour guard, instead of what they were, which was something between an escort and a threat.

She had walked alone into what Marie Blanche said was the beginning of the bears' territory.

"How can you tell?" Doctor Rapunzel had asked.

Marie Blanche pointed with her knife. "See the worn bark? That's where they mark. And look—claw marks."

She could not help rather wishing Marie Blanche hadn't shown her the claw marks. They were large, and long, and sliced deep into the trees like knife slashes in meat.

"Are you sure you want to do this alone?" Marie Blanche asked. "I could help with the bears…"

"I am entering the territory of what appears to be an extremely powerful witch. If I have the company of another woman of skill, especially one who can communicate with her familiars, it may seem either that we are intending to present a threat, or that I do not believe I can handle her by myself."

"Oh, I'm sure you can."

"Then you have no need to accompany me." She gave Marie Blanche a reassuring smile and walked into the forest.

The wind soughed through the branches, the light danced, birds sang and fussed. Deer trails ran among the undergrowth. This was familiar territory, though many miles from where Doctor Rapunzel had spent her adolescence. Somewhere to the north of here, the Rotterturm was probably now home to owls and bats, the great heavy-scented lilies that had bloomed out of season in its courtyard long dead.

Or so she hoped.

It was not long before she felt something push at her, and at the same moment spotted a small bundle of hazelwood, string and holly berries, which looked like something simply caught by accident in the branches of a tree, but was not. *Go away,* it whispered. *There's nothing here for you. Nothing of interest at all. Go away.*

She fingered the hag stone in her pocket, feeling the smoothness of seaworn rock, the indent of the hole worn through it. An old charm, but potent if you knew how to use it. *I see clearly, I pass through.*

Soon, now, she thought.

Another tug. A glimmer of copper and bronze, high up, and a faint chiming. A harder push, not at her body but at her mind. *Go away. There are bad things here, terrible things. There are teeth. Go away.*

I see clearly, she thought again, *I pass through.*

She went on.

Then, with hardly a sound, two great bears emerged from the trees, like giant shaggy shadows suddenly made solid.

Rapunzel stiffened her back and fought the instincts that were screaming at her to run.

There was nothing to show that they were not entirely ordinary bears, at least to her eyes. Marie Blanche would probably have been able to spot the signs that made them different. They sniffed at her skirts and headdress, then backed away and looked at her.

Their eyes changed, briefly, the deep brown paling, shifting to blue.

So that's how it is, Doctor Rapunzel thought. "I wish to meet the Bear Witch, Goldlöckchen," she said, "if she will permit it. My name is Doctor Emilia Rapunzel."

One jerked its head towards the east, deeper into the woods. Now *that,* she thought, was not a bearlike gesture.

They took up their positions on either side of her, and walked forward with their swaying gait that looked so lumbering and could, in an instant, become a charge no human could outrun.

DOCTOR RAPUNZEL HAD not known quite what she expected to see, but it was not a snug little cottage set in a garden abundant with flowers. *And why not?* she asked herself. *You live in a snug house with a great many flowers yourself. Really, Emilia. You expected a shack, a cave... a blood-coloured tower?*

It was embarrassing to realise how easily one fell into stereotypes.

As she drew closer, she realised the tall white-flowered plants growing close to the walls were something she did not recognise. They had the most wonderful scent, rich but not heavy, reminiscent of baking lebkuchen, so delicious she wanted to simply open her mouth and gulp it down.

The cottage door opened, and the Bear Witch, Goldlöckchen, emerged.

One might expect a Bear Witch to be a great, roaring, broad-shouldered warrior, or a green-haired, wild-looking woodswoman. The woman who emerged was barely twenty if that, and very slight. She wore a simple blue gown and the straight hair that fell over her shoulders was almost as pale as the flowers around the walls.

Her head was high, her step firm, her gaze straight.

You worked hard for that assurance, didn't you? Doctor Rapunzel thought. *Well, you are young.*

"Why are you here?" the Bear Witch said.

"I wish to speak with you, as I told these, your... guards."

"You could have left a message at the hollow tree, like everyone else."

"I thought you might have questions, and time grows short. It seemed simpler to speak face to face."

The Bear Witch stepped closer, her eyes narrowing. "There's magic around you. Who *are* you?"

"My name is Doctor Emilia Rapunzel..." But she could not finish, because there was no longer a young woman in front of her. There was a bear, and it was charging.

So this is how it will be. The thought was barely completed before she splintered, a thousand eyes a thousand wings a thousand stings, *bees,* Emilia Rapunzel held her consciousness on tiny buzzing threads—swerve, *sting,* horrible gut-rip pain, a dozen little sacrifices, each one agonising. The bear swiped and roared, then gone, in its place a slender, lethal, darting bird-shape.

Shrike.

One of the bees gone, swallowed, into hot dark and burning; another; three at once.

Every shape has its vulnerability.

Emilia converged, dropped to the ground, solid, single, sinuous, a weasel. Her body writhed and danced; the shrike paused, landed, stared. Emilia danced, closer, further, closer, further, closest and *bite.*

Blood in the mouth, *Don't let go of yourself,* her mind whispered. *You don't want to kill her, however good her blood tastes, you are Doctor Emilia Rapunzel, hold to, hold fast.*

She tasted fear, trapped bird, trapped woman.

The feathers shifted to fur, coarse and rank, now a fox, the witch shook Emilia-weasel off with ease, though blood ran down her shoulder, her eyes all pupil with a bright fierce ring of gold, ears flat, teeth bared, she pounced... and Emilia flung out wings, powerful legs propelled her up, *eagle,* she beat against the air, felt the fox's teeth scrape her foot, hot breath. Beat and *up* and *up* and hold, pause, the fox was a splash of red as bright as blood, and *stoop.*

Don't kill her, don't kill her, don't kill her... one last play, and I had better be right, or we are all in trouble.

Doctor Rapunzel strained to turn the stoop, and oh, she'd ache tomorrow. She managed, just, to go back to herself before she hit the ground, though it was a less than elegant landing and she jarred her bones. *More aches.* "Hold," she said. "Margarethe von Hesse."

The fox froze, and the Bear Witch stood there, human.

Her lip curled up, she was snarling with fear like a fox at the end of a hunt, cornered. Blood crept from her shoulder, stained the innocent blue of her dress.

"Please," Doctor Rapunzel said. "I meant it, I only wish to talk."

"*How do you know my name?*" A clenched whisper, full of terror.

"The magistrate's rolls. An... associate drew my attention to the lost children. Yellow-haired, *gold-locked*. I looked a little closer. There was just a word, here and there, a neighbour who bore witness... but she was only a sentimental old woman, and your father had powerful friends, didn't he? Such as the magistrate. Besides, everyone knows a father—or a mother—has the right to treat their children as they please. And if you ran away, why, it was because you were naughty children, who met a sad but inevitable fate."

Rapunzel straightened, eased her aching shoulders. "I guessed your name would hold you as a human. There are some things we cannot entirely leave behind. I don't blame you for choosing to be a bear," she said. "I used to dream of being a dragon. Flame is very... cleansing."

The young woman said nothing, but continued to stare at her.

"He's dead," Doctor Rapunzel said. "Your father. I'll tell you how, if you wish."

"No," the Bear Witch said. "I'd rather imagine it." She turned away. "Come in, then, and tell me what you want."

THE COTTAGE WAS as neat inside as out, the scents of baking and herbs mingling with the delicious perfume of the white flowers drifting in through the windows. More of them stood in a jug on the table, along with purple asters and loose-petalled red roses.

The Bear Witch sat, straight-backed, at the table, her hands in front of her, the window behind. The light made a halo around her hair, and in it Doctor Rapunzel could see the faint shivering of individual strands. *She's shaking, however she tries to hide it. I never meant to terrify the child so.*

"Do you not wish to tend your injury?" she said. "Goldlöckchen?" She offered the name as a reassurance.

"Tell me why you're here."

Emilia Rapunzel settled herself in the other chair, moving gently and carefully, as though she were in a room full of breakable things. "I am looking for a man who went missing in the forest," she said. "Blond, handsome, good at making himself pleasant."

"I've heard nothing. Is that all?"

"These are wonderful," Doctor Rapunzel said, brushing one of the white blooms gently with her fingertips. "I've never seen them before. You have a beautiful garden."

Goldlöckchen's face softened a little. "They're called ginger lily. My brother found them when he was studying in Cascitua, and sent tubers to me."

Doctor Rapunzel smiled. "Ah, how nice, to have such a thoughtful brother! I sometimes ask for plants in exchange for doing a casting, if I've seen something I want. I'm sure they think I use them for all kinds of wicked potions, but generally I just try to grow them. Are your ginger lilies difficult?"

"They don't like the cold. I have to cover them in winter." She looked at her hands. "You should speak to the wolf woman," she said abruptly.

"You think she knows something?"

"My brother's been gone for days. He always tells me if he's going away. *Always*. And he knows these woods as well as the bears do, but he's... If he saw a rare plant or an unfamiliar fungus, or just got lost in thought... he could have wandered into her territory. If she's hurt him..." Goldlöckchen's hands gripped each other so her nails dug in. "She'll pay if she has."

"There has been trouble between you before?"

Goldlöckchen shook her head. "I'd hardly have known they were there, until a few years ago."

"Hmm. Well, a friend of mine has spoken to her. If she has seen your brother, she certainly didn't mention it. And *she* seems to think you may have made off with her nephew."

"What? Why? What would I want with him?" Goldlöckchen looked honestly bewildered.

"The same might be said of her, and your brother."

"I don't *eat* people."

"Apparently, neither do they. They very carefully do *not* eat people. That sort of thing tends to lead to flaming torches and pitchforks."

"She could be lying."

"To be fair, so could you." Doctor Rapunzel steepled her fingers in front of her chin. "You haven't launched an attack on her."

"If he's there, and alive, he might get hurt. I can't even *scry* for him, it doesn't work here."

"You do know other men have been disappearing?" Doctor Rapunzel said. "It seems they reappear, within a month, unharmed but with a gap in their memories."

"So my brother told me, but just because the townsfolk say it that doesn't mean it's true." Her eyes immediately darkened again with suspicion. "If you think it's true, why not just wait for your friend to spring back up like a... a mushroom?"

"I cannot afford to wait that long. If we do not find him soon, it will go very badly for him, and probably me, and several others. And we do not know if all those who disappeared reappear. But you have *no idea* what may be happening to these men?"

"No. I don't speak to the townsfolk. If they want something from me, they leave a message and a payment in the hollow tree. No one has asked me to find their missing men." She gave a chilly smile too old for her face. "Perhaps they think I've taken them."

"You are a powerful witch, and you know these woods well. Are you sure there is nothing? No... odd magics? Disturbances? Random mysterious holes in the ground? Anything? Please do not think I am accusing you, I believe you don't have him hidden in a cupboard. But... Oh, the *wretched* man. Disappearing like this is so *like* him."

"These woods have always been full of magic," Goldlöckchen said. "It shifts like the tide. Five years ago, there was a... a kind of *pulse*, that made my ears ring, but nothing seemed to change, except the wolves starting to cause trouble. And that is too far back to be anything to do with your wandering man." She stared at the flowers in the jug, frowning. "My grandmother—she wasn't, not really, but that's what we called her—this was her cottage. She found us when we ran away, and took us in. She said there were threads pulled out of the weave."

"I don't understand."

"Nor did I, not really. She taught me, but I'll never have her skill at listening. I couldn't sit, like she could, for hours, days, just feeling the patterns of things. She'd have known what that change was, what it meant, but she was gone by then. But for years she said she felt someone was *meddling,* pulling the threads. Damaging the weave." Goldlöckchen glanced at the small tapestry on the wall to her left, a fruiting tree, its branches alive with birds, flowers blooming at its feet.

"She made that? She was very skilled."

"Yes." Goldlöckchen shrugged. "I'm sorry, I don't know any more."

"If you think of anything, we are staying at the Kuchenmeister, outside Felendstadt." Doctor Rapunzel got to her feet. "And if I hear anything about your brother, I will send a message." She looked at Goldlöckchen. "I will not tell anyone your true name," she said. "Trust me, I know its worth."

"And yours?" Goldlöckchen said.

"Emilia Rapunzel von Riesentor, for what good it does. It is, in fact, my true name. Knowledge of a true name only works as a control under certain conditions; if one is a fairy, or has enough fairy blood, like you."

"Grandmother said she thought I had fairy blood," Goldlöckchen said. "Most witches have a little; but you've made do with little or none, since you give your name away so easily."

"Even mortal names have their uses. I kept the name von Riesentor so that I would be taken more seriously— but now it is only a ruin where I once lived. The name Emilia Rapunzel was given to me at the orphanage. They gave them out in batches, and were running out of ideas, so I ended up named after a vegetable."

"Well," Goldlöckchen said, "I suppose it could be worse. You could be called Zweibel."

"True. I think people would take Doctor Onion even less seriously." She paused in the doorway. "I hope you find your brother," she said.

As she left, she took a deep breath of the scent of the ginger lilies.

Another Interlude

HE MEN GATHERED, yet again, in the drawing room of the silent house. It was just after midday, and the day outside was bright, with a crisp snap of autumn in the air. Hans had yet another book, and was making notes, occasionally pushing his spectacles up on his nose. Will paced and pulled at the lacings of his coat.

Charming scowled at the unreachable countryside and slumped into a chair, blowing a lock of hair out of his eyes.

"I suppose this is how women feel at a dance," Hans said. "Waiting to be chosen, not knowing their fate."

"Women at a dance don't usually get torn apart if they don't get picked," Charming said, glumly. He stared at the fire, but it made him think of the Infernal, and he turned away again.

"You don't still believe our hostess is going to tear you apart, do you?" Hans said. "She has shown no such inclination."

"Not her. Necessarily," Charming said. "Though she does rather seem to have taken a dislike to me. And I still don't know what the blasted riddle means."

"Well, part of it seems clear," Hans said. "One of us must choose to stay here."

"I *can't*," Charming said. "Even if I wanted to. House! You hear me? I can't stay, even if I wanted to stay, I simply can't! I have no choice!"

There was no response from the house, except that the nearest decanter was nudged closer to Charming's elbow. "No, thank you," he said, morosely. "I've only just recovered from my last hangover."

"Why?" Will said. "Why do *you* have to leave?"

"Because I owe a debt, and if I don't pay it on time people will die. Including me."

"Gambling?" Hans said.

"Not… precisely," Charming said. "Not in the usual sense."

Hans raised an eyebrow, but decided not to pursue it.

"You should stay," Charming said. "You like the library, she—or the house itself—appears to approve of *you*…"

"Even if it were that simple," Hans said, "and I suspect it is anything but, I do actually have a life outside these walls, and I'd like it back."

"I need to get out of here too." Will stared out of the window, craning his neck to look up at the moon.

"What will happen if *you* don't?" Charming said. *I'm fairly sure it won't involve being torn apart by a demon.*

"Bad things," Will said morosely. "I just want to get back to my family."

It struck Charming with uncomfortable intensity that he did not, in fact, have anywhere he wanted to be. He *needed* to be up a mountain with his height in gold, hoping that Mephistopheles would uphold his end of the bargain, but after that? He had no desire to go to his father's palace, even if he *wouldn't* be arrested on sight and executed for treason in short order. And there wasn't anywhere else.

But more brooding would do no good.

"Hans, you're an educated man. This"—Charming waved at the air—"situation we find ourselves in. What do you think about it, in practical terms? How do you think it operates? What are its limits?"

Hans' eyes lit up. "I have been considering the problem. There is the force within the house, that does all that is necessary here. Then there is the force that drives the roses, to act as guards and stop any escape from a window or via the main entrance. Are they part of the same thing, or are they different? I don't know."

He cleared his throat, warming to his topic. "Walking the grounds, I discovered the limits, which I assume would be the same for all of us. Any attempt to leave by a window... Well, we all saw, and *felt*, what came of that. If one leaves by the kitchen door, one is allowed to explore the kitchen garden and the stables. Leaving by the side door in the west wing, near the menagerie, allows access to the formal gardens. One is free to walk about there, so long as it is by day. I tried to go out at night and the doors simply would not open. But getting to the edge of the gardens..." He grimaced. "It's hard to describe, but everything goes... one's eyes seem to stop working properly. It's all..." He waved his hands. "It twists about. You walk away from the house, and a moment later you're walking back towards it, without any sense of having turned around. Distance and direction don't work. It's highly irritating to a rational man."

"Sounds delightful," Charming said.

At that moment one of those blasted floating candlesticks appeared, and hovered suggestively in front of Will.

"Oh, it wants me to go somewhere," Will said. "I hope it's not the library again."

"Poor lad," Hans said, once the door had closed behind him. "Can't read. Not for want of trying, apparently. He says the letters jump about and make no sense. I tutored someone like that. Perfectly intelligent, but couldn't make head nor tail of a simple sentence."

"So is that what you do in your life? The one you want to get back to. Tutoring?" Charming said.

Hans smiled. "Sometimes. In between, I live with my sister. She is excellent company. But also, I like to travel, and learn, and observe. The world is full of wonders, and I write a little. The more I see, the more material I have. I suppose I am a dilettante, but I make shift to earn my way."

"So what do you tutor in?"

"Literature. And herbalism and botany. Which has allowed me to be of use to ship's doctors on occasion. I also teach the lute, write plays, largely for my own amusement, and sometimes work in inns or mills... Really, whatever comes to hand for which I have any skills, or can learn them."

"You seem to have a great many skills. Tutor to millworker must be quite a contrast."

"I have met some fine minds in mills, and tutored some extraordinarily inept ones in palaces. As you yourself said, intelligence has nothing to do with rank. And you? Apart from your unfortunate debt, I mean. What awaits you outside these walls?"

Charming stared down at the table and shoved his hands in his pockets. "I…"

He had always told himself he loved his wandering life, saw himself as free and unencumbered.

But the trouble with defrauding people everywhere you went was that they were unlikely to want to see you again. Unless they wanted to see you *very much*, purely for the purpose of locking you up and dangling the key in front of your eyes before throwing it into the deepest ravine they could find. And the only people who might be trying to find him weren't doing it because they cared, but because they needed him alive.

He sank deeper in his chair. "Oh, you know. The open road, tra-la-la. I shall have to settle eventually, I suppose." *Where and who with, my boy? Ah, well, that's a question, isn't it?*

"No family?" Hans said. "No, ignore that. My apologies. Family is… a difficult question for some of us, I know."

Charming looked at him. *Oh ho, so, despite what sounds like an affectionate relationship with your sister, there's something there, isn't there?*

Or he was just being, what's the word… delicate. Nice. Trying to spare your feelings.

"I have one, but we don't speak."

Hans nodded. "I don't suppose," he said, "you've come to any conclusions?"

"About my family?"

"About our situation," Hans said.

"Oh. Ah. Yes, well, I mean, someone, presumably, turned our hostess into what she is now. But why? And setting her up in a magic house and having men brought here… I'd say they wanted her married off, but if that's the case, why turn her into so much less of an attractive prospect?"

"I came to similar conclusions," Hans said. "Though they barely count as conclusions, do they? So, alas, we are no further on."

"No. Dammit."

Hans sighed.

"Oh, do you by any means remember what was in that locked cabinet, in the library?" Charming said.

Hans told him.

"Wait, there's a ring that instantaneously transports you elsewhere?" Charming said. "But…"

"I was informed that I would not be permitted to use it. Not that I really want to. I distrust magical artefacts."

"Oh, for Goose's sake."

"I know. Frustrating, isn't it?"

"That's one word for it." Nonetheless, Charming thought, one way or another he had to get into that cabinet. An item like that ring was too damn useful not to have, now he didn't have his beloved boots any longer.

"So far, my thoughts have proved less than productive on how to actually get out of here," Hans said.

"Likewise." Charming sighed, and tried to ignore the churning in his stomach as yet another day wound down towards night. *How long? How long do I have?*

Hans took out his spectacles and returned to his book. Charming glowered at him when he wasn't looking. Hans could afford to relax and read. He'd probably just walk out of here with the house's blessing and an armful of books, back to his life, no demons for him.

Charming picked up a book himself, flicked through the pages for a few minutes, and decided to pace the corridors instead. There were still parts of the house he hadn't explored.

He half-heartedly tried locked doors as he went, not really expecting any of them to open. There were great wooden double doors at the end of one corridor, beautifully engraved, if he'd been in the mood to appreciate it, with all sorts of birds and beasts and twining vines. Behind them he could hear faint sounds, but they would not move under his hand.

Besides, he thought, *it's probably something dreadful.*

The Pauper and the Animals

EYOND THE DOUBLE doors, Will gaped in delight at a large bird, like nothing he had ever seen before. Its body was a brilliant yellow, its head green shading to royal blue down its back and wings. "So *beautiful*," Will said.

The bird spread its wings, showing their yellow undersides, and, rather remarkably for something without lips, made a very loud raspberry. Will blushed.

The Beast laughed. "Don't worry, he does that all the time."

"But he shouldn't... I mean... You're a *lady!*"

"Not at the moment, I'm not," the Beast said. She led him deeper into the great room. Its walls were of polished grey stone flecked with silvery mica, its roof of white-painted iron and glass—he had never seen so much glass in one place.

It was very warm, and full of plants Will could not even name: some with leaves broader than his torso, others with fat scarlet flowers whose petals were so shiny they seemed carved out of polished stone. Everywhere there was movement and chittering and the bright flicker of wings. Even as Will gasped and wondered, he worried about how sweaty he was getting in the heavy, uncomfortable clothes the house had yet again forced him into.

A delicate wrought-iron table and two matching chairs stood on the marble floor in a central space like a glade, overhung with green fronds and vines.

The Beast gestured for him to sit, and Will did so, hardly noticing the covered dishes on the table as he craned his neck to take everything in.

Something small and brown with a furry but oddly human face peered out at him. "What's *that*? Is it an imp?"

"That's a monkey. That one's quite friendly; if you stay still, she'll come to you." The Beast lifted the cover of one of the dishes. It was full of fruit. "Take an apple, and hold it out. Don't move too fast or grab for her."

Will sat like a statue, his hand with the apple resting on the table.

The monkey walked along a branch until she was a few feet from the table, looking down at them with bright brown eyes. Will hardly breathed.

The monkey hung from the branch with one hand, dropped, landed on the table, and edged towards his hand.

Quick as winking, she grabbed the apple, and leapt back for the branch, where she sat, holding the apple in her paws and taking neat little bites, in between looking around it at Will.

"Hello," he said softly. "Hello, monkey. Look at how she holds that apple, just like a person! I never knew there were such things in the world!"

As he was speaking, there was a clang and a clatter, and the Beast laughed. "Oh, you little wretch!"

The lid of another dish was on the floor, and another monkey, slightly bigger than the first, was sitting up in a tree, with a meat pasty in its paws. "They're very adept thieves," the Beast said.

"I never even saw that!" Will said, grinning. "Cheeky fella!"

The monkey chittered at him and took a big bite of the pasty.

Will ate very little of his own lunch, far more interested in feeding it to every bird or monkey he could persuade to come close.

"You're very patient," the Beast said.

"I love animals. And birds. I like to watch them. And when they decide they want to be friends it's the best feeling." He shrugged. "I'm better at them than I am people."

"You seem perfectly good at people to me."

Will blushed again and focused on feeding bits of another pasty to a small bright green parakeet that had decided he was its best friend in the entire world. He scratched it gently on the head and it closed its eyes and made little chirrups and trills.

The monkey came back and was sitting on the table, watching Will, her tail curled around her feet like a cat's.

"Do you have family, Will?"

"Yes, ma'am."

"You don't have to call me ma'am, you know."

"I'm sorry."

"Don't be. Tell me about your family."

"Umm… Well, there's my aunt. I told you about her. She's the head of the family, I suppose. And the other aunts and uncles. Then there's my cousins, Hedel and Ludek, and Ketlin and Yakob and Tylek and Hille and Ede. And Otto, he's sort of new, and Claus and Kurt. Claus and Kurt are twins. They're the handsomest of us, especially when... Well. My aunt says they're more than double the trouble of everyone else."

"I am sure you are at least as handsome," she said.

Will threw her a panicked glance, feeling himself flush even more scarlet than he was already. "Oh, no," he stammered. "They're both much taller, and blond, and older..."

She smiled and turned the subject. "Ludek is the one who plays the fiddle, is he not? Are there other musicians in your family?"

"Ede plays the flute, she says she's no good but I think she is. Tylek would like a drum but my aunt says they're too expensive. Otto says he can play the spoons, but we don't have any."

"You have no spoons? *Or* parents?"

Will shook his head. "I suppose I must have, but I don't really remember them. The family took me in when I was very little, and I don't remember anything except I was cold and hungry and scared, it was getting dark and I was lost in the wood and I looked up and saw..." He paused.

The parakeet looked up at him, accusingly, because he'd stopped scratching its head. Will made an apologetic noise and started again. The parakeet leaned into his hand.

"I saw my aunt Thelise. I didn't know... who she was. But anyway. I've been with them since."

"They sound like kind people."

"They are. They're kind and smart—well, most of them—and I'd be dead if it wasn't for them."

"Only most of them?"

"Well, Tylek's only three, no one's that smart when they're three. But Heinrich... my aunt says Heinrich could walk into a room full of gold and come out holding a... um. Something nasty."

The blue and yellow bird made another, extremely juicy-sounding, raspberry noise.

"Be *quiet,* you horrible bird," the Beast said, but there was a laugh in her voice.

Will snickered, unable to help himself. "Sorry."

"It's not your fault."

"What's his name?"

"His name's Kichka," she said. "It means 'thorn.' He's quite clever. He'll do tricks, if he's in the mood."

The bird put its head on one side and regarded Will with a bright and somehow cynical gaze.

"You were telling me about your family," the Beast said. "You miss them."

"Yes," Will said, before he thought. "I'm sorry," he said, "but I do. People get the wrong idea about them because they're... different. But they're my *family*. Are yours...?" He cut himself off.

"My family are long gone," the Beast said. "And we were not close. You said your family are different? How?"

"I..." Will looked at his hands. "I'm sorry, I can't talk about that."

"Do you think I wouldn't understand? Because they're different?" The Beast gestured at herself, the vast hairy body and toothy jaws. "You think I don't understand what it is to be different?"

"It's... I promised," Will said. "If you ever meet my aunt Thelise, perhaps she'll tell you."

"I hope I shall meet her one day," the Beast said. "I'd like that very much."

The Scholar and the Menagerie

ANS, LIKE WILL, gasped with pleasure when the doors swung open. "*Dixonia!*" His spectacles began to steam up and he whipped them off.

"I beg your pardon?" the Beast said. For the briefest moment she had entertained the ridiculous hope that it might be her that had brought an expression of delight to his face.

"Oh!" Hans bowed, but barely looked at her, his eyes immediately drawn back to the great tree fern that towered above him. "Forgive me, but I've never seen one of these in this country. And is that *Vanilla Planifolia?* And—great Goose! *Solanum lycopersicum!*" He ducked into the foliage and plucked a shiny red fruit. "May I?"

He was raising it to his lips when the Beast yelped. "Don't! It's poisonous!"

"Oh, it isn't. It's a common belief, but no. Actually, I personally believe it's very good for the constitution. The idea that it's poisonous comes from its being related to *atropa belladonna*, or deadly nightshade. And one certainly shouldn't eat any part of it but the fruit. The fruit itself, however, is highly nutritious. Its native name is *tomatl*… I'm sorry, I'm lecturing, aren't I? A dreadful habit, it comes from doing so much tutoring."

"You were, rather," the Beast said. "Are you *sure* it's not poisonous?"

"Indeed, but I shan't eat it if it makes you uncomfortable."

"Oh, no, please," she said. "Go ahead."

Hans popped the tomato into his mouth.

There was a shriek, and Hans jumped, and peered upwards.

"*Ara Ararauna*," he said. "And what a very handsome specimen you are."

Kichka tilted his head.

Hans solemnly bowed to the parrot. "I am Hans. Johannes von Behr. I am delighted to make your acquaintance."

Kichka ruffled his feathers, and tilted his head the other way.

"Not a talker, I see," Hans said. "Some of them do."

"He'll sometimes come out with a phrase or two," the Beast said. "But I don't think he knows what they mean."

"Possibly not." Hans took the chair he was offered. "I see you have several *saimiri sciureus*, too. The monkeys," he said. "How did you come by them?"

"My father had a liking for exotica," the Beast said. "In the course of his trade he travelled a great deal, and collected plants, animals, the items you saw in the library… Well, one or two of those are older, but most were my father's. And the creatures here, some will take food from your hand, if you offer it."

"I'm sure."

The Beast fidgeted with the plates, shifting them about, but not eating. One of the monkeys leapt onto the back of her chair, and she took a piece of fruit to offer it, glancing at Hans, but though he watched this interaction his troubled expression did not change.

The monkey edged closer to him. He sat quietly, his chin propped on one hand. "Hello, little one," he said softly. "You're a very long way from home."

"What is your home like?" the Beast said.

"Nothing as extravagant as yours, I fear. A cottage, where I live with my sister."

"But you have travelled about."

"Oh, here and there," Hans said, his eyes never leaving the monkey.

"I should like to travel one day. Where was your favourite place?" *If I ever get out of here,* the Beast thought to herself, *I will have enough practice at pulling teeth to set myself up in the dentist business.*

"Hmm?"

"Your favourite place," she said, fighting to keep the growl out of her voice. "In your travels."

"Oh, well, there were many," Hans said. "This little one comes from a continent far away, where there are ruined cities there that are older than our histories. One that I visited was alive with these little creatures, chattering away to each other. When I first heard them I thought the place was full of birds, from the sounds they make. They ran and jumped everywhere, and were very curious about the strange creatures that had come to visit them. Their friendliness worked to their disadvantage, unfortunately. Several were captured, and all my protests would not free them."

The Beast felt her jaw clench, and tried to loosen it. "And the city?"

"It was magnificent, but long empty until the monkeys came to fill it."

"It sounds as though there were plenty of them, and they would not miss a few," she said.

"In fact they were obviously distressed, and some of them followed us for some way when we left their territory, crying for their companions. Your handsome fellow here." Hans gestured up at Kichka. "I have seen birds like him, flying in the hot blue sky in their hundreds. They are sociable and extremely intelligent. You're a clever fellow, aren't you?" he said.

Kichka bobbed up and down.

"Oh, and they mate for life. I wonder if he had a mate. Did you have a mate, Kichka?"

Kichka opened his beak and screamed, piercingly. The Beast's ears flattened to her head.

The macaw opened his wings and flew off to the other end of the room, where he sat hunched, with his back to them.

"Oh, dear," Hans said. "I wonder how much he understood. I think I upset him."

"You are extremely concerned about the feelings of a bird, or a monkey." It was getting very hard to keep the growl in check, and the Beast heard it edging into her voice.

"Well, this is not where they belong."

"And you feel like them, caged, far from home, and with nothing here of any meaning to you?"

"My home is much closer," Hans said, watching her carefully, "and you have been a generous and attentive hostess."

And now he's watching you with that wary look as though you might rip his head from his shoulders.

It's not as though I even brought the damn creatures here!

"Perhaps I should set them all free, then," she said coldly.

"They'd die, I'm afraid," Hans said. "The winter here would kill them."

"You don't think that would be better than being so brutally used?"

"I think... that perhaps I have caused enough distress for one evening," Hans said, "and should take my leave."

"Perhaps you should."

He bowed over her hand, polite as ever, and went to the door, and waited.

After a long, horribly awkward moment, the door opened.

As soon as it had closed behind him, the Beast swept the barely touched plates from the table to shatter on the floor. Then she laid her head on her arms. Tears seeped into her fur.

Kichka looked over his shoulder at her, and muttered.

The Prince and the Parrot

HERE ARE ALL these outfits *coming* from?" Charming said, pausing in combing his hair to regard the latest offering with a cynical eye. "There must be a vast wardrobe somewhere. Or an entire room. Yellow is *not* my colour, just so you know. There are very few people who look good in yellow unless they have skin a great deal darker than mine. Not that it would make any difference how good I look. I think I've well and truly put my foot in it with our hostess."

The hose wiggled at him.

"Fine, fine, I'll put it all on and be nice." *And if she finally loses patience and tears me apart, at least it will save me being whisked off to the Infernal and turned into demon-snacks. I mean, I hope. At this point I don't even know if death will do the trick.*

He caught himself. Never in his life had he been this... *broody.* What was wrong with him? Well, apart from the threat of his imminent horrific demise, that was. *Come on, man. You've always wiggled your way out of trouble*

*before. Or at least managed to put it off until later. You're
Prince Charming. Be Charming, as hard as you possibly
can.*

He put on the fine silks and rich velvets and glared
at the mirror. "See?" he said. "Yellow. I look positively
sickly. Well, I suppose I must make the best of it."
The usual candlestick hovered pointedly by the door.
Charming lifted his chin, pasted on his best smile and
walked after it.

THE BEAST TOOK a deep breath and smoothed her hands
over the creamy satin overdress embroidered with tiny
blue and yellow flowers. As though it would do any good.

Charming being so *stupidly* handsome just made it
worse. Although he hadn't exactly lived up to his name in
other respects, so far. He wasn't perhaps the *most* jittery
of her visitors—that prize went to the unfortunate soul
who had leapt straight out of a window at the sight of
her, adding glass cuts and a broken ankle to his injuries
from the roses, and who had been a gibbering wreck for
the entire duration. After the third time she had entered a
room and he had withdrawn into a corner, whimpering,
with his arms wrapped around his head, she had given
up and left him to his own devices. It had been a relief
once the month was over and he had gone. Charming
wasn't *that* bad, but he was obviously, severely ill at ease.

Of course he was. As she herself had said, what else
could she possibly expect?

She knew she had overreacted when Charming came
to the library, but really, the sight of him, looking even
better up close (after her inadvertent glimpse of his entire
royal person when he had lost his towel in the corridor),

and the realisation of just how stupid and impossible it all was, how stupid and impossible it had *always* been, had simply overwhelmed her. She had lost control of her emotions.

She had overreacted to Hans in the menagerie, too. He was probably right, that the beasts should not be there, but she had not been the one to bring them. His disapproval had stung the more because they had been getting on so well. Or at least... *Don't fool yourself, woman. He's capable of being polite, as many have been before. It doesn't mean anything.*

Had she lost control because of the circumstances, or was the beast winning? She didn't know anymore. And at this point, did it even matter?

Stop it. Calm down. You can still control yourself. Just get through this. You can be meaninglessly polite, too. You've done it often enough, you've done it since you were twelve years old. Expect nothing, and just enjoy the view.

THE VIEW WAS, indeed, appealing. Charming paused in the doorway of the menagerie, the warm lamplight nestling in the gold waves of his hair and stroking the strong line of his throat.

Kichka gave a long, low whistle. "Who's a pretty boy, then?"

Charming's gaze flew to the bird, and he gave a gasp of laughter, and bowed to Kichka with an extravagant flourish.

The Beast could not help laughing herself, though it came out as a huffing bark.

Charming bowed to her, even more deeply, and looked

up at her under his brows while still bent low, looking absurdly like a small boy caught in mischief and trying to avoid punishment. "May I beg your forgiveness?"

"For what?"

"I'm actually not sure," he said. "But I know I offended you last time we met, and I truly had no such intentio— Yipe!"

He bolted upright, jolting the monkey that had landed on his back so it gripped his shirt with its hard little hands and chittered at him.

"Don't worry," the Beast said, "she won't hurt you. She likes yellow, for some reason."

Charming craned his neck to look at his passenger. "My goodness," he said. "Well, she's welcome to this shirt, it was *not* my choice."

The Beast tried and failed to supress the thought of him taking off his shirt. *At least he can't see me blushing.* She gestured to the little table and sat down.

Charming carefully seated himself, and the monkey settled on his shoulder and began to groom his hair. He looked at the Beast with such an anxious expression she had to laugh again. "She really won't hurt you, I promise." The idea that a man of his height, with such broad and muscular shoulders, could be afraid of a creature no bigger than a cat, was absurd.

"She won't pull my hair out?"

"No. You might lose a hair or two to her grooming, but no more than you would to a comb."

He relaxed. "If you *do* start pulling," he told the monkey sternly, "I'll be very cross."

She trilled at him and went back to grooming. The Beast wondered what it felt like to plunge fingers into that rough gold mane. *Now I am envying a monkey.*

"Not that I don't *need* a good barber," Charming said. "I promise I don't always look quite so unkempt."

"You look perfectly respectable to me," the Beast said.

"I do?"

Actually, no. A number of other words to describe him came to the Beast's mind and *respectable* was not one of them. She hurriedly turned away and took the cover off the pasties. "I should take one of these, if I were you, before the monkeys get to them."

Just enjoy the view, she told herself. *Expect nothing.*

Kichka fluttered into view again and took up a post above the table, peering at Charming, and gave another of those long, low whistles.

The Beast snorted and put her paws over her eyes. "Kichka, *must* you be an embarrassment every time I have a guest?"

Kichka shrieked and began to clean his feathers vigorously.

"Perhaps he thinks I make a good-looking bird?" Charming said. "I'm not entirely sure I should be flattered."

"I'm sure you should. I mean…" The Beast felt her insides shrink with embarrassment. She could not think of a single thing to say which would not come out wrong. "His name means 'thorn,'" she blurted. "He'll sometimes do tricks, if he feels like it." She tried not to stare too blatantly at Charming. But even the man's *hands,* reaching for a pasty, were handsome; it was absurd.

"He'll do tricks? What sort of tricks?"

"Oh, if you offer him something he wants, like an almond—he loves almonds—he'll go find something. Or someone."

"How very clever," Charming said, thoughtfully. "But you couldn't send him to find someone he didn't know, I suppose."

"You could if there was something about them he'd recognise. I got him to chase someone all around the menagerie once by showing him a hat like the man wore." The man had been one of her more revolting suitors. Father had been furious. "You didn't offend me, the other evening," she said, looking at the plate. "I was a little... overwrought, and rude. I apologise."

"Please don't," Charming said.

She looked up at him, surprised.

"You have every excuse to be more than a little overwrought," he said gently. "I don't need to know the origins of your situation to realise it must be a dreadful strain on you."

The Beast struggled to control her voice, but it was still a little shaky when she said, "It is, yes."

He held out the plate of pasties, but she shook her head. "Has it been long?" he said. "Can you tell me that?"

"Five years."

"Goose above! Five *years*? That's..." He shook his head. "That's so cruel. I'm very sorry."

Something in his face struck her strangely. He looked downcast, almost guilty.

"Is something wrong?"

"Apart from your situation, you mean? It's just... I've known people who were in similar situations to yours. In a manner of speaking."

"You have?"

Charming raised his gaze to hers for a moment—his eyes were very blue, almost as blue as Kichka's wing feathers—then looked down. "Yes, odd as it may seem, you are not the only lady I have known who was magically constrained, one way or another. And I did not… behave as well as I might, to people already in a bad way. And I hope… I'd really rather not behave badly to you."

So you behaved badly? To these ladies? I should probably worry about that. But then again, what can you possibly do that's worse than things are already?

"Yes, well, *I* would rather you didn't behave badly, too." She cleared her throat. "Let us change the subject, if you please. I don't suppose, on your way in, you saw much of the estate? I can't leave the gardens, and I worry what sort of state it's in."

He responded with obvious relief. "I'm afraid I simply stumbled on what I assume was once the main carriageway when I was lost in the woods. I was so hungry I just followed the smell of bacon straight to the kitchens, and, well…" He shrugged. "That was it. I have to say the house has looked after me *extremely* well."

"Yes, I'm sure…" she said. "Ah, well. What misfortune brought you to these woods? I assume you're not local."

"No. I was taking what I thought was a shortcut." He grinned ruefully. "I suspect I'm not the first to think that, am I? I was heading to Floriens, to deal with some urgent family business."

"I'm sorry. I hope the delay to your journey won't cause a great deal of trouble."

"Oh, I doubt it," he said. He was smiling, but his smile seemed forced. "I would rather not have to deal with it at all, but needs must when the, ah, Devil drives, as they say."

"Can no one deal with it for you?"

"Not in this particular case. I wish they could. But tell me, what concerns you, about the estate? If things"—he waved vaguely at the walls—"permit, perhaps I could have a look about for you."

She thought, *how does he move with such* grace, *even when he's just waving at the air?*

Instantly she felt twice as hulking, a great, stomping, clumsy thing. "No, don't trouble yourself," she said. "You probably won't be allowed to go any further than I am. What about your own estates?"

"You assume I have them," he said. "I could be a complete vagabond, you know. Nothing more to me than the clothes I stand in. Actually, even those, at the moment, are yours, not mine."

"Well, not exactly mine," she said, feeling a smile tug at her lips. She tried to supress it, not wanting to show him her teeth. "Even before this, they'd hardly have been suitable for me."

"Oh, I don't know. I know at least one lady who regularly dresses in a more masculine style, though not, admittedly, where her parents can see her!"

Who? the Beast thought. *What lady? Is she pretty? I expect she is. And she's only one of the no doubt dozens of pretty women he must meet all the time, in difficult magical circumstances or just in the street...*

Oh, stop it, woman. The Beast took a deep breath, and, keeping her tone light, said, "*Are* you a vagabond?"

"In a manner of speaking. I'm the heir to a rather large... estate. But only by default. It should have gone to my brother. Truly, I'd much rather it had. In any case I have kept far away for as long as possible, hoping an alternative would present itself." He seemed about to say something more, then sighed, and shook his head. "So I have been living the life of a vagabond, certainly. It has its charms."

Kichka hooted explosively. The monkey, which had been dozing off, yanked on Charming's hair as it leapt from his shoulder, chittering furiously at Kichka, and scuttled off into the plants.

"Ow." Charming rubbed his scalp. "I don't think Kichka believes me."

"Kichka, please go away," the Beast said. "I am *so* sorry," she said to Charming. "Sometimes I think he delights in being as provoking as possible."

Charming shook his head. "Don't be sorry. I actually rather like him, he reminds me of someone."

"A friend?"

"Um. Of a sort."

"Family?"

"Oh, great Goose, no. I have enough troubles."

"But how intriguing! You like him but you wouldn't want him to be family?"

"Come to think of it," Charming said, "he can't be worse than some of them. My father, for example... Oh, dear, are you going to tell me I should respect my elders? I suppose I do *respect* him, he's far better at running the... estate than I'd ever be. I just don't happen to like him very much."

"Was he unkind?"

Perhaps it was those lovely amber eyes, or the sympathy in her gruff tone, but Charming found himself wanting to answer.

"Yes. He was awful to my mother. She was a good deal younger, and she tried so hard to please him. She could charm everyone but him, it seemed. In his eyes she couldn't do anything right, apart from providing him with an heir and"—he gestured at himself—"a spare. But she was too lively, too frivolous, too interested in art

146

and poetry and not interested enough in being a Suitable Wife."

"She… was?"

"She died, trying to give him another son. Birthing two of us almost killed her, she should never… Sorry." He coughed.

"I'm sorry. You loved her a great deal."

"I did, yes."

"And she loved you."

He smiled. "I was her little co-conspirator. Planning games and amusements. She could turn any occasion into a party. She loved my brother, Auberic, too, but Father snatched him out of her grasp when he could barely walk, to educate him in the ways of… er… estate management. He was always being tutored in something, or riding around looking at farms or fortifications. Father pretty much gave up on me. I fell into some less than savoury habits. Not that he didn't have a few of his own."

He looked at the Beast. He was honestly tempted to tell her the rest. After all, he might be dead in a short time, and then it wouldn't matter what she knew about him.

But then, he might not. So he didn't tell her how the charm he inherited from his mother garnered him a great many friends—or, at least, acquaintances who enjoyed his amusing company and open-handedness.

He didn't tell her how he and the young nobles with time to spare, money to spend, and little sense of duty or direction had started thieving among the market stalls, and how this had not been enough for him. A stolen apple from a basket, a snatched cake from a white cloth: there was no *finesse* in it. Any ragged urchin could do as much.

Getting his hands on a necklace his father had bestowed on his latest mistress, however...

His mother herself, after her first tears and humiliation, had learned to at least appear to ignore the mistresses. Perhaps she was even relieved that the King's unaffectionate attentions were turned elsewhere. Charming felt the insult to her more keenly, and so took his revenge. He became quite practised at acquiring his father's gifts at one remove, and bestowed them, in turn, on any girl who took his fancy, so long as she was a very long way from his father's court where there was no chance any of those gifts might be recognised.

But he wasn't going to mention any of that.

"Then poor old Auberic goes off and gets himself killed," he said.

"Oh, what happened?"

"We don't know for sure. He decided to go off on a quest... *Not* like him. Maybe he wanted a last bit of adventure before he inherited the estate and had to be stuck running it for the rest of his life. Months go by, no Auberic. Father starts foaming at the mouth and sending people hither and yon looking for him. Eventually someone found his signet ring in the stomach of a bear they'd killed, recognised it, sent it back to Father. He hadn't even got that far from home. Poor Auberic."

"I'm so sorry."

"It hit me a lot harder than I expected. Strange, really, it's not as though we were close. He was very solemn, and studious, and serious, and I... wasn't. I might have been fonder of him if he'd had a sense of humour. Or stood up for Mother more."

Charming took a gulp of wine. "Anyway, he's gone and I end up the heir. Father wasn't exactly subtle about which son he would rather have died."

"Oh, mine hated the idea of me inheriting too," the Beast said. "I should have been a boy, you see. Or at least two boys, in fact. He made up for my disastrous lack of being a boy by shoving me at every remotely eligible man he could find."

"How ghastly," Charming said, pouring some wine into her tankard.

"He was determined to find a man to run the estate."

"I have never understood that idea. The women I've met in my, um… travels, have generally been extremely effective at whatever they wanted to do. Running kingdoms—why aren't they called *queendoms*, anyway? I mean…" He waved his glass. "If it has a queen, it should be a queendom."

"You've met queens?"

"One or two. Anyway, tell me more about your family."

"Must I?" she said.

He laughed. "Only if you want to. But having listened to me bore on about mine, you have the right to revenge."

The Beast found herself more and more drawn to him, his wit, his interest in her and her family—even his occasional evasiveness only made her want to find out more about him.

She realised, with a suddenness that made her fumble her tankard—fortunately it was almost empty—that they were simply *talking*. As though he had forgotten what she looked like. Or didn't care. He was talking to *her*, not her appearance.

His appearance, on the other hand, was affecting her far more than the wine. That hair, the breadth of his shoulders, the way he moved, a dancer's grace and a fighter's strength. *I wonder what it would feel like if he picked me up,* she thought, *as I was before. He's tall enough and strong enough, I bet he could pick me up and spin me off my feet in the dance…* That smile—oh, dear, his smile did things to her insides, the way it pulled up slightly more at one side than the other, making her want to stroke his lips with her finger.

Stop it, she told herself. *You're staring. You'll do nothing but break your own heart again. Just be… nice.*

"Eventually, though, you will inherit," she said. "What will you do then?"

"Find other people to do the work. Responsibility doesn't suit me," he said lightly. "Other people are generally *so* much better at it."

"Surely that's not a choice. If one has responsibilities, one has them, like it or not." Guilt jabbed at her. *And how well have you dealt with yours?*

"Ah, but my brother was trained to it. I was not."

"Perhaps he didn't want them either."

"Oh, he did. Thoroughly ready to step up and take the… responsibility, my brother."

"Or he just thought it was his duty."

"I don't like being in charge of people," Charming said. "Last time it didn't go so well."

"But those people often don't have a choice," the Beast said. "*Someone's* going to be in charge of them, and if they're lucky, that person will look after them. If they're unlucky… things can go so terribly badly for them." She almost choked on the words.

"I've upset you, haven't I?" Charming said, after a moment. "I don't know what I said, but I'm sorry. Again."

The Beast dashed tears from her eyes. "It's not your fault," she said.

"It does seem to be, though."

"No, it really isn't," she said, slumping in her chair, suddenly tired all the way through.

Kichka squawked.

The Beast hunched her shoulders, but didn't say anything.

"Oh, stop it," Charming said. "Can't you see the lady's tired? Leave her be."

Kichka made a very loud raspberry and cocked his head at Charming, with rather too much intelligence glittering in his eyes.

Charming got to his feet. "You look exhausted. I shall let you rest. Can I do anything? Or will the house see to your needs?"

The Beast shook her head. "I'll be fine, thank you."

"Could I ask you a favour?"

"Of course," she said, dully.

"Could I take Kichka with me? He reminds me strikingly of that old acquaintance I mentioned, and I can be rude to him without you having to suffer either of us. With any luck, I'll have worn out all my faux pas on him by the time I see you again."

The Beast managed to dredge up a ghost of a smile. "By all means," she said. "If you really want to listen to him shriek. But I warn you, he'll keep you awake."

"Oh, it will be just like old times," Charming said. He took her paw, and instead of bowing over it, held it a moment, pressed between his hands. They felt very warm. "I hope… Well, I hope you find my company less upsetting next time."

"It isn't you," she said. And that was at least partly true, but once he left, she raised the paw he had held to her face and pressed it against her cheek, hoping that perhaps a little of that warmth might still be there. But if it was, her fur would not allow her to feel it.

Stupid, she told herself. *A man like him would never have cared about you, even before. Put it out of your mind.*

KICHKA WAS AMAZINGLY quiet as he rode on Charming's shoulder back to his rooms, peering at things in the corridors and only making the occasional soft whistle or chirp. Occasionally he lifted his wings and stretched them out, ruffling Charming's hair.

Charming, too, said little, until they were back in his room. He looked at the bird, and shook his head. "I don't suppose you're actually an imp in bird form, are you?" he said.

Kichka whistled and cocked his head.

"I'm honestly not sure if that's a 'yes' or a 'no.'"

Charming slumped in the nearest chair and started tugging off his boots. "I'm trapped in a house with a beast, and talking to a bird."

Kichka bobbed up and down, fixing him with a bright gold-ringed eye.

"Although I'm not scared of her. Not anymore. As a matter of fact, I rather like her." He paused with a boot in one hand, smiling to himself. "I should like to see her smile, with her own face. I don't suppose *you* can tell me the answer to the riddle?"

Kichka screeched twice, ruffling his feathers.

Charming waited, but the bird simply snapped its beak at him. "Well, that was helpful," he said. He poured himself a glass of water then said, "Hello, House? Can I get a pair of slippers? It's obvious I'm not going anywhere, so I would like some slippers. Oh, and whatever our friend here needs for the night?"

A perch, a bowl of water, and a plate of sliced fruit shortly appeared, along with a pair of red velvet, gold-embroidered slippers lined with sheepskin. Charming eased his feet into them and groaned with pleasure. "Thank you, House. Damn, I shall miss this place."

Kichka blew another raspberry.

"Well that's nice, after I got you your supper."

The parrot, slowly and deliberately, turned his back.

"Fine, be like that," Charming said. "I'm going to go have *my* supper."

An Interlude

CHARMING FOUND HIS fellow captives in the dining room. Hans, inevitably, had a book, but was not reading it. He was tapping his spectacles against his hand, looking at the object that lay next to Will's plate. Will was alternating between chewing his thumbnail and pulling his collar away from his neck.

"Ah," Charming said. "So…"

"It's a rose," Will said, unnecessarily, eyeing the flower as though it were about to bite him.

"Yes, I can see that," Charming said. "So you've been favoured, have you?"

"I… suppose? I'm still not really sure what it means," Will said. "Did you see the menagerie? Isn't it wonderful? Hans doesn't like it, though."

"I don't like seeing things in cages," Hans said. "Any more than I like being in one myself."

"I thought you wanted to stay on?" Charming said.

"There's a difference between staying somewhere because you want to and staying somewhere because you have no choice," Hans snapped. "When I made that foolish remark I had just found the library. I was overexcited. We are as much prisoners as those poor creatures in the menagerie! And my sister will be worried. I do not want my sister to be worried. She…" He broke off. "It's not good for her," he said. "Or anyone else, frankly."

"Sounds like my lot," Will said.

"Yes," Hans said. "And who exactly *are* your lot, young Wilhelm? Because you aren't from the town, are you?"

Will looked wary. "Not… exactly," he said.

"No. And you've been just as evasive since the moment we arrived. So where, *exactly?*"

"It's just a place. In the forest. It doesn't have a name."

"And who lives there?"

"My family lives there!"

"What is this, Hans?" Charming said. "You're acting as though you suspect the boy of something."

"Not him, or not him alone. His family, as he calls them. Or would *pack* be more appropriate?"

"What have my family ever done to you?"

"Wait, what?" Charming said. "Did you say *pack?*"

"They're werewolves," Hans snapped. "And they've been bothering my sister for…"

"You're the *Bear Witch's* brother?" Will jumped to his feet. "Bothering *her?* She sent her bears to attack us!"

"Gentlemen," Charming said. "Please. Can someone explain to me…? In fact, we'll start with Will, since he'll use nice simple words I can understand. Will. Are you a werewolf?"

"No."

"Well he would say that, wouldn't he?" Hans threw up his hands.

"But I'm not! I asked to! My aunt said it wouldn't be right. Everyone else—the adults, that is—got turned by accident. She wasn't going to do it to me on purpose."

"Your *aunt* is a werewolf, but you're not?" Charming said. "I mean, how...?"

"She found me in the forest when I was little. She took me in and looked after me."

"So not officially your aunt, then. I see." Charming turned to Hans. "And what was that about bears?"

Hans stuffed his hands in his pockets and scowled. "My sister has an... influence... over the local bears. They act as her... um..."

"Familiars," Will said. "She's a witch."

"Ah," Charming said. "I see. No, actually, that's a lie and I don't see at all. A witch with *bears* for familiars? Not just one but *lots?*"

"Not *that* many," Hans said.

"I shouldn't imagine one would need *that* many," Charming said. "They're *bears.*"

"They don't *hurt* anyone," Hans said. "Not unless someone threatens her." He glared at Will.

"Well, my family don't hurt people either! It's people who hurt *them*—or tried, until my aunt stopped it."

"It was your family who started trespassing into my sister's territory," Hans retorted.

"No it wasn't—your sister sent her bears after our hives!"

"You shouldn't have built them so close to her territory! Besides, they didn't know the hives belonged to someone, they were just after honey."

"They were *wooden hives*. Made of wood and nails. They thought the *bees* built them? With, like, tiny bee hammers and stuff? Of course they knew!"

The two men were almost nose to nose now, fists clenched. "Ahem," Charming said, loudly. "Look down, gents."

The men looked down.

Charming's blade was gleaming between them.

"Now," he said. "I think we should all sit down, in chairs a good long way apart, and discuss this *calmly*. Because like it or not, we are all in this together, and you two beating each other to a pulp is not going to get any of us any closer to getting out of here. Yes?"

Hans threw up his hands, and flung himself into a chair. "*Fine.*"

Will backed gingerly away from the blade and sat rather more cautiously in another chair. "I spent *ages* on those hives," he muttered. "And the bees were properly upset."

Charming sighed, sheathed his blade, and took a chair between the two of them. "All right," he said. "Now I understand why you were both worried about what might happen in your absence. Will, what is it you fear, exactly?"

"That my family will think the townspeople or the Bear Witch did something to me, and they'll do something stupid and someone will get *hurt*. Maybe lots of people. They can mostly choose whether to change, after their first time—it's just easier, closer to a full moon—but if they're really upset it can happen anyway. And if they go after the townspeople they'll get hunted down; there's way more people in the town than there are of them. If they go after the Bear Witch... She's..."

"She's not a bad person," Hans insisted. "It's just... A lot of bad things happened to her. Well, both of us, but she got the worst of it. At first I didn't like leaving her there alone, but she said I needed to have a life among people, to get out and see the world. She says she's happy where she is. I don't know." He looked down at his hands. "I think I *wanted* to believe it." He gave Will an apologetic glance. "She needs people to be scared of her," he said. "It's the only way she feels safe."

"How long has this been going on?" Charming said. "Your two... er... clans at odds."

"About five years," Hans said.

"So not nearly long enough to establish a generational feud, at least. So one day, Hans, your sister's familiars just decided to rip up some hives, yes?"

"No! They found them, like I said." Hans spread his hands apologetically. "Look, bears are very intelligent, but honey is... something of an addiction. They might break them up first and ask questions when they've finished guzzling."

"And this never happened before?" Charming said.

"They never built hives verging on our territory before!"

"How was I to know?" Will growled, sounding rather more wolfish than usual. He obviously had strong feelings about his hives. "It's not like there's *markers*. And there'd been hives there years back, it was a good place for them. It wasn't a problem *then*."

"Interesting," Charming said. "So, Hans. You have more to do with the nearest town than Will, yes? What's the place called?"

"Felendstadt." Hans shrugged. "A little. They'll serve me in shops, but they don't talk to me much. They're scared of my sister. I don't go there unless I have to."

"But you've heard the gossip about the missing men."

"Yes. Mostly when they didn't think I was listening."

"And they started disappearing when?" Charming said.

"About five years... Oh."

"What?" Will said, looking from one to the other.

Hans rubbed his brow. "It's obvious, isn't it? Only it wasn't, until our friend here pointed it out. The men started going missing around the same time that your aunt's clan and my sister's bears started to clash."

He started counting his observations off on his fingers. "We know now that the men have been coming *here*, trapped by the house to attend on the Beast. Which suggests that whatever it was befell this place, presumably including our hostess's affliction and the start of the abductions, also occurred about then. And there were no difficulties between our families until then, which"—he looked up triumphantly—"suggests that prior to that time, it provided some sort of barrier, or at the very least *distance*, between the two."

"And now it doesn't," Charming said. "The enchantment keeping us *in* is presumably keeping everyone else *out* in the same way. So far as the clans are concerned, this place isn't even here." He shrugged. "So we are not only trapped inside this house, we may somehow be trapped outside the world altogether."

Will went as pale as his tan allowed. "Outside... the world?"

Hans took off his spectacles and polished them, frowning. "But then why the rose barrier? Our escape would hardly be worth preventing if there was nowhere to escape *to*. I think perhaps it's more a question of, shall we say, misdirection?"

Charming felt a moment of disappointment. Leaving the world entirely behind would have had its advantages.

Will put his hands over his face. "But we can't get out. I don't care, we'll make it up with your sister somehow, I just want to go *home*."

Hans sighed, put his spectacles on, and went and patted Will on the shoulder. "We will."

Supper was, as always, excellent, but the conversation was somewhat strained. Both Will and Hans were increasingly anxious and distracted. Hans frequently shifted in his chair, or got up to peer out of the windows at the sunset painting the roses.

"Bored, Hans?" Charming said. "Even you can't have finished every book in the library already."

"Forgive me," Hans said. "I'm used to travelling. Even when I stay with my sister, I walk a great deal. The grounds of this place may well be extensive, but being limited to the formal gardens is making me most dreadfully restless."

Charming tugged at the waistband of his breeches. "I fear confinement is having an effect on me, too—or at least my waistline. I really must practise my forms. If either of you would like to give me a bout…"

"Swordplay?" Hans smiled. "I am a competent amateur at best; but yes, a little practice would undoubtedly do me good."

Will shook his head. "I've never used a sword in my life. I'm as likely to stab myself in the leg as anything."

"I could teach you a few moves, if you like," Charming said. "It would give us both something to do."

"I'm horribly clumsy," Will said. "I don't want to stab *you*."

"I shall endeavour to avoid that. Let me know if you feel inclined. Hans. I had a look around and felt the same effect you mentioned. And if one can be kept prisoner so easily, why in the name of Goose did whoever it was feel the need to have those unnecessarily vicious roses as well?"

"I wish I knew," Hans said. "I suspect something prevents the place from being perceived at all from outside, otherwise we'd have heard *something* of it."

"Have you seen anything at all go in and out?"

"Oh, yes," Hans said. "Birds fly over quite regularly." He shrugged. "Nothing else so far."

"At any rate, I'll be in the gardens," Charming said.

WHEN CHARMING GOT back to his room that night, Kichka had settled on his perch and appeared to be asleep.

Charming tried to concentrate on making plans. He had always been good at wriggling out of difficult situations, even *without* the help of Roland, but he had to admit that life had been a lot easier, if slightly more pungent, with Roland in it.

But his mind kept wandering to the Beast.

Those eyes. So pretty, and so sad. Were they the same colour when she was herself? Had her smile lit them up, when she was human?

He shuffled the covers off, then back on, then got up and poured himself some water, got back into bed, and eventually managed to fall into an uneasy sleep, haunted by wolf howls and sad eyes and roses red as blood. The flowers appeared in his room, hundreds upon hundreds of them, filling every corner, and when he opened the door the entire corridor was packed with roses and he could not get out.

The Witch and the Players
(The First Part)

URLY WATCHED THE wagon being shuffled into a barn. "I think he keeps chickens in there. If there's chicken poo on everything when we get back, or they eat the stores, I shall be *peeved*. Assuming that innkeeper doesn't sell it or break it up for firewood the minute we're out of sight. *And* the horses."

"I don't think you can break horses up for firewood," Gilda said, wrapping one arm behind her neck to ease her shoulder muscles. "Too soggy."

"Ew, *Gilda,*" Mouse said, fidgeting with her jacket.

"Mouse, she's a *witch*. She's going to know those knives are there. Curly, love, I *said* you could stay with the wagon," Dance said, combing his fingers through his beard. "I still wish you would."

"You're not going to deal with a witch without me," Curly said. "Also I'm not sure I want to stay here on my own. *I'm* not the one whisking their sons away, but you wouldn't know it."

"It's the provinces," Dance said. "Sooner we're back in

a decent-sized town, the better. So how do we *find* this witch?"

"We just follow our noses," Cassia said. "My nose, that is. Oh, and there are bears. Try not to scream at the bears, it upsets them."

"What?" Mouse said. "What do you mean, there are bears? How *many* bears? Magic bears? Or just the perfectly ordinary rip-you-to-shreds sort of bears?"

"The bears won't hurt you. Unless…"

"Unless *what?*" Dance said.

"Unless we seem like a threat to the witch. Just look unthreatening." She glanced up at the troupe. "You won't have to work that hard."

"What about me?" Gilda said, hurt.

"Listen, darling, if we were dealing with your average robber or something, you'd be very scary. But this is a witch we're talking about."

"You're not making it seem like any better an idea," Dance said. "And the second it looks like anyone's in danger, we're getting out of there. No messing. You understand? And if that means leaving you behind, Cat, we're doing it."

"Fine, fine." Cassia trotted off into the wood, tail high.

"Well she *looks* like she knows what she's doing," Curly muttered.

"Of course she does," Dance said. "She's a *cat*. They always look like they know what they're doing until the moment they fall off the table, and then they pretend they meant to. And don't forget she's also one of the Good Folk. And what do we say about the Good Folk?"

The rest of the troupe sighed, but muttered, in unison: "Wholesome as an arsenic stew, straightforward as a bent corkscrew, keep one hand upon your brass and use the other to cover your…"

"Cats have *very* good hearing, you know," Cassia called back.

THE WOODS WERE lovely, dark, and deep... "What I wouldn't give to see a paved street," Mouse said, glaring at the trees as though they had personally offended her. "Shops. *People*."

"A decent tavern," Gilda said, wistfully. "Or three."

"A pie shop," Curly said. "I'd do a number of illegal things for a proper game pie, about now. Nice puffy crust..."

"Oh, stop it, you're making me hungry," Mouse said.

"After this," Dance said, "we'll head straight to Wohlhabendberg. Streets. Walls. Roofs. All the buildings you could wish for. *Audiences*."

As they moved further into the woods the troupe became more and more silent. Rain began to spit down. They drew closer together and began looking over their shoulders. Cassia seemed entirely untroubled by either the rain or the woods.

"Look, when we get out of here..." Dance began.

"*If* we get out of here," Curly said.

"Yeah," Gilda said, looking around. "This place is giving me the twitch. Reminds me of when we got ambushed outside Avarre."

"Or that theatre in Maledetta," Dance said.

"Oh, don't," said Curly, shuddering. "That place was *bad*. I've never been so glad to finish a run."

"The forest is full of go-aways," Cassia said. "She's good."

"Go-aways?"

"Charms to make you feel uncomfortable and want to leave."

"Well, they're working," Curly said. "Wait. Is that a bear? Up ahead, in the trees…"

"It's a rock, love," Dance said.

"On the other hand," Mouse said, in the careful voice of a woman trying very hard to sound calm and staring straight ahead, "there are definitely two bears pacing us. Either side. They're really quite big."

"On the other-other hand," Dance said, in an equally controlled voice, "they're not currently attacking us. Which is probably a good sign, I think? Cassia?" As an actor, he was generally good at making his voice more penetrative without it seeming louder, but under these particular circumstances he sounded as though someone had their fist wrapped around his vocal chords. "Oh, where is that blighted cat?"

CASSIA HAD SOMEHOW slipped across the path, and was now in front of one of the bears and walking towards it. The bear paused, looking at the small stripy creature in its path, and shook its head, as though confused. It looked across the troupe at its companion.

The other bear also stopped, and returned the look.

They both focussed on Cassia. Dance was aware of a strong desire to simply take his troupe and sneak off while the bears were otherwise occupied. How much of that was due to the go-away charms and how much was sheer common sense he was not certain.

"We're here to see Goldlöckchen," Cassia said. "We have information about her brother."

The Jealous Blade

CHARMING WAS IN the garden, practising his forms. He had not been able to persuade Will to join him at swordplay—the boy seemed terrified of accidentally injuring him, which, while laughable, would make for a tedious time of it. Hans was in the library, writing something, and had waved him away irritably, muttering about interruptions.

Charming hoped the exercise would calm his churning mind a little, and let him sleep without dreams. Or at least without such thoroughly unpleasant ones. And having something occupy his body might help his mind get to grips with the wretched riddle of this place. *Stay, but willingly.* Well, one would have thought Hans had that one in the bag, except that he was getting restless. If a willingness to stay was all it took, the moment he had wondered aloud about the possibility of staying on should have broken the spell.

Too simple, of course.

Charming began to go over the spells he had encountered in his chequered career, to see if any of them matched up. There had been that dungeon in Stierstadt, with the maze guarded by a monster. Normally one was supposed to fight monsters, but just occasionally they required you answer a riddle.

What had it *been?* He'd spent long enough trying to find out the answer before he went in... Had he actually solved the riddle? No. No, he hadn't—he'd managed to dig through part of the maze and get in behind the monster, get the treasure and have it away before old horny-head even realised he'd been there, no riddles required. Which, while he was quite proud of it, was hardly useful in the current circumstances.

There was the odd and unsavoury fellow he'd acquired various artefacts from over the years, who demanded payment partly in verbal form, but it was usually dirty stories and bad jokes, and you could get a good deal for a limerick if it was really filthy and made him laugh. Only if it was original, though.

Charming's brain seemed determined to throw up everything except what might be helpful. He parried and thrust faster, occasionally imagining a particular opponent just to spice things up a little. *Not* Mephistopheles—so far as he knew nothing short of an enchanted sword of the highest quality had even the slightest chance of working on a demon, and he didn't trust enchanted swords anyway. They had a bad habit of making gnomic pronouncements or, worse, yelling out challenges just as one was trying to sneak out of somewhere quietly *without* a fight.

He had worked up a reasonable sweat by the time he heard voices on the other side of the hedge.

The Beast's laugh... He knew it by now. There was something appealing about that half-bark, half-cough.

He wondered what her laugh would sound like if she transformed back to herself.

If. The thought actually made him pause. What if she was stuck like that? He stopped, and looked down at his sword. Stuck in this place, only to face an endless parade of potential—well, suitors, he supposed. There must, surely, have been *some* of them who'd have been willing to marry her just for the sake of the wonderful house and whatever treasures it contained—but if there had been, they hadn't broken the spell.

He imagined some ruffian, some lunkhead, who would declare his willingness to stay, only to then ignore the poor Beast and spend his time on every possible indulgence.

Even though it had obviously never happened, he found himself getting infuriated at the thought. Then the other voice came clearly through the hedge, a laugh in return.

Will. What had that boy said to make her laugh? His laugh, Charming decided, was a particularly irritating one. More like a dog barking than the Beast's. One of those large, bouncy, excessive dogs who assumed everybody wanted to be their friend.

Charming frowned. Had Will deliberately turned down a chance at practising swordplay, just to be alone with the Beast?

Well, it wasn't as though she'd look at him twice, was it? He wasn't sophisticated enough for her. She was probably just being nice, pretending to laugh at some foolish joke he'd made.

Hans, on the other hand… with his love of books and his education and his endless knowledge of this, that and the other…

Charming went back to his practice with renewed vigour, skewering imaginary ruffians and lunkheads with every thrust, and if occasionally he might imagine smacking Will or Hans with the flat of his sword, it was surely only because he was tired of the sight of them, and not for any other reason.

Cwo Ladies Go to Cown

AM *DYING*," Nell declared, fluttering her eyelashes to full effect, flinging herself onto the nearest chaise and posing dramatically.

Bella Lucia shook a curl out of her eye and blinked. "What...?"

"Of *boredom*. We have been kicking our heels in this inn for *ever*. If I spend any more time in the kitchen the cook is going to hand in her notice out of sheer irritation. Everyone else has something to do. The good doctor is cooking up spells and chatting up demons, Marie Blanche is off somewhere, I can't think where, but she's obviously entertaining herself quite happily, or perhaps entertaining someone else..." Nell's eyebrows were able to look remarkably salacious all by themselves.

"You think she's met someone?" Bella said.

"Bella, dear heart, have you *looked* at her recently? She's lit up like a winter fair!"

"She did seem happier. Oh, I do hope it's someone

nice." Bella's mouth drooped a little. "She deserves someone nice, after…"

"Don't we all, love," Nell said. "How's *your* tender little heart, these days?"

"I'm doing well enough, Nell, don't worry about me."

Nell gave her a shrewd look, but left it alone. Bella had perhaps been hurt most by Charming. Having been surrounded by genuine love and affection for all her short life, she had had no defences against the Prince's fake version. But she had already proved herself tougher than one might give her credit for. She probably just needed time.

Nell, on the other hand, had grown up in circumstances that inclined her to be cynical, and her encounter with Charming had done nothing to make her less so. This had stood her in good stead when she came into her inheritance, but it did leave her eyeing potential suitors with more thought to the future of her kingdom than any personal dreams she might still have hidden away.

And once this was over, back to her kingdom she must go, to see what sort of mess they'd got themselves in while she was away. Not too bad a one, probably, with Godmother keeping an eye on things, but still… There would be paperwork. And meetings. And all the tedious business of ruling. When she was a little girl she'd thought princessing mainly involved gorgeous dresses, sparkly jewellery and towering desserts covered in whipped cream—and not having to scrub *anything*.

The scrubbing part, at least, was generally true. But, perversely, nowadays she actually quite enjoyed giving things a good scrub; it helped her think. And no one beat her if she stopped.

"I wouldn't mind going out myself," Bella confessed.

"I can't stop worrying about whether we're going to find Charming in time. I've found out everything I can from the townsfolk and, well… It's getting a bit awkward."

"I noticed several young men sitting on the bench by the inn door, with their hands full of flowers and little parcels. And a chicken. What is it with this place and chickens?"

"Oh, dear, that would be Bartolt, from the mill. I've tried to explain that I'm not… That I can't…"

"They're not going to listen. Their ears are all stuffed up with desire. They're not giving you trouble, are they?" Nell said.

"Oh, no. Nothing I can't handle." Bella was a diplomat both by training and as a result of the gifts she had been given, but should diplomacy fail, she was also exceptionally skilled with a sword.

Nell, when she was being Nell and not Her Royal Highness, was more inclined to rely on her fists. Or, when necessary, a well-placed knee. Though, come to think of it, even Her Royal Highness had been forced to make use of the Royal Knee on occasion.

"It's getting tedious, though, isn't it?" Nell said. "Hah. There was a time when I'd have given anything for male attention. *And* almost did. Now, though…" She made a little flicking gesture, as though chasing away a fly.

"I know," Bella said.

Not that you've ever had to give anything for male attention, Nell thought. *Poor woman. Lack of it would probably be a relief.* "Right, then," she said. "Let's go out by the kitchens so we don't get an entourage of lovesick young men."

"But where are we going?"

"I heard there were some strolling players in town. Shall we see if we can find them?"

"Oh! Yes, let's!" Bella clapped her hands. "I do love a play."

"It probably won't be anything terribly sophisticated," Nell said. "Not out here."

"I don't care if it's a play about turnips. I just want something to do."

"WE'VE MISSED THEM? Oh, what a shame," Bella said.

"I'm so sorry, miss." The man she was talking to had the sort of battered leather bag of a face that suggests the world and everyone in it is a massive but entirely predictable disappointment. Now, however, all his disappointment was focused on the fact that he could not instantly present Bella with not just the strolling players, but the best strolling players in the land, together with velvet seating and free drinks at the interval.

Nell was watching this byplay, her eyes glimmering with resigned amusement, when a shout rang out.

"That's them, Officer! Them right there!"

She turned, mildly curious to see what little local difficulty might be taking place, only to find herself face to face with two middle-aged women and one man, quivering with self-righteousness, pointing outraged fingers in the direction of herself and Bella.

"Wh...?"

"*They're* the ones," one of the women shouted. "They've bewitched our boys, every one of 'em!"

"Um..." said Nell. "Bella?"

"What did you do with our Joest?" the man said.

Nell drew herself up to her full height. This was not in fact very tall, but she made the most of it. "Sir," she said. "I do not know anyone named Joest."

"Lies! You've taken him!"

"Nell? Is something wrong?" Bella gave their accusers the benefit of her enchanting smile. "Is there some sort of trouble?" she said. "Can we help?"

"You've done enough. Wachtmeister, arrest these women!"

The Wachtmeister turned out to be a man of middle years and expansive moustache, who was trudging by on the other side of the muddy track that passed for a road. He sighed and crossed over to them. He had the sort of stolid weariness common to law enforcement officials who might once have cared, but now just want to make it to their pension with as little trouble as possible.

"Now then, what's all this about?" he said. "Herr Rumpf?"

People who had been passing paused to watch. In a place like Felendstadt—where, until recently, a double-yoked egg was news—you either had to make your own entertainment or hope other people would provide some.

"They've bewitched our boys!" one of the outraged women said. "All day my Henrich's been outside that inn, *mooning*."

"Mooning?" Someone snorted. "Sounds like *he* should be the one under arrest."

"She means spooning."

"No, I don't! I mean *mooning*. And he wrote a *poem*."

"Literature," the Wachtmeister said, "isn't an offence." He thought a moment. "Generally, that is. Was it a poem about the Duke?"

"No! It was about one of *them*." The finger of outrage quivered in Bella's direction.

The Wachtmeister sighed. "If you ladies could tell me who you are and…"

"What's going on?" Several young men were pushing their way through the crowd.

One of them was carrying a chicken.

"Oh, no," Nell muttered.

"Bartolt!" the accusing woman shrieked. "Don't look at them! They've put you under a spell!"

Bartolt, a lanky young man, immediately went scarlet and clutched the chicken harder. The chicken squawked and flapped.

"Please," Bella said, "we don't want any trouble."

"I'm *sure* you don't," Bartolt's mother said, in dark tones.

"We were just looking for the strolling players," Bella said. "We seem to have missed them. I promise you we haven't put any spells on anyone."

"I bet those players are in on it!" said an elderly man. "*Actors.* What sort of a job is that, *pretending* stuff all day?"

"Aaah," someone said. "And going from place to place all the time. People should stay put."

Bella's normally reliable smile and tact seemed to be having very little effect, but then, charm—even charm granted by the Good Folk—has its limits. These were people whose sons and grandsons and brothers had disappeared, even if most of them had come back. They did not look at all friendly, and some of them had farming implements. *Pitchforks,* Nell thought. *Never a good sign.*

"Are they *bothering* you, miss?" said another young man, who stepped in front of Bella, facing the Wachtmeister.

Two other young men lined up beside him.

Nell decided the Royal Knee was probably not going to cut it. "Wachtmeister," she muttered, "is there somewhere we could go and talk this over with these good people?"

The Wachtmeister gave her the sort of look a certain kind of man gets when he thinks a woman is telling him how to do his job.

"Get along, the lot of you," he shouted. "Go on. Go about your business."

"Arrest them!"

"Witches!"

"He's in on it too!"

"*Don't you dare touch her!*"

"Don't you talk to your mother like that!"

The babble was spreading, drawing in more onlookers. The Wachtmeister put a hand on his sword.

A stone flew from the back of the crowd and hit the Wachtmeister's helmet with a penetrating *clonk*.

"Oh, *arse*," Nell muttered.

No one noticed the small figure who was standing on the verge of the crowd with a half-eaten sausage in one hand, who took in the scene, shook his head, and left abruptly.

(No one except the keeper of the sausage stall, who was looking bemused, and wondering why he'd just been paid enough gold for his bratwurst recipe to buy all his bratwurst, his stall, his donkey, and probably his house. "Tourists," the sausage-seller muttered to himself, and becoming slightly more aware of his surroundings, began to swiftly pack up his stall.)

The Witch and the Players
(The Second Part)

HAT'S... NOT WHAT I expected," Curly muttered, looking at the small, pretty house with its full flowerbeds. "Nice vegetable patch, too."

"Cosy," Mouse said. "Apart from the bears. No offence," she said.

One of the bears huffed at her.

"You all know better than to go by appearances," Dance said, tugging nervously at his beard. "Remember Ombreville? Pretty as a picture, that place. And the local lord was *so* friendly, and *so* generous, and housed us in his own castle..."

"I'd rather *not*," Mouse said. The others nodded fervently.

"You'd better," Dance said. "All it took was picking the wrong play and—oops! Jail, chains, and a big chap in a mask polishing his axe. We got out of there by the skin of our teeth and *only* because Mr Friendly-and-Generous was so bad his own citizens decided to riot and break open the jail, and he had other things to focus on than the troupe of idiots who'd accidentally insulted his ancestors."

"Bet they weren't even really *his* ancestors," Gilda grumbled. "Nobs always think the hero in a play is their ancestor, even when—"

"What I'm saying is, Do Not Insult the Witch," Dance said.

"We wouldn't!" Mouse said. "We're not that daft!"

"He's got a point, though," Curly said. "It's not like we meant to insult the lord of Ombreville, either."

Dance drew his hand down his face and sighed. "Look, just… let me and Cassia do the talking, all right?"

"Who are you, and what do you know about my brother?"

Curly yelped as Goldlöckchen appeared, just suddenly *there,* her feet hovering a few inches above the grass, one hand resting on the head of each bear. Her white-blonde hair drifted about her shoulders, her ice-blue eyes scanning them in a way that should have chilled the most buoyant spirit.

"*That's* the Bear Witch? She's only a baby!" Mouse said, in a whisper that was not nearly inaudible enough.

Dance winced.

All Mouse's knives, and there were a lot of them, cascaded to the ground, some landing point first in the earth. Mouse narrowly missed them when her legs collapsed under her. "Umm…"

Gilda's knees buckled, and she thumped to the ground. "Hey!"

Curly backed away. "I don't know what you're doing but please don't…" He sat down abruptly. "Ow. There's a *rock*."

Dance held up his hands, folded his long legs and sat down, keeping eye contact with the witch as he did so. "Bad knees," he said. "I'd rather do this myself than limp for a week."

Cassia cleared her throat. "Don't damage them, dear," she said. "They're useful. And harmless."

"She has a great many knives for someone harmless." But Goldlöckchen wasn't looking at Mouse; her gaze flicked between Dance and Curly, endlessly. "And why would I trust them, *or* one of the Good Folk?"

"Because we can help you get your brother back," Cassia said.

"*How do you know about my brother?*" Now Goldlöckchen's gaze focussed solely on Cassia, like a blue flame, and her fingers tightened in the bears' fur. One of the bears whined.

"I saw him," Cassia said, keeping one eye on the bear. "I was out in the woods, and I saw him wandering along the old track, and I recognised him, but I couldn't get his attention even if I yelled, and if I've ever seen anyone under a 'fluence... there he was, then there he wasn't. Because there's a big fat spell and he walked right into it."

"You just happened to wander into my brother, in the middle of these forests," Goldlöckchen said.

"It's my 'gift,' if you can call it that." Cassia flicked her tail. "It's a fairy thing. I get a lot of luck, generally. Good luck, bad luck. Often I don't know which till afterwards."

"And you can get him back? And in return?"

"I want to be my own shape again," Cassia said.

"And what do *they* want?" Goldlöckchen said.

"Nothing much," Cassia said. "Just a script or two from your brother. I was in Sperita and saw his *The Traveller's Servant*, and..."

"Wait, he's *Johannes von Behr?*" Mouse said. "Oh, I loved that play! So clever, and I'd kill to play Gera, *such* a great part..."

She subsided under Dance's glare.

"*And…*" Cassia said in pointed tones, "at the end he came on stage and everyone cheered. I was going to tell him I liked his play, but he was gone before I reached him. I tried to find him, but there are at least five different families of von Behrs in this region, none of them with a young man the right age or, so far as I could find out, anyone more creative than a brick. I thought I was out of luck until I heard a rumour that the Bear Witch of the Scatovald and her brother went by that name. Still didn't think I'd see him again, but then, there he was. And now I also just happened to really need a witch."

"*Plays?* That is all you want?"

"We'll do your brother's work justice," Dance said.

"They probably will, at that," Cassia said. "They're actually not bad, but they do desperately need some decent material."

"Not *desperately*," Curly said. "I mean, we get some laughs, right?"

"Yeah," Gilda said. "'Specially that time I put my foot in a bucket *someone* left in the wings. I mean, that's why we kept it in, bit of business like that, it's gold."

"So you're planning on spending the rest of your lives waiting for happy accidents?" Cassia said. "Or would you rather have someone who already knows which bits should be there and *puts them in?*"

"You don't have to be so brutal about it," Dance muttered.

"If you've quite finished…" Goldlöckchen said. A rumble of thunder accompanied her words and the troupe looked up apprehensively.

"Sorry," Cassia said, "but they're what I've got."

"Oy!" Gilda said, without much conviction.

Curly held up his hand.

Goldlöckchen frowned at him. "What?"

"Can I move? At least, like, sideways? Only this rock is getting very *personal*."

"And my backside is damp," Mouse said. "I wouldn't mind, it's not as bad as that place, what was it, Dumpfigburg? You remember, Gilda, the one by the river, I mean, the walls were *running*, only my only other britches are filthy, and…"

"Quiet," Goldlöckchen said.

The troupe obeyed.

Goldlöckchen looked at Cassia. "Tell me what you know about my brother. And hurry, or I'll put a mute spell on you all. For a year and a day."

"He's being held in the manor house," Cassia said.

"*What* manor house?"

"The one whose lands stand between your territory and Red Cap's."

"There *are* no lands between our territories, that's why—"

"There are, only they've disappeared, and you've all forgotten they existed for the last five years, because of the *spell*."

"If they've disappeared, where is my brother?"

"They've *disappeared*, not *gone*," Cassia said. "They're still there, it's just you can't get in, and they can't get out. But *I* can."

"And how exactly do *they* come into it?" Goldlöckchen gestured at the troupe.

"Because of what they are," Cassia said. "I need them to get in."

"Hang on," Dance said. "Let me get this right. Only young men get pulled into this spell. So won't someone notice if a bunch of us, neither all young nor all men, suddenly turn up?"

"Hello," Cassia said. "You are *actors,* yes? Or am I labouring under a basic misapprehension here?"

"Oh, I get it," Mouse said. "And who isn't young, anyway?"

"Me," Dance said. "Me and my knees are feeling older by the minute. They think about all the sudden frantic running away they'll have to do when this *inevitably* goes horribly wrong, and they feel positively *ancient.*"

"Oh, bull… bosh, you're not old," Curly said. He turned to Goldlöckchen. "He only pulls this old man act when he's grumpy."

"Yeah," Gilda said. "Or when he's trying to get us to behave. If you thought it was this bad an idea, Dance, why'd you agree to come?"

"Because I know when I'm outnumbered, that's why."

"*Stop talking!*" The thunder boomed louder.

Muttered apologies echoed through the garden.

"And how exactly will actors help you get my brother out?" Goldlöckchen said.

"It'll help with the spell."

"So," Goldlöckchen said. "I've heard that the young men who have disappeared reappear after a certain time, apparently unharmed. Why shouldn't I just wait for my brother to come back? Why risk entangling myself in the Good Folk's business?"

"Well," Cassia said, "for one, not all of them *have* turned up again. Joest Rumpf and Ludolf Winman never came back to the town, nor did Otto Muller. You can ask, if you want. As for those who did, who says they're unharmed? Have you *talked* to any of them? Some of them, their families say they're not the same. And there's a reason they're being drawn there. There's a purpose to it. Just because whoever's behind it hasn't got the person they want yet, doesn't mean it won't be your brother."

Goldlöckchen stared at Cassia with her ice-blue eyes. Cassia, in the way of cats, became uneasy under that direct gaze, and started washing her shoulder.

"All right," Goldlöckchen said. "I will take your offer. But under three conditions. Firstly, my brother returns, unchanged and unharmed. I will give you something to help with that. Secondly, *he* decides whether to give you any of his plays, and which ones. And thirdly..." She looked at them, one finger pressed against her lower lip. "You owe me one piece of information," she said. "I decide whether or not it's of use to me."

The troupe looked at each other. "What sort of information?" Dance said. "Because I could talk to you about how to stage a fight scene, but..."

"We know where the good inns are in most towns between here and Sperduto," Curly said. "Well, the ones that will let us in, anyway."

"*And* most of the worst ones, which is more useful a lot of the time," Mouse said. "I mean, a good inn is all very well but a bad one can ruin a whole tour."

"Oh, yeah. Food poisoning," Gilda said. "*And* a fight. When both your romantic leads have black eyes and have to keep rushing off stage to throw up very loudly in the wings it does take the edge off your tender love scenes."

"*Do* shut up, you lot, before you get us all muted for a year," Dance said. "Although on the other hand I can see advantages to running a troupe of mimes."

"I will think about it," Goldlöckchen said. "And decide when you come back. *With* my brother, safe and sound." And she was gone, as suddenly as she had appeared.

The bears sat and glared at them, and with a massive reverberating crack of thunder, the rain came drenching down.

THE TROUPE RETURNED to the inn, dripping and bedraggled, to find their wagon undamaged, although they did have to extract a hen who had decided one of the baskets full of stage cloth was a perfect place to brood on a clutch. "At least we got some eggs out of it," Curly said.

"And we weren't turned into anything," Gilda said. She shifted some boxes to better balance the wagon, her wet shirt plastered to her muscles.

"Except drowned rats. You know," Mouse said thoughtfully, "I forgot how young she was. I mean, she was like this powerful figure, like a warrior queen, all the time we were there, and then, as soon as we were out, I thought, wait a minute, she was barely more than a *child*. So... was that magic?"

"Partly," Cassia said. "Well, she needs people to see her as powerful. That's part of a witch's stock in trade, darling. Personally, I much prefer being underestimated."

"I wonder what happened to the ones who didn't turn up again," Dance said. "Honestly the more I think about this, the worse an idea it seems."

"Oh, you needn't worry about *that*," Cassia said. "Joest Rumpf had his eye on a girl over Devil's Head Mountain way he'd met when the fair came through. His parents didn't approve. Not that they approved of much. So he took the chance when he got out of the mansion and simply went to find her instead of going home. Ludolf Winman got lost, wandered around for a bit, and got taken up by some travelling folk. I'm sure they'll find a use for him. Otto Muller, ah, well. He ended up with Red Cap's lot. Bit unfortunate, that, but it could have been worse."

"How do you *know* all this?" Mouse said.

"And how do *we* know it's not all complete pigeon droppings?" Dance said.

"I get lucky, like I said. Also, I'm nosy and I pay attention. You never know when something you just happened to find out will turn out useful"—she grimaced—"or dangerous. As for how you know I'm not lying, well, you'll just have to trust me."

"Not reassuring." Dance looked mournfully at the sad, soggy object he had removed from his head. "This hat is ruined. Cat…"

"Cassia."

"Cassia, then. How *exactly* will we help you with the spell? Because this is sounding more and more like a con to me."

Cassia jumped up onto the driver's bench.

"You're actors. You just have to act. Act like you're *exactly* what the spell's looking for, and *believe* it."

"But we don't *know* what the spell's looking for!" Dance yanked on his beard in exasperation.

"You don't have to. Just, you know, act like you're the most golden, glorious, fabulous, desirable young men to ever strut the earth. Emphasis on *desirable*. Have your heads full of *you want me and you know it*. Yes?"

The troupe looked at each other. "Makeup," Mouse said. "And lots of it."

"Oh, not beards," Gilda said. "I *hate* beards. Only on me," she added hastily. "They *itch*."

"You get a beard, Gilda," Dance said. "As for *you want me and you know it*…"

The troupe looked at each other for a long moment, and even Dance began, reluctantly, to grin. "Like she says," Curly said, "we are *actors*..."

"Well, get your kit on then, darlings," Cassie said, "it's nearly sunset. I'll show you where the old road to the manor is."

"So we're going to fling ourself into the equivalent of a magical flytrap, just as it's getting dark. Lovely," Dance said, gloom descending once more.

"Cheer up," said Curly. "At least once we're in, we'll have a captive audience."

The Tale of the Werewolf

 ARIE BLANCHE HELD her hands out low, away from her knife-hilt, and waited patiently for the wolves to sniff at her. A pair in human form appeared through the trees, so alike they must be brother and sister, both stocky and bronze haired. They escorted her silently to Red Cap's hut.

"Well," Red Cap said, lounging in the doorway. "Did you find him?"

"No," Marie Blanche said. She held out a parcel. "I brought you some tea. It's a blend we drink at home."

"You didn't like my tea?"

"No, I... It was very good tea. I just..."

Red Cap grinned at her. "It was extremely ordinary tea. It's not the easiest thing to get around here. I'll be glad to drink something better. Come in and drink some with me."

Marie Blanche entered the hut and sat down. The green gloom, the quiet crackle of the fire and the gentle bubbling of the kettle already felt familiar.

"So," Red Cap said.

"I wondered if you'd remembered anything," Marie Blanche said. "Anything at all that might help."

Red Cap shrugged. "Sorry. I asked the clan, too. None of them knows a thing, except that five years ago things changed, and no one is quite sure why."

She got up and poured tea. Marie Blanche watched her. She had the unselfconscious grace of someone utterly at home in their body. "How—" She cut herself off.

Red Cap turned around, mugs in hand. "What?"

Marie Blanche stared at the table, feeling herself blush.

"You want to ask me about the Change? You needn't be embarrassed, it's a natural enough question."

"I wanted to ask how you ended up here," Marie Blanche said. "You're not local."

"Hmm. What gave me away?"

"The way you speak. There's an accent—not much of one, but a little. And it's silly, but it sounds *familiar* to me. Not quite that of Macqreux, where I'm from, but..."

"Ariens."

"Ariens? But that's only a few miles over the border from my home! How in the Goose's name did you end up here?"

"It's a long story. We might need more than tea."

"Oh well, in that case..." Marie Blanche pulled out her hip flask and put it on the table.

"I WAS BORN Thelise Fournier, only child of Arnaud and Verane Fournier. We were"—Red Cap gave a slightly twisted smile—"comfortable, shall we say. A little too comfortable, perhaps. Once my parents had resigned themselves to the lack of a male heir... Ah. You know that particular tune, I take it?"

"A different tune, but the same instruments," Marie Blanche said.

"They made token efforts to marry me off. I was not enthusiastic. My father was happy to leave such things to my mother while he wrote a book on the ancient civilisation of Gralia. It would have been at least thirty volumes if he ever finished it. He also left the running of the estate to Mother, and she taught me. Then, when I was eighteen, a fever took them both within weeks of each other."

"I'm sorry."

"Thank you. Fortunately for me, Mother had managed to drag Father out of ancient Gralia long enough to set up the estate so that I could inherit. Unfortunately, a distant cousin, Gustau, heard of their deaths, and came riding in six months later, all set to grab this unexpected windfall. I had no idea of his existence until he turned up with his entire entourage in tow.

"He was *not* pleased to discover that my inheritance could not be legally broken. He hired lawyers. Then more lawyers. Eventually one of them discovered a sub-clause which allowed for the estate to be transferred, if I should become incapable of managing it by means of a curse. Why the wretched thing was in there, and how my mother missed it, I will never understand.

"A few days later, a werewolf was captured on the estate. Strange, that. There was no history of their presence in the entire region. By some dreadful misfortune, that night it escaped into the house, and, even *more* unfortunately, happened to find the door of my chamber open, and—Oh, such a series of terrible, unlucky coincidences... Someone had managed to leave a piece of raw meat on my bed! Perhaps I had meant to feed the dogs and forgotten.

"Now, I did not know, at the time, a great deal about werewolves. But I did know dogs. And I had seen a dog that had got into a wisewoman's herb bed, and eaten a number of things it should not have, and had to be captured and killed. The wolf looked remarkably similar: it was wall-eyed and foaming.

"Cousin Gustau happened to still be awake, and hearing the commotion, ran to my chamber. He got there remarkably quickly, considering he was staying in a room on the other side of the house. He killed the werewolf. No doubt he acted out of pure concern for others' safety, and it had nothing at all to do with the fact that she might have had something to say when she became human again."

Red Cap—Thelise—shrugged. "So. I was locked up. Again, I'm sure, purely out of concern for everyone's safety. My mothers' lawyers managed to insist that we wait until it was certain I would transform at the full moon, before handing over my inheritance. I should explain: for us, the full moon only sparks the first change. After that, it is at will. Mainly. And as the moon fattened, I could tell that something was different, I could feel the change getting ready to take hold. And I guessed that Gustau would arrange for me to escape, and I would thus be a danger to everyone, and someone, perhaps my so-brave cousin himself, would kill another werewolf.

"I was very lucky. The head cook and her husband— she had been with us since I was a child—arranged for me to disappear. Their daughter had moved here, near the Scatovald, when she married, and they knew there were rumours of werewolves hereabouts. They thought that I would be better off with others of my kind. In their way, they were right. I found this pack, if you could call them that, and realised they desperately needed organisation and a steady hand. In the end, after a certain amount of persuasion, they realised it too. So. Now I am running another estate, of sorts. Or possibly a school, or an orphanage, or a home for wayward wolves. I'm never entirely sure."

Here is a woman who puts her hands to what is in front of them, Marie Blanche thought. "You seem remarkably… sanguine about it all."

"When I am human I am generally too busy to brood. In the Change, well, a wolf doesn't think of might-have-beens or vengeance. In its own way, it's quite cleansing."

"And your nephew?"

"Oh, Will! He's not one of us, just an abandoned child I came across. He's not been bitten. I've been trying to work out what to do with him, now he's grown. And you," she said, tipping her mug at Marie Blanche. "What was your tune?"

"My…? Oh. It's a long story."

"I have time if you do," Thelise said. "And also beer."

So Marie Blanche told her about her father, and her stepmother, and a poisoned apple, and how Charming had rescued her and promised marriage, and then…

"Wait, wait…" Thelise held up a hand. "You're the *Princess Marie Blanche of Macqreux?*"

"Ah, yes. Did I not mention that?"

"Not as such, no. I heard the dwarves call you Your Highness, but I didn't make the connection. I've heard your story, of course—or a version of it, at least."

Marie Blanche felt a little chill of disappointment at the use of her title, and the sudden change in what had been such easy conversation. Now she was a princess in a story, and no longer simply Marie Blanche. "And you," she said, "are the dread Red Cap, blood-soaked leader of a vicious gang of werewolves, no?"

"Ouch. Touché."

"We are more than the stories that are told about us," Marie Blanche said. "And less, too."

Thelise hesitated a moment, scanning Marie Blanche's face. Then she grinned. It was a wide, understanding grin, and if it had something of the wolf in it, that didn't make it any less appealing. "Beer," she said, and took out a stoppered jug and poured two foamy mugs.

She sat down again and pushed a mug towards Marie Blanche. The yeasty smell twined pleasingly with the woodsmoke and jerky and herbs. "You're sure this Charming hasn't simply bolted?" Thelise said.

"He's utterly untrustworthy, but he's also very concerned with his own skin. He knows that if he fails, the curse will find him wherever he is. I really wouldn't care, except that others will suffer—including, probably, the four of us."

Thelise shook her head. "Why does a demon *want* all that gold, anyway? Are there shops in the Infernal?"

"I really have no idea," Marie Blanche frowned. "Whatever would they sell?"

"And it seems an awfully roundabout way to go about getting gold. Surely he could just magic it up? Or rob travelling merchants like any other bandit? Or, I don't know, set up his own bank."

"He's of the Infernal. Straightforward isn't generally their way of going about things."

"Sounds like my dear cousin."

"Yes," Marie Blanche said. "But I think perhaps something can be *done* about your dear cousin, if you're willing. Unless you want to stay here?"

"What do you mean?" Thelise said.

"As you point out, I am the heir to the throne of Macqreux. Rank, as they say, has its privileges. And its lawyers. Also, should the lawyers prove inadequate, my friends have a number of skills of their own which I think I could persuade them to use on your behalf."

"If lawyers employed by *royalty* might be inadequate in comparison, how scared should I be of your friends?"

"I don't believe you are scared of anything," Marie Blanche said.

"Everyone has their weaknesses," Thelise said, looking at her over the rim of her mug.

Roland's Warning

OCTOR RAPUNZEL BECAME aware of the smell of sulphur and automatically reached for her amulet, her fingers beginning to glow.

"No need for that," said her visitor.

"Good. I have a sufficiency of problems. Did you want something, Roland? Because I'm very tired and would rather you came straight out with whatever it is."

Roland peered at her. "You are, en't you? Not found Himself yet?"

"No. But there is definitely *some* sort of powerful magic going on in this area, pulling things out of shape."

"Yeah, there is, and not just here. Any road, I just came through town, if you can call it that, and there's a little trouble."

"More disappearances?"

"Not *yet*."

"What's going on?"

"Lady Bella and Queen Nell. They kind of started a riot."

"What in the... why didn't you tell me that immediately?" The doctor leapt to her feet and began gathering things into her capacious shoulder bag.

"Just did," Roland said, jumping down. "And the only person there to stop it is the Wachtmeister. He's not the brightest, but even he's managed to work out that they're posh, so he's not eager to risk his pension by being overzealous. But he's also a coward, and he's not exactly keen on women, if you get my drift."

"Do you mean he prefers men?"

"In every way *other* than bed, yes."

"That is hardly unusual in this world, Roland. What exactly is your point?" Doctor Rapunzel asked as she hurried down the stairs.

"Thought you might need an intermediary. Get on his good side. Mano a mano—or impo, I guess."

"'Mano' doesn't mean—nevermind."

Doctor Rapunzel glanced at his face, which struggled to be anything other than unsettling at the best of times. He was trying so hard to look innocent he could only be up to something.

"I see," she said.

The Language of Birds

ARIE BLANCHE LOOKED down at her hands, because she was spending too much time staring at Thelise. She was not sure if the beer on top of brandy had been a little too much. Years of celebrating trade deals with a clan of dwarves who made the best stone brandy in Macqreux had toughened her constitution, but she was definitely feeling a little light-headed. A little light-everythinged, in fact. As though the blood running in her veins had been replaced with some bright and airy fluid.

A moment of silence had fallen between them, both companionable and tense, building with possibilities that she was not yet ready to look at too closely.

Into it fell a sudden gabble of sparrow-speech right outside the window of the hut, so loud and odd she blinked.

…loud big bird… bigger than a raven… over to sunrise way, near the big oak where the bats live…

…a stranger from far, far away…

...so loud, *it doesn't even sing, it just* shouts...

...such bright plumage!...

"What is it?" Thelise was on her feet, her eyes going to the window.

"I'm really not sure," Marie Blanche said, and got up herself, half-reluctant, half-relieved. "But I should check. The sparrows are terrible little gossips, but there is occasionally something useful in all their chatter."

"You speak the language of birds?" Thelise said, her eyebrows shooting up. "You're full of surprises, Princess."

"Oh, not all—although as many as I've been able to. The language of sparrows is one of the easier to learn, because they talk so much—walk past a hedgerow of an evening and there's a free lesson, once you've made a start. But *they're* talking about an unfamiliar bird. Large and bright-coloured."

Thelise followed her out of the door.

"They said a big oak where bats roost, east of here," Marie Blanche said. "Would you know...?"

"Oh, yes. I know. Bats have a very distinct smell. One thing one tends to keep, outside of the Change, is a heightened sense of smell." She set off at an easy trot, and Marie Blanche followed her.

They did not have to go very far before they heard a piercing shriek.

"Is that...?" Thelise said.

"I don't know. It's calling for... a doctor? Maybe someone is hurt?" The voice was extremely loud and sounded more excited than in pain.

"There is a word in the language of bird for 'doctor'?"

"There are words for most human concepts. *They* listen to *us*, after all."

Marie Blanche looked up.

Above her the most brilliantly coloured bird she had ever seen was bobbing up and down and spreading its wings. It warbled and shrieked again.

"I'm not a doctor, no," Marie Blanche said. "But I know a Doctor of the Arcane. Will she do?"

Shiny fingers! He says she's scary!

Marie Blanche snorted quietly. "Yes, that's the one. If you'll come with me, I'll take you to her."

The bird flew down and landed on her shoulder.

My name's Kichka. Thorn thorn stabby thorn. Pretty boy let me out.

"Oh, did he, indeed," Marie Blanche said. She glanced apologetically at Thelise. "I must go."

"It sounds as though you have your clue," Thelise said.

"Yes." Marie Blanche stood there, feeling slightly absurd with this large, impossible bird sitting on her shoulder, and more than slightly awkward.

"I'll lead you back to the path."

"I know the way from here. You could come back with me," Marie Blanche said, so abruptly she felt as though she had just put her foot in a hole. "We could talk about dealing with your cousin."

"I think you and your friends have other things to deal with right now," Thelise said. "But let me know if I can help with retrieving your prince."

"Thank you," Marie Blanche said. "And... well. Thank you."

Thelise grinned, and was gone, a shadow among the trees.

A Poor Boy Comes to Dinner

HIS COSTUME IS *the worst yet,* Will thought gloomily, as he allowed himself to be dressed. The collar was so high he felt it dig into his neck whenever he turned his head. The sleeves and breeches were enormously puffed, the shoulders of the outer coat padded so he looked even more broad-shouldered than he actually was. At least the shoes weren't pointed this time. A reluctant glance at the mirror showed him a figure he thought, personally, was ridiculous. He would swear he was wearing enough cloth to dress his entire clan.

He did rather like the necklace: heavy gold links interspersed with engraved plaques, set with gleaming green stones. In the middle was a great pendant set with a larger green stone surrounded by pearls. He stroked it gently, imagining it on Hedel's strong tanned neck. How her eyes would widen if he gave her such a thing! She'd probably laugh at him, having nothing to wear it with but her usual shirt and breeches—or her fur. It would look splendid either way, he thought.

He knew why Aunt Thelise didn't want him to get close to Hedel. But if *he* didn't care that she was sometimes a wolf, why should anyone else?

His musings were interrupted by the door opening, and the candle jiggling up and down. "Oh, all right," he said.

He seemed to walk the length of his clan's whole settlement before he got to another set of double doors. Did the house actually *grow* when they weren't looking?

The doors swung open, and Will found himself faced with a vast table. Empty chairs lined either side, but the table itself was anything but empty. The light of dozens of candles splashed back from candlesticks of gleaming brass, and glowed on platters piled with different breads, some round, some twisted into knots, some sprinkled with seeds. Other platters were heaped with apples and pears and cherries, which at least he recognised, but also with little brown wrinkled things and small smooth pale green things and shiny pink things. Were they fruit? Was he supposed to eat them? Or were they just to be looked at?

He had never in his life seen so much food in one place. Or so many glasses and knives and small spoons and huge spoons and some strange little flat metal things with thin poky bits, like miniature pitchforks, and what looked like hundreds of glasses and jugs. In all that gleam and richness it took him a moment to even notice the Beast, seated at the far end. "Oh! Good evening!" He remembered that he was supposed to bow, and did so. The necklace swung forward and clanged loudly against one of the jugs. Will winced.

"Good evening," she called back.

Will glanced around at the table, wondering if anyone else was to join them. He half-hoped they would, then there would be someone else to make conversation with the Beast while he tried to negotiate all this fanciness. On the other hand, anyone who did join them would probably know what all this stuff was and make him look even more of a fool. He hoped he wasn't expected to eat his way through all these mountains of food; the mere thought made his appetite curl up in a corner of his stomach and refuse to talk to him.

With so much cutlery and glassware on the table he was not entirely sure where he was supposed to sit, until the chair in front of him drew back with a horrible scraping sound. He eyed it uncertainly, then cautiously perched himself on it. It moved back. Now he could barely see the Beast at all; several candlesticks and a silver tureen large enough to be a bath for a healthy six-month-old child were in the way.

A jug filled one of the glasses by his plate with a pale yellow liquid.

The glass was even worse than the ones in the library; it looked as thin as a bubble. He saw that the Beast had her usual tankard, and wished he could have one too.

Before him was a bowl, sitting on a plate, sitting on yet another plate. All of them were decorated with colourful, stylised representations of birds and beasts, trapped beneath the shining glaze. Surely they would chip if he so much as *breathed* near them, never mind did something so crude as *use* them.

A napkin flicked itself out of a napkin ring and settled itself on his lap; linen so fine it was translucent, embroidered with a crest showing a wolf and a bear either side of a post, and some words he could not read.

The tureen floated towards him, and he ducked.

"It's soup," the Beast called.

"Oh, right."

A vast ladle tipped a green liquid into the dish that appeared in front of him. It smelled of leeks, and who-knew-what other things. It was a pleasant enough scent, but Will looked at it with trepidation.

He picked up the spoon, then put it down again. A basket piled with breads hovered by his elbow; he took one of the seeded rolls, his hand shaking so that he knocked two more onto the floor. "I'm sorry," he said.

"What was that?" the Beast said.

"Nothing, sorry," Will shouted, then cringed as his voice echoed in the huge room.

The soup steamed before him, a swamp of social inadequacy waiting for him to fall in.

"Do start, please," she called.

Will picked up his spoon. It looked tiny in his hand, but clinked loudly against the bowl. He managed to scoop up a tiny amount of soup, leaning far forward, afraid of spilling it on the fine clothes.

How did one eat soup without making a noise? Every clink and slurp seemed to echo from the ceiling. He couldn't hear the Beast at all. Perhaps there were special lessons rich folk took that allowed them to eat in silence. Or perhaps she had left already. He glanced up, suddenly absurdly afraid that he had been left alone in this room full of terrifyingly breakable things, but she was still there. If he strained his ears, he could hear the very faintest clinking as she dipped her spoon in the bowl, but even though she had a muzzle, she seemed to manage not to slurp.

"How is the soup?" she asked.

"Very good, thank you," said Will, though he had put the spoon down after a bare three mouthfuls, too scared of spilling it everywhere, and had no idea how it had actually tasted.

He saw her bowl float away and felt a sense of relief, knowing his would be next—perhaps the next course would be something less dangerous.

He waited for his bowl to float up off the table, like hers. There was a long moment while he gazed vaguely into midair, trying to look pleasant.

Then there was a clinking noise. He looked down.

His necklace was being lifted out of the soup. He must have leaned too far forward, and hadn't even noticed. "Oh, no..." He dabbed frantically at the dripping pendant with his napkin.

"Is everything all right?" the Beast said.

"I... The chain... The soup... Um." He peered at the pendant. Nothing too dreadful seemed to have happened to it, but he took it off and laid it beside his plate, just in case.

She probably hadn't seen what happened. Should he confess? What if he didn't and the house picked up the necklace and presented it to her in all its soupy horror?

He dropped his napkin over it. An accusatory stain seeped through the fine linen.

The next course seemed to have started out as eggs. At least, the outsides were recognisably egg, but the insides bore no resemblance to yolks as he knew them. They were full of fluffy brown stuff.

The flavours were odd, and if he hadn't been concentrating so hard on not letting the middle bit fall out before he could get it into his mouth, he probably wouldn't have liked them very much.

Next came something about the size of his fist, which might have been a very small chicken or a very large blackbird. He stared at it despairingly. At home you ate what you could get, because there wasn't usually much of it, but he'd never been fond of eating something that seemed to give you thirty bones for every mouthful of meat. He picked it up and a napkin flicked the back of his hand. He yelped, and dropped the bird. The napkin tapped meaningfully at the thin pokey thing.

"You can use your fork," the Beast said.

"Excuse me?" To Will a fork was a great long thing you held stuff over the fire with.

"You use it like this."

He peered through the candlesticks at the Beast. She cut a small piece off the bird, then stuck it with one of the thin pokey things, and lifted it up. She waved it at him encouragingly.

Will looked at the fork warily. The handle was engraved with the same picture that was embroidered on the napkin. The pokey bits looked very sharp for something you were supposed to *put in your mouth*. What if he stabbed himself in the tongue?

In desperation he grabbed for the wineglass, wishing it were proper beer, in a proper tankard, and took a large swallow.

It was unexpectedly and shockingly dry. He felt as though his mouth were reversing in on itself and was going to emerge out of the back of his neck. When he got his breath back, he put the glass down hastily.

He wasn't looking. The glass missed the tabletop almost completely, but hit the edge on the way down.

Spink.

Splash.

Tinkle.

Will stared at the stem in his hand. One vicious shard

poked up from the end, as though inviting him to put himself out of his misery.

"I'm awfully sorry," he said.

"I'm sorry?"

"No, I mean, I broke your glass."

"Oh, dear. Well, never mind." She waved a hand and another glass floated into view, just as fragile as the first.

Will looked at it, and at the array of food still before him, like a man contemplating the scaffold. He thought of home—the firelight in the hall, the jugs of beer, the laughter, the twins trying to outboast each other, Hedel rolling her eyes at their nonsense—and all the silence and splendour seemed to crush in on him.

"I'm sorry," he said again, and scrambled up from his chair, knocking it over in his haste. "I can't, I... I'm sorry." He rushed from the room, cheeks burning.

The Scholar at the Feast

ANS RAISED HIS eyebrows and pushed his spectacles up on his nose when he entered the great dining room, but gave no other sign of his mood or opinion. He bowed over the Beast's hand as politely as ever. *As though I were a distant elderly relative,* she thought. *Someone he doesn't want to offend, but doesn't have the slightest reason to like.*

He took his seat at the other end of the table and raised his glass to her, paused, and turned it in the candlelight. "Crosera glass," he said. "Quite lovely." He pitched his voice to be heard—he was obviously used to dining in spaces like this.

"I'm glad you like it," she said. "My..." She bit down on the remark. Crosera glass had been another of the things her father had discovered in his travels. "Have you been to Crosera?"

"I was stranded there once, during a storm," he said. His voice took on something of a storyteller's pitch; perhaps it was simply the need to project. Unlike poor

Will, who had either muttered or shouted. She actually *liked* Will, but he was entirely hopeless. And from the way his face lit up when he talked about her, he was almost certainly in love with that girl he'd mentioned—Helle or Hegel or whatever her name was.

"That sounds exciting," she said.

"It was rather more exciting than I cared for," Hans said. "I was horribly seasick." He chuckled. "But the city is wonderful. Built on the sea, a marvellous feat of engineering."

The Beast contented herself with leaning back and listening to him talk, at first. He was certainly pleasant enough to look at—that hair was almost the colour of the winter-pale wine, and unlike some of the studious men she had encountered, he had a traveller's tan. The contrast was striking. Pallor might be the fashion among the nobility, but it had never been particularly to her taste. Too like herself—when she *was* herself. Red hair and pale skin that speckled like a song thrush at the first glimpse of sunshine. Even his spectacles gave his face interest.

He ate with casual ease. She got the impression he would be as much at home at a harvest feast as he was here, so long as he found something to interest him—a rare breed of turnip, perhaps, or a farmer's child with an interest in literature.

She could provide him with enough to interest him, certainly. The estate, the library… and there was enough money that he could travel as he wished, without having to support himself.

She realised, with a sinking heart, that she wouldn't mind terribly if he did want to travel. For months.

But it didn't *matter*. What *she* felt didn't matter at all. And she wasn't making enough effort.

"Did you watch them make the glass?" she said. "I understand it's a fascinating process…"

And off he went, talking about cristallo and silica and lattimo and flux, waving his glass or a leg of chicken in the air, and occasionally pausing, as a polite guest must, to apologise and ask her a question and then go off again about some other subject.

I can bear this, she thought. *I can bear this if I must.* And she smiled and lifted her glass and nodded in an interested way and laughed in what seemed the appropriate places.

And at the end of the evening, where he had spoken cheerfully and with enthusiasm and had even got slightly—though only very slightly—drunk, he seemed to have warmed a little, and bent over her hand with slightly less formality than he had at the start, and she bid him goodnight and went outside and paced the garden under the fattening moon, tearing rose petals from the bushes and crushing them between her paws.

An Interlude

O H COME ON," Charming said, clutching at his hair. "I said no yellow. And as for *that*…"

The latest collection of clothes was a festival of saffron velvet slashed to show plum satin beneath. The doublet had a flat front but massively puffed sleeves. The breeches were short and wide and striped, and once on would give the impression that the wearer had shoved their legs into a pair of giant humbugs. And in the middle of the breeches was an… object. It was large, and padded, and positively jaunty.

"No," Charming said firmly. "Absolutely *not*. Apart from any other consideration, I have no need to be boastful in that area. Take it *away*. Something *simple*, do you understand? Simple and elegant and without the… ah… groinal exaggeration. Simple elegance will show off that very splendid necklace to much better effect. Also, I'll be able to walk without feeling as though I'm shouting, 'wahey!' with every step."

The clothes did not move. Charming folded his arms

and stared into midair, trying to maintain his composure while feeling more than slightly ridiculous and imagining what Roland would make of that... object.

Eventually, the house gave in. The clothes were whisked away and replaced with a costume of deep blue satin with black velvet trim, and black hose. The breeches were a sensible width and had no unnecessary additions. Even the shoes, though square-toed and adorned with large, heavy buckles, looked comfortable.

Charming nodded. "Thank you. That's much better."

He put the outfit on, and picked up the necklace; a really lovely chain of heavy gold links and enamelled pendants showing scenes of dancing couples. He paused, as always, to look over the chain with an eye to its value. What Roland would no doubt have called 'a lovely piece of flash.' For all the imp's many, *many* faults he had a good eye for jewellery.

Something about the dancing couples caught his eye, and he lifted it to look more closely. He realised that each of the enamelled plates showed a different step of the dance. The tiny dancers appeared to be concentrating fiercely rather than enjoying themselves, desperate not to make a mistake, as though their very lives depended on it.

He frowned, discomfited, and dropped the necklace over his head.

Last was a soft, wide-brimmed black velvet hat with blue satin trim, decorated with ostrich feathers dyed blue to match. He nodded at himself in the mirror, took a deep breath, and followed the patiently waiting candlestick.

The Three Ladies and
the Wachtmeister

BELLA LUCIA DREW a deep breath and shoved a stray curl back inside her snood. The Wachtmeister was bellowing orders no one was listening to and waving his arms, one of which had a sword at the end of it. Someone was going to get hurt very soon. Several young men were now lining up between her and the older townsfolk. Nell was backed against the wall, her eyes wide, and though Bella knew Nell was extremely tough, she was only one small person and was actually looking scared for the first time since Bella had met her.

The trouble with being given fairy gifts that make you very good at a lot of things is you don't always know if you are *actually* good at anything. Bella had the gift of poise—but she had still trained in dancing and swordplay almost every day since she was seven years old, because what the Good Folk give, the Good Folk can whisk away on a whim. She had the gift of wit, but she worked extremely hard to understand people, because as the heir to the city-state of Caraggia she could not afford for fairy-given wit to be her only means of dealing with them.

She had the gift of beauty, and people generally liked her. But was that because she was beautiful? Or was that the gift of grace? Was there any of Bella there at all?

She took a deep breath. Fairy gifts or no, she was the daughter of the Duke and Duchess dei' Sogni, and if she couldn't deal with this, she had no right to be in charge of a state that held the financial security of half the world in its hands.

"Bartolt," Bella said, pitching her voice to be heard, "would you be so good as to introduce me to your mother?"

"Uh… yes?" Confusion swirled over Bartolt's features. "Mum? This is…" He looked back at Bella in desperation.

"Bella Lucia dei' Sogni," Bella said, and curtsied.

Bartolt's mother started to curtsey in return, stopped herself partway down, and straightened up. "I don't know what you think you're doing!" she said.

"You must have been worried about your son," Bella said. "Bartolt, I hope you understand your mother is only concerned for you."

"I can look after myself," Bartolt said.

"I'm sure you can, but it's still natural for your mother to worry about you. My own parents worry about me all the time." She smiled, while becoming aware that some of the other young men were now looking at Bartolt with expressions ranging from envy to pity to outright rage. The chicken clutched under Bartolt's arm glared beadily at everyone.

"That is a very fine chicken," Bella said. "Does it have a name?"

Its owner blushed furiously and looked down, shaking his head.

"That's one of my best layers, is that!" Bartolt's mother said. "What were you going to do with her, Bartolt?"

Bartolt muttered something and hunched his shoulders.

"Was it for me?" Bella Lucia said. "Well, that's very generous, Bartolt, but I think you should give her back to your mother, don't you? I'm travelling and I can't really look after a chicken just at the moment." She exchanged a glance with Bartolt's mother that was both sympathetic and faintly amused.

Nell watched appreciatively and somewhat amazed as Bella, not yet thirty years old, by some extraordinary alchemy of voice and words and posture became a motherly figure. All around her young men who a minute ago had been lovestruck and furiously protective were now in various stages of shuffling adolescent embarrassment, and their previously furiously protective parents were eyeing their offspring with exasperation, and Bella with something verging on sympathy.

Nell was standing near the Wachtmeister, and saw his mouth open. Strongly suspecting that he was about to throw a very large spanner into these delicate works, she flung a hand to her brow, said "Oh!" loudly enough to make him look, and performed a dramatic and—if she said so herself—elegant swoon at such an angle that he either had to catch her or let her fall in the mud.

She forgot he was still holding his sword. So did he.

There was a loud ripping sound. Nell shrieked.

"Nell!" Bella rushed to her side. "Are you all right?"

"Yes, I think so," Nell said, looking at the blade poking through her cloak.

"Are you hurt?"

"No… My cloak isn't going to be the same, though."

"I didn't… I thought…" the Wachtmeister stammered.

"Oh, the poor lady," one of the townswomen said. "Herr Wachtmeister! What were you *doing?* You almost stabbed her!"

"Please, I'm quite all right," Nell said, wavering to her feet and clinging heavily to the Wachtmeister's arm.

"I… ah… Let's… um… get you a…" The Wachtmeister looked around frantically.

A stool, a mug of water, a flask of something very alcoholic, and a pie of uncertain origins were all thrust at Nell. She accepted the water, and had just given back the mug when Doctor Rapunzel's voice cut through the crowd. "Nell! Bella! What *is* going on? Are you…?"

"*Doctor* Rapunzel," Bella said hastily. "I know you have been working very hard to find out where these young men have been disappearing to. Have you found out anything? Many of their parents are here and *extremely anxious* for their safety."

"Ah," Rapunzel said, taking in the scene. "Yes. I hope I may have found out some information that will lead us to the perpetrators of these crimes. You are the Wachtmeister of this place, yes?"

"Yes?" he said. "I mean, yes. Yes, I am. I am responsible for the safety of this district, and—"

"Of course, the very person I needed." She laid her fingers gently on his sleeve. "May we speak in private, Wachtmeister? I have information I cannot entrust to any lesser authority."

Nell spotted the figure peering out from behind the doctor and said, "*Roland?*"

"'Ello, ladies," Roland said.

* * *

"WHAT EXACTLY DID you *say* to him?" Bella asked Doctor Rapunzel as they made their way back to the inn.

"I told him that I had come across information that recruiters for the Lantambahte are working the area, but that they had, in an excess of eagerness, decided that instead of simply getting potential recruits drunk, they would dose them with laudanum."

"Enough for them to get lost for *weeks?*" Bella said.

"That seems expensive. And inefficient," Nell said.

"And the Lantambahte have generally no need to get potential recruits drunk in any case," Rapunzel said. "It was the best I could come up with on short notice, but makes no sense whatsoever given even the slightest thought."

"You've met the Wachtmeister," Nell said, rolling her eyes. "I don't think that'll be a problem. And even if any Lantambahte do happen to turn up in the vicinity, he's hardly going to risk asking them potentially awkward questions."

Since the Lantambahte were highly trained, highly regarded mercenaries eagerly employed by various extremely powerful people, she was probably right.

Roland, his attempt at rescue having been pre-empted, was in a sulk.

"So, Roland," Bella said. "How lovely to see you again! Are you well?"

Her obvious sincerity threw him for something of a loop. He was used to being greeted with disgust at worst and wary exasperation at best.

"Yeah, I'm all right," he said. "You've not been having much luck finding Himself, then."

"No." Bella frowned. "And the deadline…"

"Cutting it finer than a butcher's ham, en't you?"

"Not by any means willingly," Rapunzel said tartly. "I hope Marie Blanche—"

At that moment a large, loud bird exploded from the inn's upper window, shrieking.

"What in the name of *Goose*…?" Roland yelped.

Rapunzel's hands came up in a defensive gesture, and the ends of her fingers began to glow.

"Don't hurt him!" Marie Blanche yelled from the window, waving her hands. "That's Kichka. He's looking for Rapunzel. He knows where Charming is!"

The bird flew around Rapunzel's head, crying and hooting.

"The bird asked after me?" the sorceress asked. "How?"

"He, uh…" Marie Blanche cleared her throat. "He's looking for the 'scary doctor shinyfingers.'"

Nell, possibly a little overloaded by recent events, gave a strangled hiccup and dissolved into laughter. "Scary doctor shinyfingers! Scary doc—"

"Yes, most amusing," Doctor Rapunzel said.

Nell got herself under control, and wiped her eyes. "I may have to learn embroidery just so I can make you a sampler!"

"Please don't put yourself to the trouble on my account," Rapunzel said. "Shall we get inside before we attract any more unnecessary attention?"

Several faces were, indeed, peering down from the windows of the inn, and two stableboys had paused in their never-ending work to gawp.

Bella, meanwhile, was staring at Kichka. "You are *so* beautiful!" she said. "And what a clever bird!"

Kichka landed on her shoulder, took one of her curls in his beak and tugged gently, then pressed his cheek to her face.

They proceeded into the inn, Kichka perched on Bella's shoulder while she continued to tell him how special and beautiful he was. Roland slouched along behind, glaring at Kichka.

The two stableboys looked at each other. "Gentry," one said.

The other grunted in agreement, and went back to shovelling manure.

A Prince Goes to Dine

HARMING ENTERED THE dining room to see the Beast standing by the window. She was even more extravagantly dressed than usual, and positively rattled with jewellery. She turned around when he entered. Her head was lowered and her ears flat to her skull, and she would not look directly at him.

"Good evening," he said, gently. "Are you well?" *Oh, dear, I've never felt quite so in danger of being bitten by a dinner companion.*

Well there was that lady in Vallefascino, but... He shoved the memory of that lively and somewhat bruising evening hastily to the back of his brain.

"Yes, thank you," she said. "And you? I hope you've had a pleasant day?"

"I have, as always, been looked after extremely well." *Apart from overhearing you and Will giggling at each other, that is.* He drew out her chair for her, then looked down the vast gleaming length of the table at his own place setting at the far end. "Oh, I don't think so," he said. "I'd like to be able to actually *talk* to my dinner companion, not shout like a town crier. House, would you be so kind as to move my place next to hers?"

"Oh, no!" the Beast yelped.

"No? I'm sorry, was that rude of me?"

"No, no, it's just… No. Never mind." The Beast made an effort to smile.

The place setting was duly moved. Charming poured wine into her tankard, and set himself to be pleasant.

Stuffed eggs were followed by chickens with saffron. Charming found himself yet again thinking of Roland and how much he would have enjoyed this meal, even if he'd been sitting below the salt, snarkily commenting on everything and disconcerting his dinner companions.

But he realised that the Beast, while she had allowed herself to be served, had not eaten a mouthful. Nor had she eaten when they met in the menagerie. And whenever she drank, she turned aside. "Is something wrong?" he asked. "Do you not like the food? Surely the house knows your tastes by now!"

"No, no, I'm… not very hungry." She looked away.

Charming watched her for a moment. Then he put down his cutlery and picked up a leg of chicken with his fingers. "This is so good," he said, "I am going to revert to more traditional methods." He bit into the chicken, dribbling a little sauce onto the table, and ate the rest of it with gusto, while she watched him wide-eyed.

"Forgive me," he said, wiping his mouth. "My hunger overcame me. But then again, I have dined with people who are far messier eaters than either of us could possibly be."

The Beast dropped her gaze to her plate. "I… oh." She glanced sideways at him. "Really?"

"Really. I have shared boar stew with a literal Imp of the Infernal. An... *enthusiastic* eater. I believe they had to wash the walls."

She huffed amusement. "I don't believe you."

"Regarding what I ate, and with whom, the story is entirely true, I assure you. And if they didn't wash the walls afterwards, they certainly should have." He held out a plate of little medlar tartlets. "Do eat with me. These smell so good, and I hate to dine alone."

She took one of the tartlets. It looked barely bigger than a coin in her paw. And though she still turned her head aside when she put food in her mouth, at least she was eating.

Enter, Stage Left

O ALL APPEARANCES, four handsome and self-confident men lounged fabulously in the wagon. Even that seemed to have gained a certain plumptious gloss. Cassia—who was a cat, and therefore already over-blessed with self-assurance—jumped down from her perch and trotted towards a thickly tangled patch of brambles.

The sun was already setting, and the trees cast long shadows.

"Ready?" Cassia said.

"Are you *sure* this is it?" Dance tugged his beard. "The wagon won't make it through that."

"Trust me, not your eyes, dear. Now hush, please."

Cassia sat down and lifted her chin, and the air in front of her took on a shimmer, like a heat haze but tinged with pink and slightly sparkly.

"Coo," said Not-Mouse, looking up from sharpening one of 'his' knives.

"Pretty," said Not-Gilda, watching the pink light play

over 'his' muscular arms.

Dance pressed his lips together, but continued to radiate *I'm too sexy for any possible item of clothing* with every grain of his being.

The haze split down the middle. An opening appeared, through which they could clearly see a carriageway. The opening parted with painful slowness. The evening light on the other side did not quite match the light that surrounded them. "Soon… as it's big enough…" Cassia grunted, "*move*. Can't… hold it long."

"I'm *exactly* what this place needs and—This is *such* a terrible idea," Dance said.

"Oh don't be a stick in the mud, love," Mouse said. "We've played worse venues, and they didn't deserve us."

"*Go!*" Cassia yowled.

Curly clicked to the horses. The wagon rumbled through the opening. Gilda reached out to touch the pink shimmer and Dance grabbed the reaching arm. "Like those fingers, do you?" he said. "Want to keep them?"

"But it's so *shiny*."

"So's blood."

The opening snapped shut behind them. Cassia wobbled slightly as she got to her feet, and took two tries to jump into the wagon.

"Are you all right?" Mouse said.

"Fine. Let's get a move on," she said. "Look, there's the house, at the end of the carriageway. See?"

"Er…" Curly said.

"What?"

"Nothing, nothing."

"Yes, something, you're looking at… My tail! My tail's bald!"

"It's only the last bit," Curly said. "Less than an inch. I'm sure it will grow back."

Cassia curled herself into a loaf with her abused tail tucked out of sight under her paws, and the wagon trundled forward. Gilda stared at her fingers, caught Dance smirking and shoved her hands in her pockets.

An Exchange of Confessions

HARMING TURNED HIS glass around in his fingers. His signet ring caught the light, and the Beast watched the movement of his hands, half-hypnotised. His voice was low and caught a little in his throat. "I have a confession to make," he said. "Well, to be honest, I probably should make rather a lot of them, but that would be tedious conversation for the dinner table."

Oh, dear, the Beast thought.

"I'm afraid Kichka escaped," Charming said. "I opened the window. I didn't think."

"I hope he has the sense to come back, at least before it gets too cold. From what Hans said, he may not survive the winter."

"Ah. I really am sorry, I didn't... Well, perhaps he will turn up; he seems an exceptionally intelligent bird. Disconcertingly so." He glanced at her. "And... Well. I mentioned my manservant, Roland? He was rude, and smelly, and food-obsessed, and, rather like Kichka, disconcertingly clever. And I... The thing is, he couldn't

224

really help being smelly, because he was an imp. It's the sulphur. Gets ingrained. And he'd just been released from servitude, after years. Decades, actually. To a truly awful person. And I bound him to my service. Magically. I happened to find out his true name. Eventually he got free of me, but it wasn't my doing.

"So…" He looked at her again, and sighed. "I was thinking about what you said, last time we spoke. About responsibility to those in your power. I didn't want to upset you again. I do seem to be very good at doing that, but just so you know, I'm probably worse than you. Whatever it is you did, that made you unhappy to think of, it probably wasn't as bad."

The Beast sat in silence for a while, staring at her own tankard. Then she downed what remained in one go. "I didn't do it on purpose," she said. "It happened when"—she waved a paw at herself—"*this* happened. And this *was* my fault. But they got caught up in it. Every single member of the household who was on the estate when the curse came down. Rendered invisible and silent, and unable to leave. Because of me."

Charming sat back, his face rigid with shock. "They… oh, *Goose*. They're still here!" He groaned aloud. "I'm an idiot. They've been serving us and choosing our clothes all this time." He reached out and took her paw. "I'm so sorry. For you. And them. I'm sorry," he said to the air. "I'm really sorry."

"It was my fault," the Beast said, drawing her paw away. "I brought down the curse on us all."

"No," Charming said sharply. "It absolutely was not. It was the fault of whoever cursed you. What did you do, anyway, that was so terrible? Walk in a fairy ring? Speak the wrong name aloud?"

"I turned down a proposal," the Beast said.

"Oh, really? A wizard?"

"No, just a baron. But his mother was of the Good Folk. She was furious, and did... this." She made a flat, ugly sound that might have been a laugh. "He wasn't bothered, himself. He only proposed because she told him to. I saw the relief on his face when I turned him down. I didn't even know he had fey blood."

"And this was what she chose to do: punish you and all those you care for? Seems I got off lightly," he said. "One of them tried to force *me* to marry. Put a love spell on me. They appear to have an obsession with trying to marry us off."

"You escaped that, though."

"Not by my own efforts, again. Her protégée didn't want to marry me if it wasn't true love."

The Beast jolted in her seat. Had he noticed?

"I'm sorry, are you all right?" He was looking at her intently.

Words jammed in the Beast's throat. *I can't tell you! I can't tell you!*

"Water?"

She nodded. Charming poured water into her tankard. The Beast drank.

"Anyway, she was a smart woman," Charming said. "Apart from falling for me in the first place, obviously. And I found out later that one of her companions offered the fairy in question something she thought might be more useful than a forced marriage. So we got away with it."

"I've nothing I can think of to offer," the Beast said.

"Oh, I disagree," Charming said, smiling that smile that melted her bones. "But I am getting frightfully tired of us all being pushed about at their whims. Try not to be so sad. You couldn't know, any more than Bella... Well, you couldn't know."

Bella? The one he didn't love enough to want to marry? Or someone else, someone he did love?

Stop it, she told herself—again. It worked about as well as it had every other time.

"Let's talk of more pleasant things," Charming said. "What will you do, when the curse is broken?"

"If."

"Oh, never mind *if. If* is a stupid little word. What do you most look forward to?"

"Riding," she said. "Oh, and dancing. I do miss dancing."

"A horse I can't immediately come up with," Charming said, "but dancing I can do." He pushed his chair back and stood up.

"Oh, no," the Beast said. "Like this? No, I can't..."

"You can, you know," Charming said. "You move with grace, and I admire how hard you must have worked to do that, being suddenly transformed into such a different shape. Please," he said, "dance with me?"

He held out his hand, and said, "House? Er... sorry. Steward? Whoever? If you happen to be here? Could we possibly—Is there any chance of some music? I'd hum"—he grinned at the Beast—"but you really don't want such a dreadful noise in your ear."

"I don't think... There's a piano," she said, "but no-one to play it." Relief and disappointment churned so hard in her she felt sick.

"Was there one in the ballroom? I don't remember... Shall we look?"

"No! I mean, no, not the ballroom, please."

"Then we must simply imagine the music," Charming

said, but at that moment a fiddle floated into view, shortly followed, closer to the ground, by a wooden whistle.

"Frederich," the Beast said. "Oh, Frederich, can you still… I didn't… This is Frederich," she said to Charming. "And his son Pawel." She stood up.

Charming bowed. "I'm honoured to make your acquaintance," he said.

The fiddle and the flute bobbed in the air.

"Do you have a favourite tune?" he asked the Beast.

"Frederich knows," she said. "It's a folk song, not a court song, but…"

"Perfect," Charming said.

The bow touched the strings, an introductory note. Charming bowed. The Beast took a deep breath, started to curtsey, realised she would look ridiculous, and simply stopped where she was, closing her eyes, unable to move.

The music leapt into life, *The Wild Thyme A-Blowing*, a song she had loved and danced to since she was a child, when what she looked like didn't matter and dancing was only for fun. She felt Charming take her arm, and opened her eyes to see him smiling. "You'll have to forgive me," he said, "I'm a little out of practice…"

He didn't seem out of practice. He was confident and neat-footed as a cat. He guided her without force or pressure, so that she moved more easily than she expected, and each step came smoother than the last.

He was shorter than her—they all were, now—but it didn't matter. She looked down at his hair and wondered again what it would be like to plunge her hands in that tumbled gold. He tilted his head up, smiled a merry, easy smile, took her hand and spun her away from him, and back again, and she felt *light*. Light for the first time in— oh, so long.

Wild Thyme was followed by *Girdle 'Round the Earth* and *Moonlight Revels, Airy Spirit* and *Merry Wanderer* and *Pipes of Corn,* dance after dance until she was out of breath and laughing. "Let the poor men rest!" she gasped. "And me!"

"One more," Charming said. "Please? Something a little slower, hmm?" He turned to where the instruments seemingly hung in the air, and it was almost as though she could *see* them, Friederich and little Pawel, as they should be. "Do you know *Take Hands With Me?*" he said.

She couldn't remember the song, didn't care. Charming put an arm around where her waist used to be. The fiddle wailed sweet as honeyed wine, the flute spun silver through the air, and he was close and warm and smiling and she danced, danced, danced until the door opened and the sound of a clanging bell broke all the music into smithereens.

"Visitors? At this hour?" Charming said, still standing with his arm around her. "I don't remember any bells ringing when I arrived."

The Beast felt a cold clenching in her chest. *Not yet, not yet, it's not for days yet!*

"I suppose I'd better go and see," she said, all the lightness draining away, her feet once more planted heavily on the hard reality of the floor.

"Do you want me to come with you?" Charming asked.

"No, please, stay. Finish your wine."

It seemed so unfair for this moment to end so soon, and as long as Charming was still here, in this room, the remnants of the meal spread out before him, it hadn't quite ended.

An Interlude

HE BEAST FOLLOWED the sound of the bell straight to the kitchen and paused on the threshold, almost as startled as the group who leapt to their feet as she appeared.

At least it was only more men. But there were *four* of them this time, not three, and before the last lot had even disappeared. *Someone's trying to up the odds. I suppose I should be grateful*. One was distinctly older than usual, though not as old as some of the men her father had tried to marry her off to. All of them stood with their mouths open, but—unless you counted a small squeak from the one with the tight black curls—none screamed.

The one with the neat little beard stepped forward, and bowed. "Ivan Prokhor, at your service. Everyone calls me Dance. You must be the—ah, lady of the house?" He had a slightly *blurred* look, to the Beast's eyes; as though he were a painting and someone had smudged a cloth over his features while they were still damp. In fact, all of them did.

"Mostly," the Beast said. "I assume you found yourselves lost in the woods?"

"Yes. We're actors. We were looking for a place to perform and…" He spread his hands.

"You were all *together*?"

"Well, yes…" He looked bemused, as well he might.

The Beast sighed. "You might as well make yourselves at home. You will be provided with rooms and meals, and you won't be able to leave for a while. Don't try and go out of the window, the roses will stop you."

"The… *roses*?"

"Yes. Unless you want a skinful of thorns, really, don't go out of the window. You can walk the gardens if you leave through this door." She sighed, and braced herself. "As to why you are here, I cannot tell you more than this. 'When the moon has run its course, some of you, or all of you, will be going free, and one of you, or none of you, will be bound, but willingly.'"

A cat hissed, startling her. She hadn't even noticed it. Its fur was standing on end, which made the naked ratty bit at the end of its tail even more obvious.

The rest of them looked at each other. "Well, I suppose, since it's full moon very soon, we won't be here that long…" the small one said.

"And there are other guests," the Beast said.

"There are?" Dance said. "Well, perhaps if we're all going to be here for a while, we could put on a little performance? If you've no objection."

"A *performance*? A play? I've just told you you're stuck here in a place guarded by magical and vicious roses, and with, well, *me*, and you want to put on a *play*?"

Dance shrugged. "It's what we do."

"Got to keep in practice," the muscular one said.

"Can't get stale," the little one said.

"Nope, it's bad. Staleness. Like bread," the curly-headed one said. "Not good for much, stale bread."

"Well, it's all right for toast," said the muscular one. "So long as it's not too hard. And no mould."

"Why's mould all right on cheese, but not bread?" the little one said. "Is it, like, all the same mould? Or is it different mould, do you think?"

"I think it's different, gotta be," the muscular one said. "It's different colours, mould. Blue, green…"

"I saw pink once," the little one said. "Don't eat it if it's pink. Trust me." Their voices didn't seem to sound quite the same as they had to start with, but they were strangers, and the Beast knew she had drunk a little more wine than she was used to.

"I apologise," Dance said, wearily. "They *forget themselves*." He glared around at the others.

They quietened.

The Beast looked at them for a moment.

Four, not three. And all together. And a cat. No animal bigger than a bird has appeared here since this began.

Something has changed. Something is happening.

Is it good? Or is it bad?

I don't know. But it's change.

That feeling that did not quite dare to be hope rose in her chest, like a light in the distance that might be the sunrise, or might be a forest fire.

"Ah, Charming." Hans looked up from his book, candlelight gleaming on his spectacles. "It appears we have some new companions."

"We do?"

"The spell seems to have trapped a group of travelling players."

"Oh, so *that's* who rang the bell," Charming said. "Well, I hope their timing is better when they're onstage."

"What do they do?" Will said, tugging at his jacket.

"What do they *do?*" Hans blinked at him.

"Yes, is it like… playing? Like cub—children?"

"No…" Hans looked at Charming, who had slumped into a chair and was staring into the fire. "Charming?"

"Hmm?"

"How would you explain travelling players to someone who's never encountered them?"

"People who pretend to be someone they're not, to tell a story," Charming said. "For money, usually. And because it's fun, I suppose." He scowled down at his hands.

"You dislike them?"

"What? No, not at all. Thinking of something else." Charming smiled, though it looked more effortful than usual. "I think you might like them, Will. And it will break up the monotony, at least."

"Don't you think it's odd?" Hans said. "That they should get caught up in this… net?"

"Maybe one of them's the youngest son," Will said.

The other two looked at him.

"You know. In the stories the Beast was reading to me, it's the youngest son who succeeds where the others have failed, wins the fair lady and gets the kingdom."

"Huh. You might have something there," Hans said.

Charming scowled again. "Strolling players. Of all things. Oh, by the way, I found out about the curse."

"You *solved* it?" Will clapped his hands. The sound rang out like a shot.

"Sorry, Will, nothing so splendid, I'm afraid. Just what happened. She turned down a marriage proposal from the son of one of the Good Folk, and this is what they did to her for it."

"Wait, they did this to her because she wouldn't…" Will looked both horrified and puzzled. "But *why?*"

"The fairy really, *really* wanted the Beast married to her son, for some reason," Charming said. "Oh, and it wasn't just her. The staff. They're all still here. The curse made them silent and invisible, but they're still here."

"It's *people?*" Will blushed so hard he could have hidden among the most crimson of the roses. "People have been *dressing* me?"

"I'm sure you've nothing they haven't seen before, my boy."

"It's not *that,* it's just… Oh, I'm so *stupid*." He looked wildly around the room. "Are any of them here? If you're here, I'm sorry I've been so stupid."

"Now, Will," Charming said. "I'm sure they don't think badly of you. Or no more so than the rest of us, at any rate. Hans, you're having a thought, aren't you? You always polish those damned spectacles when that great brain of yours gets going."

"Hmm?" Hans looked up, spectacles dangling from his fingers. "Why *us?*"

"What?"

"Why *us?* There have only been a few men taken from the town, and if they just wanted healthy young men, they should have gone through hundreds by now."

"Perhaps there are limits on how many they can pull in at a time."

"It's more than that," Hans said. "I'm *sure* it's more than that. There's a reason they picked the people they did. And why *now?* Will and I have both been within easy reach all this time. Were we further down the list? And again, *why?*" He sighed, and shoved his spectacles back on. "All I have is more questions and no answers."

"Well, it can't be much longer," Will said. "I've been watching the moon. It's almost a month."

"I want to *know,*" Hans said. "It's maddening."

"It's not just maddening," Charming said. "If we don't know why it's happening, what's to stop it happening again? Although I suppose it's unlikely one would get chosen twice... My head hurts. I'm going to bed." He got out of his chair and left the room.

"What's wrong with him?" Will said.

Hans shrugged. "He's probably just tired of being locked up here. We all are."

The Cat That Leapt Out of the Bag

O HOW DO we approach this?" Curly said, buttering a slice of bread. "I mean, we can't just go up and say, 'Oh, anyone here happen to be a playwright?' can we? Bit obvious."

"This beard itches," Gilda said, her face muscles twitching.

"They *always* itch," Dance said, stroking his own beard with slight but undeniable smugness. "You know they always itch."

"I'm just *saying*. Anyway, how would you know? Yours doesn't itch."

"Mine itches after I shave it and it's growing out. And I know the false ones always itch because you complain about it *every single time*. And to answer your question—"

"Say the script you were going to use got lost. Or burned. Or something," Cassia said. "It's not beyond the wit of man, surely." She was curled up with her back to everyone, mournfully licking the bald bit of her tail.

"But we don't use a script every time. We've *learned* stuff: there's at least seven plays we could do from memory," Mouse said. "Gilda, stop *twitching*. We're in now, give me a minute and I'll get rid of it properly."

"They won't know that," Cassia said.

"*He* will, the witch's brother—whatshisname, Hans," Mouse said. "Gilda, if you don't stop, I won't take it off, I'll use the *other* glue and you'll have a beard that won't come off until spring."

Dance rolled his eyes. "I've *thought* of what to say, for Goose's sake. Just do what you're told and try not to mess up."

"GENTLE LORDS," DANCE said, bowing. Hans looked up from his book, and Will turned from the window.

"Oh, I'm not a lord!" Will said. "Not a bit of one. Hans has been telling me about what you do. I can't wait. I've never seen a play."

"Then I hope we can fulfil your expectations," Dance said. "But that, gentlemen, is my dilemma. We have been touring the provinces for a long time, and are out of touch with what is the fashion in theatre. I wondered if perhaps either of you knew what they are doing in the cities, and might advise us, but it seems…"

"Oh, I might be able to help," Hans said. "In fact, I would be delighted."

"Then if you would be so kind as to join us after supper, and give us the benefit of your experience?"

"By all means," Hans said. "It's a shame our companion isn't here. He *has* probably seen a play or two, and might have a different perspective."

"Your companion?"

"The third of us. Three is usual, apparently. You and your troupe are a new development. Has anyone explained the situation to you?"

"Well, our... hostess, as you say, gave us some idea. It's all rather odd, but we're making the best of it. We haven't encountered your companion yet."

"Well, I hope you will be able to cheer him up, he's become rather glum. Fellow by the name of Charming."

"Oh," Dance said. "Really? Hmm. Well, if you'll excuse me, I should get back to my troupe, make sure they're not getting up to mischief..."

THE QUARTERS IN which the troupe had been housed were far more elegant than were usually allotted to strolling players, on the rare occasion they were allowed indoors, but Dance was not in the mood to appreciate them. "We've got a problem," he said. "One of the three men trapped here is Prince Charming."

"What? The one who was in *Eingeten*?" Curly said.

"The same *one*?" Gilda said around a mouthful of beef.

"Leave some for the rest of us, Muscles. How many people called Prince Charming can there possibly *be*?" said Mouse. She was curled up in a massive chair, an empty plate before her, practicing juggling her knives. The blades gleamed and flashed.

"Interesting," said Cassia.

"Interesting my arse," Dance said. "What if he recognises us?"

"Well, you had about three inches of face paint and a long wig last time, and no beard," Mouse said. "I think Curly was the only one who looked anything like himself.

Besides, he's a *prince*. How likely is he to recognise mere commoners like us?"

"He's a *conman*," Dance said. "They notice things. If they don't they get caught."

"A conman?" Hans said, from the doorway. "Would you care to elaborate?"

The players looked at him, then at each other. Cassia kept looking at Hans, and purred.

"Um," Dance said. "First of all, perhaps we'd better explain why we're here. Gilda, the door, if you would."

An Invitation to a Fairy Ball

ANS WAS WALKING in the garden, his hands clasped behind him, pausing to examine an interesting plant, or gaze up at the sky. Will came out to join him. "You look as though you have something on your mind," he said.

"Hmm. Yes, I do rather. Oh, there's our companion. Good morning, Charming. How are you?"

Charming shrugged. He looked a little shadowed under the eyes, and kept glancing upwards, then back towards the house. "At least the wretched roses are staying in one place," he said, eyeing them suspiciously. They were still in full glory: scarlet, crimson, claret, ruby, magenta and cerise, gold and saffron and amber and apricot, filling the air with their scent.

"Beautiful, but not to be trusted," Hans said.

"Indeed," Charming said gloomily.

They turned as one when the Beast appeared. She looked different. Still massive. Still something between a bear and a wolf. But instead of the endless layers, and ruffles, and jewels, she wore a gown of bronze satin, simply cut, that glowed like an ember in the sunlight and deepened the colour of her eyes. Drop pearls hung from her ears, and an amber pendant on a plain gold chain hung at her breast. When she drew closer, Hans realised that she was no longer drenched in perfume. She smelled perfectly pleasant, like any clean and healthy animal.

"Good morning," she said. "I trust you all slept well?"

Hans noticed how her gaze kept going to Charming. Each of them smiled and bowed over her outstretched paw. Charming held it longest, looking into the Beast's eyes. To Hans, his smile seemed artificial, but then, perhaps all of them were.

"So have you met our latest visitors?" the Beast said.

"The players? Yes, they are interesting people. Widely travelled," Hans said. He kept an eye on Charming. "Sperita, Crosera, Eingeten…"

Charming did not appear to react, or even notice.

"They come at just the right time," the Beast said. "Four days from now, there will be a masked ball, to mark my birthday. They said they wanted to perform, so the players can be part of the entertainment."

It was hard to tell, but Hans thought she was operating under some strain. But then, he thought, how could she not be?

"A masked ball?" Charming gave a slight laugh, and gestured at them all. "How will we ever guess who anyone is, among so many?"

"Oh, there will be other guests," the Beast said. "Plenty of them. Good Folk, among them the one who did this." The Beast gestured to herself. "It happens every year. I think she likes to gloat."

"That's awful!" Charming burst out. "Of all the…" He closed his lips tightly but took the Beast's paw. "I'm sorry."

She tried to smile. "Well, you will at least meet those who have served you so well. They reappear, for one night. Every year I have pleaded for their freedom. Perhaps this time…" Her voice trembled.

"Perhaps," Charming said.

The Beast said, "Just for this one night, the barriers open, to allow the visitors in. And you will be free. You have been gracious guests."

"And you a most excellent hostess," Charming said. "But let's not anticipate the end of our stay just yet, shall we? And it *is* a ball, so we shall have an excuse for dancing!"

"I've never danced, not properly," Will said. "I shan't know what to do."

"Hans, you must have done some dancing, in your travels?" Charming said. "Surely between us, you and I can teach Will a few steps."

Hans nodded. "I think that can be managed," he said. "I have, indeed, learned a few things. Some of them quite recently."

"No," THE BEAST said, as yet another dress appeared in front of her, a magnificently ugly concoction of maroon silk. "No, not that one. No. And no. *No*, Maria. Pink? Really? And definitely not yellow. He… Not yellow."

She was humming, she realised. *Wild Thyme A-Blowing.* Surely that was one the fairy musicians would know; she would ask them to play it at the ball. They could hardly refuse, could they?

Foolish, foolish, her mind whispered at her. *And they'll choose what you wear for the ball, too, as though it mattered. They always do.*

Nothing's going to happen.

At least I will get to dance with him one more time.

"No," she said, as another dress whirled past. "No. No."

The knock on her door startled her.

"Who is it?"

"Hans. May I speak with you?"

Hans? Whatever could he possibly want?

"Let him in," she said.

The door opened. Hans bowed, and glanced at the dresses piled everywhere, but did not comment.

"Was there something you needed?"

"I…" He coughed. "I have something to tell you, but I fear… Perhaps you would like to sit down?"

She laughed. "I am not a frail creature, Hans, I am sure nothing you can tell me can be so shocking."

He sighed heavily. She frowned at him. He looked— not so much embarrassed as *sad*. Older, and sad, and looking at her with a kind of detached pity.

She felt cold, suddenly. She wanted to say, *No.* To push him out of the room, and shut the door, and hide in here for four more days, until the ball.

But she had never been in the habit of turning away from hard truths.

"Tell me," she said.

An Interlude

HARMING WAS PACING the walls of his room when Kichka landed on the sill in a great flutter of wings. The bird preened, fluffing his feathers.

"Kichka!" Charming rushed to the window. "Did you find them?"

The parrot cocked his head and looked at him reproachfully. Charming decided to take that as a 'yes.'

"Listen, I have to tell you something. There's a ball. In four days. Saturday evening. But I haven't discovered how to break the curse."

Kichka hooted and made his raspberry noise.

"I know, I know! The ball, the Good Folk will be here, and the manor is accessible, just for one night. That may be a way for me to get out. But tell them, I want to know how to break the curse as well. Can you tell them that?"

Kichka let out a scream of such piercing intensity Charming clapped his hands over his ears. "What was that for?"

The parrot screamed again and took off around the room. "Oh. *Oh*. You know, don't you? You know how to break the curse?"

Kichka hissed.

"Go tell them," Charming said. "Go and tell them about the ball. And talk to the doctor, she's very smart. Tell her what you *can* tell her. She might be able to work out how to break the curse. Please?"

"So IN FOUR days," Doctor Rapunzel said, rubbing the tips of her fingers together, making little purple sparks jump and fizz, "we have a chance to get into this secret manor house and get Charming out."

Kichka sat on Bella Lucia's shoulder, half-hidden by curls, pressing his cheek against her face. She skritched the top of his head, and he made a strangely feline purring sound.

"Not natural," Roland muttered. "Talking birds. 'Sweird."

"You're only cross because he said you weren't a pretty boy. And as for natural, you're an *imp*," Nell pointed out, her eyes sparkling.

"So? Being an imp's natural where I come from. Talking birds ain't natural anywhere."

Kichka blew a raspberry at him.

"All birds talk," Marie Blanche said.

"Oh, never mind." Roland retreated into a sulk. He was an extraordinarily efficient sulker. He could sulk like an entire schoolful of hormonal teenagers.

Kichka clattered his beak and chittered.

"He—that is, Charming—wants to break the curse," translated Marie Blanche. "He says he wants to break the curse, he says Doctor Shiny—Rapunzel will know."

"So there's a woman who is under a curse," Bella said. "And Charming seems eager to break it…" She stopped.

The other three glanced at each other.

"Bella," Nell said. "I don't think…"

"Can we warn her?" Bella said.

"Ah. Maybe? But then again," Nell said, "this isn't like before, is it? He's not there voluntarily. He hasn't planned it."

"No," Marie Blanche said, "but we all know he is an opportunist."

"He is not going to have *time* to run away with her treasury, if there is one," Doctor Rapunzel said. "He knows what will happen if he does not meet Mephistopheles."

"And, I hate to say it, but he's been there for *weeks*," Nell said. "I don't know about the rest of you, but I fell in love with him in the course of two pavanes and five minutes on a moonlit balcony."

"We're probably too late, then," Bella said. "Oh, the poor woman."

"Yeah, let's hope the mask doesn't come off before we can get him away," Nell said. "Because the poor woman is currently quite capable, by the sound of it, of ripping his princely head right off his shoulders if he upsets her. Sorry, Bella. But if that happens, we're *really* in it."

Bella Lucia shuddered. "Yes. But even if we can get in and get him *out*, we have to get him to Devil's Head Mountain the next day! How?"

"Doctor?" said Nell. "Any ideas?"

"Full moon *and* the equinox?" Roland emerged from his sulk long enough to shake his head and whistle. "Enough wild magic swirling around to power a hurricane."

"Yes, and that makes any large working… problematic,

to say the least," Doctor Rapunzel said. "Even smaller ones will take considerably more power than usual."

"What about the Fox Queen?" Bella asked Marie Blanche. "She was able to help move you a long way very fast."

Marie Blanche shook her head. "She won't come into the Scatovald. I had to do a lot of negotiating just to get the dwarf guards to come with me, and they bolted for home the second I told them they could go."

Doctor Rapunzel turned to Nell. "Your Grace…"

"Oh, you want something," Nell said. "You lot *never* call me 'Your Grace' unless you want something."

"I think we may need your godmother's help. If she would be willing."

"Ah. I did *tell* you she doesn't have anything to do with the Good Folk, didn't I? I mean, I did mention it? Several times? I'm fairly certain I did. And you want me to ask her to get us into a fairy ball *and* maybe help whisk Charming—who she does *not* like, at all, because I *am* her favourite goddaughter, and he *did* rob me and abandon me—to his meeting with Mephistopheles?"

"She might be quite happy to hear he's being whisked to meet Mephistopheles, if she doesn't like him," Bella said. "It's not likely to be a *pleasant* experience."

"I hmm. Well, I could try that angle, I suppose."

"Would she do it?" Rapunzel said.

"I don't know. She won't be happy about it. But I can ask. I'll have to do it by magic, too, because there won't be time for a normal messenger."

"I can help you with that," Rapunzel said.

Kichka chattered and squawked again. "He can't lie to break the curse," Marie Blanche offered. "No tricks and no lies? I don't… You're getting too excited, Kichka! He says… he says, none of them know."

Rapunzel frowned. "What does he mean, none of them know?"

"There's three," Marie Blanche explained as Kichka chattered. "One pretty boy, one clever—yes, Kichka, just like you—and one nice one." The parrot whistled three falling notes. "Nice one smells like—I'm not clear on this, I don't think there's a word for it in the parrot language."

"Can he say what they *look* like?" the sorceress asked.

More squawking.

"Yes, we know about the pretty one," said Marie Blanche. "What about the other two?"

Kichka flapped and chattered.

"*Yes*, Kichka, but can you tell us—?"

"Kichka, what colour feathers do they have on their heads?" Nell said.

Kichka stopped and gave her a look so old fashioned it was practically fossilised. He croaked and Marie Blanche laughed. "Birds do know what hair is, you know."

"Sorry, sorry, yes I know. Hair, then. What colour hair?"

Kichka tilted his head to one side, then the other.

"The clever boy has… yellow hair," said Marie Blanche. "Like *Minschterkaas*. Right down his back."

"And *Minschterkaas* is…?" Nell said.

"Cheese," Roland said. "Excellent stuff, *Minschterkaas*. It's *pale* yellow. Almost white. And pongy. Good pongy."

"Hair like pongy cheese," Nell gulped.

"*Long* pongy cheese hair," Roland added helpfully.

"Well, I think we know where Goldlöckchen's brother is," Doctor Rapunzel said, ignoring Nell's snickering. "And the other? The nice one?"

"Smells like—there's that word again. I think it's an animal," Marie Blanche said. "But it's not native to where Kichka comes from, so he's made up his own word for it."

"What *sort* of animal?" Doctor Rapunzel was a patient woman; she'd had to be. But her patience was beginning to wear thin.

Kichka tilted his head again, then opened his beak and *howled,* making the women jump and setting every dog within three miles into a frenzy of barking.

"*Please,*" Nell said, clutching her chest. "Give a girl some warning before you make a noise like that!"

"And now we know where Red Cap's young protégé is, too," Doctor Rapunzel said, when she got her breath back.

Kichka eyed her fingertips, which were still glowing, and tucked his head down apologetically.

"Yes, well, perhaps a *quieter* form of information would be better next time," she said. "In the meantime, Marie Blanche, if you would speak to Red Cap—"

"Thelise," Marie Blanche said. "Her name is Thelise."

"—and I will talk to the Bear Witch. With their help, I think we can get Charming away, *if* we can get in."

"Then what?" Nell said. "If only we had those damn boots."

"I will think about it. Kichka, I have forgiven you. Please do not nibble my ear."

KICHKA HAD DECIDED to accompany Rapunzel to her room and was hopping about the desk, peering at things with his head on one side or the other, muttering to himself.

Doctor Rapunzel poured over her maps, and charts, and instruments. She had managed to gather much of what she needed, though some of it was still at her cottage in the Trübenholz. For a moment she missed her home furiously: the quiet, the regularity of her days, knowing exactly where everything was and having it all to hand. Her own well-aired bed and good sheets. Her garden, which would be so lovely now, colourful as embroidery, every turn of the path bringing a new delight, a new bloom opened, a drift of scent. Her fingers itched to pull weeds; the mundane magic of helping nature create beauty.

But time was running out, in more senses than one. Now that she knew of the hidden manor's existence, she had been able to work out its rough location. Though scrying could not penetrate the forest's increasingly thick wild magic, she had been able to get some sense of the spell in operation there. Not in any detail, alas, but even without Kichka's information about the ball, she could feel that it was building, very rapidly, towards its conclusion. What that would mean for Charming, or the other victims, she did not know.

"All right?" Roland said, plumping himself down on the desk, pointedly ignoring Kichka.

"Roland, the maps. Please move your... self."

Roland took himself over to the windowsill and perched on it like a gargoyle, his arms wrapped around his shins. "All right, all right. Everyone ain't half snappy today. Even Queen Nell, all that giggling. 'Snerves."

"Very astute, Roland. But I am sure Bella Lucia is not *snappy*."

"Lady Bella wouldn't know snappy if it sat on her, but she's worried. You all are."

"Time is short. And I would like to break this poor woman's curse, if at all possible."

Kichka cackled, and opened his beak wide.

Doctor Rapunzel pointed a glimmering finger at him. "Do *not* scream. I mean it."

Kichka eyed the finger warily, and closed his beak. He hopped up and down, muttering and pulling at things on the desk.

Doctor Rapunzel watched him.

"He doesn't half go on," Roland said. "What does he mean, about the curse? No tricks and no lies?"

"I think perhaps it means the curse can only be lifted with something that is real, and true," Doctor Rapunzel said.

Kichka leapt up with an excited squawk, scattering papers as he took off in excitement.

"Lots of things are real. My toes are real. Don't mean they can lift curses."

"I think I understand, Kichka. But it doesn't help us at all. Oh dear, that poor woman," Doctor Rapunzel said.

The Beast and Her Treasure

HARMING HEARD THE knock and smoothed the front of his shirt. It was a deep forest green, the velvet surcoat a darker green, almost black, like the shadows in the heart of the forest. He peered into the mirror and anxiously fidgeted with a lock of hair that was failing to lie exactly as he preferred.

He took the rose that had been lying next to his plate at lunch time and tucked it into his buttonhole.

"Do I look all right?" he asked whoever bore the floating candle. "Er, I know you can't precisely answer, but—you know—bob the candle up and down or something. Up for yes, down for no. No, wait, that'll be confusing. Up and down for yes, side to side and I need to change into something else."

The candle wavered, then bobbed upwards.

"Are you sure?" Charming said. "You don't appear very sure. Is it the hose?" He looked down. The hose, too, were dark green. "Do I look like a plant? I do, don't I? I look like a bush or something. Or some sort of thing with a stem."

The candle moved from side to side.

"Two stems. You're not helping, you know. Oh, I know you can't. Sorry. I just... Well, there's no point fretting, is there? Let's go, then."

The candle began to drift away. Charming tried to tell himself that it wasn't really moving with reluctance, that he was imagining its progress was slower than he had become used to. Nonetheless his nerves only increased. *It's probably some old servant*, he told himself. *Ancient retainer, grown stiff in the service of the family, that style of thing, and not someone reluctant to lead a man to his fate.*

How he wished Roland were here. Roland with his sarcastic quips and cynical attitude. Roland would bring him down to earth.

Charming really had no idea why he was feeling quite so... whatever he was feeling. Anxious. Uneasy. But at the same time, as though every colour was brighter than usual; as though the feel of his feet on the floor, his clothes against his skin, the breath going in and out of his lungs, were all somehow polished, bright, more intense than usual.

Perhaps he was coming down with something. He slowed. "I may have a fever. I shouldn't risk infecting the Beast, should I?" he said. "I mean, do I look feverish? I don't even know if she can catch things from me, in her current state. I know mostly animals can't catch what people have, but I'm fairly sure swine fever is one they can, only neither of us is a swine so... What do you think?" he pleaded with the unseen candle bearer. "Do I look sick? Should I excuse myself?"

The candle moved from side to side, the flame wavering and flattening.

"Oh, all right. If you're sure."

It was the library, again. Oh, dear. The site of that unfortunate earlier meeting. But maybe it was good to meet there, to wipe away that memory and replace it with a more pleasant one.

He shook his head. How could he feel so muddled and so very clear at the same time? All he knew was that he wanted to see her. Perhaps he could ask her why he had upset her so, that first time, and how he could make it up to her. Or would it be tactless to bring it up? Perhaps he should wait, and see if she mentioned it herself.

What in the name of the Goose is wrong with me? I am Prince Charming, always in control of every social situation, the master of the right word at the right time... until now.

He was startled when the doors of the library appeared in front of him. The candlestick hovered.

"I feel as though I should tip you," Charming said. "Perhaps when I next have some money..."

The candlestick moved from side to side again, so rapidly that the flame went out entirely. The many, beautifully wrought wall sconces, each in the shape of a pair of hands holding a torch, still lit the corridor, but there was something about that small light going out that chilled Charming's skin.

"If I insulted you, somehow, I apologise," he said. "I seem to be rather good at putting my foot in it, lately."

The candle did not move. Charming felt as though someone were regarding him intently.

"Is there..."

Then the candle was moving away. He almost called it back. Suddenly the corridor seemed too empty. The sconces hissed and crackled, and he shook himself. He was about to see the Beast, and that thought chased the shadows away.

The door opened.

There she stood, in a gown of heavy grey satin that fell in sculptural folds. The effect was oddly magnificent, like a statue of a goddess from an ancient land, strange and almost mythic.

"You look…" He stopped, and shook his head. "Really quite wonderful."

"Why, thank you," she said. "Though truly you may thank my poor maid, who has the task of dressing me."

"I'm sure your own taste informs her choices," Charming said.

"When I can persuade her away from yards of ruffles and acres of lace, yes," the Beast said. "I am not always so fortunate."

"I like that colour on you very much. It brings out your eyes."

"Those, at least, remain the same," she said. "Now, you, too, look the very picture of a noble prince."

"Ah, for that you must thank my… manservant? Valet? Whoever it is who chose this outfit. I was slightly worried about it. I'm glad it meets with your approval."

"How could it not? Please," she said, gesturing, "sit. Take some wine."

He seated himself in one of the comfortable, deep-padded chairs, but he did not feel comfortable. There was something different, tonight. She was distant, polite, social, with that kind of brittle, superficial politesse he had encountered at everything from massive court gatherings to intimate dinners: a woman concealing herself behind social niceties. "Is there…?"

"I thought perhaps," she said, "we should come back here. It is where we started, is it not?" She settled herself in the other chair.

Her fur, now he looked closer, seemed to have dulled a little. Her eyes, though still that bright hazel, were weary-looking.

"Is something wrong?" he asked.

"No, what could be wrong? Everything is happening just as it was meant to, is it not?"

"I'm not sure I understand…" Something *was* wrong, something was very wrong. The ground seemed to shift and turn beneath his feet, unstable.

"Don't worry, I do." She smiled, and for a moment it looked as dangerous to him as it had in the beginning, all nerves and teeth. Then it was all smoothed away, and she seemed as calm as a lake on a still day. But there were cold depths in that lake, he could sense them.

She leaned forward, her chin on her paw, and smiled again, a polite, impenetrable smile. "Tell me some more about your adventures," she said. "I have been here so long, and I am so very bored. I like to hear of things outside these walls."

If that was what she wanted, he would do as she asked, and perhaps he could make her laugh, and relax a little, and tell him what was really going on.

He reviewed his stock of stories. All of them over the years had been edited and polished to show him in the best light, so even he sometimes had trouble remembering what had really happened.

And while he wanted to entertain her, part of him— that new, uncomfortable part of him—also wanted to tell her the truth. But that would not make her laugh, would it? That would not make her relax and trust him.

He was taking too long. Was it obvious that he was sorting his memories like a pack of cards?

"Come," she said. "There must be something you can tell me! You have had such an interesting life, after all!"

"Well, yes," he said, "though I suppose most people's lives are more interesting than they appear from the outside. Still, there is one incident that might amuse you, though I warn you, I look a complete fool. You'll never see me the same way again."

"Oh, don't worry about that," she said. "Tell me anyway."

"Once upon a time..." Charming said.

The Tale of the
Poet and the Woodwose

NCE UPON A time there were two brothers. The older brother was serious and hard-working and spent his time studying useful matters. The younger brother was light-hearted and easy-going, and spent his time dancing and riding and writing love poetry.

One day he discovered a poem, thrown away in a corner, that had been written by his older brother. The younger brother read it to himself and laughed. It was obvious that his brother had never attempted poetry before. It had a rhythm as heavy as a troll's footsteps and rhymes that hit the ear like a hammer striking a cracked bell. He tucked it in his pocket, planning to tease his brother with it later, and went on his way.

The next day he went hunting, and chased a hart deep into the woods. He and his horse were wearied, so he dismounted and sat upon a mossy bank. Finding the poem in his pocket, he read it aloud to amuse himself.

Unknown to the young man, a woodwose, a wild man of the woods, happened to be nearby, and leapt out upon him, causing the young man to leap to his feet in startlement. For the woodwose was very large, and covered all over with muscles and thick shaggy hair.

"Don't fear me!" the woodwose said, waving his hands. "I only want you to write a poem for me. I am in love with a fairy, but I am too wild and uncultured and will embarrass her. If I can give her a beautiful poem like that one, I can surely win her heart!"

Now the young man was caught in a dilemma. For a woodwose knows ancient wisdom, and while the young man was rather vain and foolish, he at least realised that he could definitely benefit from a bit of wisdom, ancient or otherwise. If he did the woodwose a favour, he could ask for some of that ancient wisdom to be revealed to him in return.

But the young man knew that this poem was very bad. If he wrote one like it for the woodwose, then surely the fairy would laugh and turn him away, and the woodwose would be furious with him. Not only would he refuse to tell him any wisdom, he might tear him limb from limb. For though he had told the young man not to be afraid, he looked extremely strong—and he was, after all, a wild man, so what was to stop him?

But if the young man wrote him a proper poem, with rhythm that danced and rhymes that sang, the woodwose might not think it was a proper poem at all, and again would be furious.

What to do, what to do?

Then the young man had an idea, which would solve his dilemma and also amuse him. "I will make a bargain with you," he said. "It is hard to tell someone's tastes, when you do not know them. What *you* like, *she* may not, and what *she* likes, *you* may not. I will write you two poems, one in the style of this one, and one in a different style. Take them to your fairy, and let her hear them both. Let her choose which she likes the best, and you may claim it for your own. Only tell me her name and the things you like about her, and I will do it. And in return, you will tell me a piece of that wisdom for which woodwose are well renowned."

The woodwose frowned, and sighed, and tugged at the long hairs on his arms, and in the end said, "Very well, very well." And he went on to tell the young man the things he loved about his lady, from the colour of her eyes to the sound of her laugh and the things she delighted in, and that took quite some time.

When the woodwose finally ran out of things to say in praise of his beloved, they agreed to meet again, by the mossy bank, in three days' time.

So the young man went home and wrote two poems, one in his own very refined style, and one in his brother's most amateur fashion. He even took phrases and sentiments from his brother's poem, to make it as similar as possible, grinning to himself the while.

The young man went to the mossy bank on the appointed day, smugly certain that he knew which poem the fairy would choose. The woodwose took them from him, and promised to meet with him in three days' time.

"Good luck with your wooing!" the young man said, and rode away quite happily.

The appointed time came, and the young man returned to the mossy bank. At first there was no sign of the woodwose, and the young man wondered if that meant his wooing had gone well, or badly, and what that might mean for himself. But in the end the woodwose appeared, and said, "Well, well, you have come for your reward."

"Were you successful?" said the young man, with some anxiety, as the woodwose was looking at him frowning.

"Why, yes," the woodwose said. "My lady was very pleased."

"I am delighted to hear it," the young man said.

"She chose the very poem I would have chosen myself," said the woodwose.

"Oh, really?" said the young man.

"The one that sounded most like the one I heard you reciting when we met. She said that it seemed it had been written with an honest hand, from an honest heart. And I could not deceive her, and said that I had not written it myself, but that it described how I felt. And she took my hand and said that she was very happy to hear it."

"Oh, really," said the young man. "Well, I am delighted for you." And he concluded that both the fairy and the woodwose had terrible taste in poetry, but at least they had the *same* terrible taste, and would probably be very happy together.

"AND WHAT WAS the wisdom the woodwose told the handsome prince?" the Beast said.

"Did I say he was handsome? I don't think I said he was handsome," Charming said. "Or that he was a prince."

"But they are almost always handsome princes, in stories, are they not? Come, tell me what the woodwose said."

"You know, I'm not sure I remember," Charming said. "Perhaps it was too profound for such a shallow fellow as I was, and my mind would not hold onto it."

In fact, he remembered perfectly well what the woodwose had told him: "An honest word is better than a fancy word with no heart behind it." And he had been very cross, because that did not seem to him, at the time, like ancient wisdom, but merely the sort of annoying, moralising thing his older brother might say. And now he could not tell the Beast that. Maybe one day he would be able to admit it.

"Well, that is a shame," she said. "Still, it gave you a story to tell, to add to your collection, didn't it? Now I have a collection to show you."

She walked over to the cabinet in the corner, which Charming had almost forgotten was there, and took out a key, and opened it. He realised her hand was shaking a little. "Are you well?" he said. "You don't seem quite well. Please don't worry about this now."

"I am quite well," she said. "And I must show you my treasures."

The first was a shabby green coat. She draped it over his shoulders, smiling. "Well, you don't look quite as fine as usual, but the pockets are always full of gold, so you may soon buy more coats."

"Beast…"

A ring, heavy and dark, with an oily shimmer. She pushed it onto his finger. "See? It fits you perfectly. Turn it three times, and it will take you anywhere you need to go." Her voice was bright and brittle as fine glass.

"But I don't want to…"

The harp made a plaintive sound as she lifted it out of the cabinet, sending a chill along Charming's nerves. "Please," he said, but she did not even look at him.

"The harp speaks only the truth," she said. "I don't know if you'll find it useful. He can't solve the riddle for you, though. Please don't ask him. But I don't suppose you care about the riddle, do you? I know now that these

are what you came here for, so here it is, all my treasure.
You may take it all, and go."

He took her paw. "Stop, please! Listen to me!"

She snatched her paw away, scraping him with her
claws, and snarled, actually snarled, and he was face to
face with a beast in her fury, the candlelight gleaming
gold on the tears standing in her eyes.

Then in a whirl of satin and the slam of a door, she
was gone.

The Werewolves and the Witch

HELISE AND HEDEL sat in the hut, watching the shifting leaf patterns on the wall.

"You've got the most sense," Thelise said. "And they listen to you."

"Some of them," Hedel said.

"There will always be some who are stubborn. But I'm asking if you're willing."

"Are you really going to leave?"

"Whether I leave or not, one day someone must take over. I wouldn't ask if I did not think you were more than capable."

Hedel drew a pattern on the table with her forefinger, then looked up. Her eyes were hazel, sharp in the green gloom. "All right. But if…" She swallowed. "If he's alive, and we get him back, I want Will with me."

Thelise sighed. "Hedel…"

"I know you think it isn't suitable. And I don't want to turn him. He's fine as he is. And *as* he is, he'll be good to negotiate with the villagers, if we need to. People like him."

"*You* certainly do, I know."

"Come on, Aunt Thelise, *everyone* likes Will. Who else can walk into a fight and pull people apart and no one bites him? You've seen it. And they'll trust him more because he's *not* one of us."

"I was going to try and get him an apprenticeship. He should have the chance at a normal life, if he wants it."

"Well, of course he should! I'm going to *ask* him, not *tell* him."

"Hedel, if you ask him, he'll say yes without thinking twice."

"You don't give him enough credit. He's got a mind of his own, and he's smarter than you think. He's smarter than *he* thinks." Hedel straightened her back, and looked Thelise in the eye. "You think he should have a 'normal' life, because you miss yours," she said. "Not everyone wants that."

Thelise drew breath to answer and they heard the yelling, smelled the raw, compelling reek of torn flesh and the cloudy stink of bear. She flung open the door of the hut and of *course* it was Claus, in human form, his blond curls flat to his head with sweat and blood, leaning on one of the boys, his shoulder ripped open almost to bone. "Where's Kurt?"

"I made him go the other way," Claus said. He was pallid and sweating.

"Come, sit. And shut up until I've stopped the bleeding," Thelise said. "No, first, tell me why in the Goose's name were you in human form? Did you *want* to be torn to pieces before you could heal?" She turned to Hedel, who already had bandages out of the chest. "Get that little barrel, in the corner."

"Is that wine?" Claus said, rousing.

"Yes. It's the stuff we made last summer. It's not for drinking, idiot." She slapped his hand away. "It's for washing the wound out. Only thing it's good for."

"Can I have some anyway? I don't care what it tastes like."

"No, you cannot. Not until you *stop bleeding*. And tell me why you were in the Bear Witch's territory, in human form, in broad daylight."

"We weren't! We were hunting. You know we don't like going near there. Feels horrible. Ow!"

"Hold still. So what happened?"

"So we got a couple of rabbits, and then this *bear* turns up, and just *goes* for me!"

"Female?"

"Yes."

"Did you get between her and her cubs?"

"There *weren't* any cubs! We'd have smelled 'em! We're not *stupid*."

Thelise exchanged a look with Hedel over Claus's head. Hedel shrugged.

The door of the hut slapped against the wall. "Claus!"

"Kurt! You got away!" Claus leapt up, or tried to, but Thelise and Hedel slammed him back into the chair. "Ow!"

"*Sit down*," Thelise snapped, not bothering to keep the snarl out of her voice.

"I was just telling 'em how this bear attacked us out of *nowhere!*" Claus said. "And we were nowhere *near* the witch's place!"

"Yeah," Kurt said. "Just, like, we weren't doing anything. Just after rabbits."

"You're *sure* there weren't cubs?" Thelise tightened the

bandage around Claus's shoulder and tucked the end under.

"Didn't smell 'em, or see 'em."

"And the bear gave no warning before it attacked?" Thelise said.

"You think I'd have stood there?" Claus said.

"Go to your hut, both of you. Claus, don't use that arm, and come back to me immediately if the wound swells, or starts to stink. I'll check it tomorrow."

Hedel made tea while Thelise slumped at the table.

"So," Thelise said. "What do you think?"

Hedel scowled at the tea. "I don't know. I mean, you know those two. But I don't know why they'd have gone into the witch's territory. We can all feel it, it's like your skin shouting at you to run away. And the bears, well, before, there's been some snarling, some territorial stuff, you know. This, though…"

"You think something's changed? Why now?"

"That woman who came here, with the dwarves. Maybe she and her friends stirred things up."

Thelise rubbed her forehead. "Dammit."

BY THE TIME Doctor Rapunzel was nearing Goldlöckchen's cottage, her head was pounding and her fingers stung with magic. Knowing the keep-aways were there should have been enough to dampen their effects, but they had been renewed, and strengthened, and her hair was crackling with static and her muscles aching with the tension of forcing her forward against their shrieking to turn back, to leave, that she was in terrible danger.

The bears emerged from the trees sooner than they had on her last visit, and were obviously riled up, huffing and clacking their teeth at her. She stood very still to let them investigate her, and was not sure, at first, that they would even let her pass.

When she reached the cottage, Goldlöckchen stood in the doorway, her arms folded, huge bears on either side. She should have looked fragile, so pale and small and young, standing between the great dark shaggy beasts, but instead she looked like the focus, as though they were mere firedogs and she was the flame. The air around her rippled faintly. "What do you want?" she said.

Doctor Rapunzel found herself briefly speechless. She contemplated Goldlöckchen. The young woman was rigid, holding her arms like a shield across herself, her blue eyes like all the winters of the north.

She had been defensive the first time, but now, she was barricaded. In her stance were broken carts and sandbags and burning rubbish and weapons pointing over the top.

Doctor Rapunzel stopped where she was and held out her hands, palm up. "We have found where Charming is, and the likelihood is that your brother is there also. We have a plan for getting in, but we would appreciate your help."

"You're too late."

"What?" Doctor Rapunzel's hands went cold. "What happened?" Her mind began to race. Was Charming *dead?* If he was, what could they do? She was aware of a brief, complicated regret at the thought, amid all the other thoughts, and fears, and plans that began to crowd her brain.

"I made my own arrangements," Goldlöckchen said. "You were taking too long. Hans will be home soon."

"I… What arrangements?"

"What does it matter?"

"Do these arrangements include freeing the other young men, as well as your brother?"

"I don't *care* about them! I want *Hansel!*"

One of the bears whined. It was a strange, piteous sound from such a huge beast, not a sound Rapunzel even knew a bear could make. "Go away," Goldlöckchen said. She stepped back. The door snapped shut, and one after another so did the shutters, *bang, bang, bang, bang, bang.*

"I don't suppose *you* can tell me what happened?" Rapunzel said to the bears.

They simply stared at her, and moved forward.

"Very well," Rapunzel said, and, slowly, carefully, with no sudden moves, turned and walked away, refusing to break into a run, feeling with every step hot brown eyes and cold blue ones boring into the back of her neck.

MARIE BLANCHE KNEW the instant she stepped into the wolves' territory that something had changed. The air bristled. She flexed her hands and touched the hilt of her knife.

Thelise came out to greet her, but it was obvious she was distracted, her eyes constantly on the move, the corner of her lip lifting to show her teeth.

"Something's wrong," Marie Blanche said. "What is it?"

"The Bear Bitch decided to escalate. If she has made up her mind that we are a threat, I will have to consider moving the whole camp, but there are few places we would be safe. The villagers here don't exactly trust us, but they have learned not to make a nuisance of themselves. Anywhere else...? And going further into the forest is too dangerous. There are things there that would make even the Witch run screaming."

"Can you tell me what happened?"

"Two of my pack were attacked, without warning. They weren't even in her territory."

"It wasn't just a bear they startled?"

"No. Any bear for miles around is under her..."—Thelise flicked her hands—"influence? There are no strays. Those leave, fast."

Marie Blanche tried to concentrate on Thelise's words, distracted by the desire to take one of those strong, scarred hands, press it to her cheek and tell Thelise that everything would be well, that she would make *sure* of it, if she had to go up against the legions of the Infernal herself to do it. The thought of Thelise and her pack disappearing into the depths of the forest, or setting up near some village or town where they would be hunted down...

"Please do not do anything yet," she said. "We will talk to her. Find out what is happening, and why this change."

"She is dangerous."

"I have dealt with dangerous people before. I am friends with some of them. We can deal with the witch."

Thelise looked her in the eyes. "You need something from her."

"Yes. We need her help, to get that wretched man out. And yours."

"If it was just me," Thelise said, "I would, you understand? But I can't risk the pack."

"I know."

"Yes." Thelise shoved her hands in her pockets. "Well, try not to get yourself turned into anything unpleasant."

"I'll do my best."

"And come back."

"Yes."

Marie Blanche walked away, feeling the weight of unspoken words in her chest.

An Interlude

AVE YOU SEEN the Beast?" Charming said.

Will shook his head. "No, not since yesterday. Oh, your hand! Did you try and get past the roses again?"

"No. I... No."

"Is something wrong?" Will said. "You look as though something's wrong."

"No, yes, everything. If you see her, will you tell her...? No, never mind."

Will watched Charming disappear down the corridor towards the menagerie, and shook his head.

"I think Charming's going a bit strange," he said to Hans.

Hans was seated in the parlour, a book in his lap, but instead of reading it he was staring out of the window, a frown on his face. "Oh?"

"He was asking me about the Beast, then he sort of ran off. I thought he must have seen her already; wasn't he summoned to the library?"

"I believe so," Hans said.

"It's being shut up here," Will said. "It's enough to make anyone quarrelsome."

Hans looked at Will, who was biting at his nails and gazing longingly out of the window, and decided not to tell him what he had learned. The boy's face was an open book, written in large, simple words; he would never be able to hide that he knew.

"I know, Will," Hans said. "I think, if we're right about how long each—ah—*visit* lasts, the ball should mark the end of it. It's only a couple of days now."

"Yeah," Will said. "Only…"

"What is it?"

"Well, I've been thinking. And the thing is, what if one of us *is* chosen?"

"I understood that *we* had to choose," Hans said.

"'…bound, but willingly.' Yes, I remember. But what if *that's* a spell, too? I may not know much, but I know about love spells. Horrible things. What if there's others, that can make you *think* you want to do something, when you really don't? What if… whatever it is… decides that one of us is the right one, and we wake up all happy to be here and not wanting to leave? It's not like we *wanted* to come here in the first place, is it?"

"Ah," Hans said. "Oh, dear. You may be right. Will, I don't understand why you think you're stupid. But I'm sure there's a way out. I can't tell you, yet, but I promise, we have one."

"I hope you're right," Will said, mournfully. He wrapped his arms around himself. "I can't wait. Poor Beast, though. She'll be stuck here, and we won't even remember her."

"What?"

The shout made them jump. Neither of them had noticed Charming come in. "What do you mean, we won't remember?" he said. "How could we possibly not *remember?*"

"The men who turned up afterwards, they didn't remember where they'd been, or anything about it," Will said. "We told you."

"We won't remember." Charming looked distraught. "But I don't *want* to forget. I mean, what if I wanted to come back, after..."

"You *want* to come back?" Hans gave him a piercing look. "Why would that be?"

There was a light tap on the door. "Herr von Behr?"

Charming ignored the interruption, and sank into a seat beside the fire, shoving his hands into his hair, yanking at his blond locks, then covering his face.

Hans glanced at him, glanced at Will, shook his head and followed a heavily-disguised Mouse into the corridor.

The Catspell

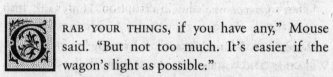RAB YOUR THINGS, if you have any," Mouse said. "But not too much. It's easier if the wagon's light as possible."

Hans thought briefly and reluctantly about the books that were still by his bed, and his chair, and sitting unread on the shelves in the library... "I want to bring the boy," Hans said.

"Right, well, go grab *him*, then. Only *hurry*, before someone catches on."

Hans stuck his head back through the door. "Will? Come with me a moment, would you?"

Will came happily enough, and smiled at the players gathered in the stable yard. He'd been expecting something more colourful, but they all looked rather dimmed, and slumped—and they all seemed to be women. "Hello. I've never met players before. Have you been doing this long?"

"Long enough to know when an engagement's run its course," the one with a scarf wrapped lumpily around

275

her chin said. "Everyone into the wagon, and don't forget, this time, we're all sad, miserable, unwanted creatures, no one would look at us twice. Hup!"

"Wait, are we going? How? What about Charming?"

"I'll explain later," Hans said. "Please, Will, just get in the wagon. And it might help if you tried to feel... um... the way you feel when you try to read, all right?"

"Oh, it's a pusscat!" Will said. "Now, who put you in boots? That's not kind."

"*I* did, and I'm perfectly happy with them, thank you," Cassia said.

Will blinked, opened his mouth, shut it again, and sat down.

"That's Cassia. She's not really a cat," Hans said. "I'll explain—"

"Later. Yes, I know. Where did you get your boots?" Will said. "Did you have them specially made?"

"These? No. I found them. They used to belong to a chap called Charming."

Hans and Dance exchanged alarmed looks.

"*Him?* But they wouldn't have fitted," Will said.

"They adapt to whoever's wearing them. They carry you out of danger."

"They do?"

Dance said, "Brace yourselves." He flicked the reins and the horses started to trot forward.

Cassia sat next to Dance, staring ahead. The wagon rumbled towards the entrance to the stable yard, but the gate never seemed to get any closer. Looking at it made Will's eyes feel odd. He decided to look at Cassia instead. Her small body was tensed hard, her ears back.

Pink shimmering sparkles swirled in the air, danced, clustered, spread. Through the gap Will could see the carriageway, and beyond it, the lovely familiar forest. His heart leapt with delight, then he thought of Charming, and the Beast, and the poor servants, all left behind, and glanced over his shoulder. But already the trees had closed in. He turned around.

They drove on. Cassia stared ahead, occasionally blinking, and twitching her tail.

After a while, Dance said, "Where were we headed?"

"Out," Cassia said. "I told you."

"Yes," said Mouse, "but... did we come this way?"

"We must have, there's only one road," Cassia said. "One way in, one way out."

"Is there?" Mouse said. "Right. Only this doesn't look the same. Hey, we haven't been in there for, like, a hundred years or something, have we?"

"The road would have grown over," Dance said. "Probably."

Gilda stretched and eased her shoulders. "I'm hungry."

"You had breakfast about five minutes ago." Dance peered into the woods, rubbing his eyes.

"Breakfast was *hours* ago."

"Nah. Wait," Mouse said, "was it?"

"*Feels* like hours,"

"It does," Curly said. "Must be the anxiety. Bound to make you hungry. Dance, can you see something?"

"Not sure. We didn't pass any buildings on the way in, did we?"

"Not after we left the witch's cottage. Is it that?"

"No..."

Curly peered. "No, it isn't, is it? That place is much bigger. We must have come a different way..."

"No, we didn't," Cassia said, her voice flat. "We came the same way. We're still going the same way."

"I don't understand," Will said.

"Oh, dear," said Hans.

The gate to the stable yard—the very stable yard they'd just left, or left hours ago—stood wide open in front of them.

"Bugger," said Cassia.

With a small, sad, *floomph* she collapsed onto the boards.

THE PLAYERS GATHERED in the kitchen. Comforting scents of bacon and bread warmed the air, but the atmosphere was more like overboiled cabbage.

"It's only a couple of days," Curly said. "Look, at least we're being well fed. It'll be fine, I'm sure."

"Not if Hans here gets picked, it won't," Dance said. "And maybe trapped here permanently. Then his sister's going to be *very unhappy* with us. And from what I understand, that unhappiness may mean everyone within a fifty-mile radius suddenly discovering their amphibian side. There are not many parts for toads."

"It won't necessarily be toads," Curly said. "Toads are a bit of a cliché, after all."

"Are you trying to be comforting?"

Mouse and Will both hovered anxiously around Cassia. Will kept reaching out a hand to stroke her and pulling it back.

Finally she sputtered, sneezed, and opened her eyes.

"I suppose you're going to tell us you meant to do that?" Dance said.

"Go eat a thistle," Cassia said.

"Do you want some milk?" Mouse said.

"So I can add an upset stomach to my problems? *Why* do people keep giving cats milk?"

"Because most of them are dumb enough to drink it," Dance said. "You, of course, are far too smart to do anything like that, right?"

"Oh, leave her alone, Dance," Mouse said.

"She got us into this mess. She was supposed to get us *out*."

"What happened?" Hans said.

"You saw what happened," Dance snapped.

"Cassia," Hans said patiently. "You got through before. What was different this time?"

Cassia looked at him mournfully, and butted his hand. He found himself, rather to his own surprise, rubbing her ears. She leaned into his hand briefly, then slumped. "I suppose it's my fault for thinking actors could imagine themselves as insignificant."

"Oi," Mouse said indignantly. "That place you found us? We've had *worse* gigs than that. We've sat in the rain watching our wagon be taken away by debt collectors. I had to sell my *knives*. I *used* all that."

Curly said, "I was the ninth child of a farm labourer. How significant do you think I grew up feeling? Went right back to that, I did."

"So you were all acting your little socks off. I still failed."

"Did it feel different to you?" Hans said.

"*Must* we dissect this like a mouse's innards?"

"Indulge me, please?" Hans said. "If we know the detail as to why your spell failed to work this time, we may be able to find a solution."

"Oh, very well." Cassia sat up and began to wash her face. "It's a spell of revelation," she said between licks of her paw. "With a spell of opening. Can't get where you're going if you can't *see* where you're going. Coming in, well, it was hard, but…" She paused in mid-lick. "Not this

279

hard. I am weaker. I could feel it. Maybe it's being out of my natural shape. But the magic surrounding this place is stronger, too—and wilder. Less inclined to be controlled."

"Is it the moon?" Will said. "Lots of things get stronger with the moon."

"Could be."

"It's also very nearly the equinox," Hans said.

Cassia slumped bonelessly to the boards and laid her head on her paws. "Full moon, equinox, wild magic all over the place and stupid cat shape. That's probably it. And all that's just going to get worse until after the ball. And who knows if I'll have any magic at all left by then." She flung herself over on her back. "Kill me now."

"Oh, the melodrama," Dance said. "Maybe we *should* hire you, if we need some rampant overacting."

"Go eat another thistle. And maybe some—"

"Stop it," Curly said. "All of you. I say, whoever, could we get some tea? Please?"

"Beer?" Gilda said.

"Hemlock," Cassia moaned. She eyed Hans. "Well, I might be able to force down a morsel of salmon. If someone were to feed me."

A plate floated into view and landed in front of her. Hans looked at the fish, and looked at her. "It's an inch from your nose, I think you can probably manage."

She made huge eyes at him. "So cruel, after I wore myself out trying to help you escape."

"I appreciate it. I am still not going to hand-feed you salmon you are perfectly capable of eating by yourself."

"You've still got your boots," Will said. "So you could leave and maybe get help."

"Unless they think I'm in immediate danger, they won't work."

"They may not work here anyway," Hans said. "Remember the ring from the library cabinet?" He turned to Dance. "It's supposed to take you where you want to go, but even under ordinary circumstances I wouldn't trust it, and here…" He gestured around them.

"Oh, fabulous, so now even if my life's in danger, I can't get away," Cassia said. "I hate everything."

"May I remind you that all this was your idea?" Dance said.

Hans took off his spectacles and began to polish them. "I believe we're the problem," he said after a moment. "Me and Will. It simply isn't going to let us go. And I'm certainly not enough of an actor to believe I'm someone else, even for a few minutes."

Will said, "I don't think I can pretend to be anyone else either. Not well enough to fool the magic."

"But Herr von Behr, getting you out was rather the *point* of this ridiculous exercise," Dance said.

"If you can get out," Hans said, "you can tell my sister that I am safe, and that Will's people were not responsible for my disappearance, and also speak to Will's aunt. And soon one or both of us will reappear, one way or another."

"Are you sure about that?" Dance said.

"No, of course I'm not; how could I be?" Hans said. "But this is our best chance of ensuring that things between our families don't escalate any worse than they are already, and since you will still be in the area, I suggest that is also in your best interest."

They tried again, Will and Hans watching anxiously.

The pink shimmers were fainter this time, and the gap barely opened before it snapped shut. As it did so, every window in the Manor did too, hundreds of them, with a sound like mocking applause.

Cassia took far longer to wake up, and when she did was too weak to stand.

"No more," Mouse said. "You're going to kill yourself."

"Unless you try going alone," Hans said. "At least that way *someone* gets out."

"And then I get skinned by the Bear Witch because you aren't with me. No, thank you." Cassia shut her eyes and lay looking like a discarded rag.

Mouse picked her up, and they all trooped back to the kitchen, and slumped disconsolately around the room.

Gilda picked up an apple, looked at it, and put it down.

"I'm sorry," Hans said. "But at least you should be out of here soon in any case, since none of you were actually chosen."

"So what are we going to do in the meantime?" Mouse said, propping her boot heels on the table. A spatula immediately flew through the air and smacked them off again. "Yikes! All right, all right, sorry, no feet on the table, I get it."

The spatula flew to the sink and was ostentatiously scrubbed.

"Well," Curly said, "young Will here has never seen a play…"

Will's face immediately lit up like a sunrise.

"You're not seriously suggesting we actually put on a performance," Dance said.

"You said you wanted to," Mouse pointed out.

"That was a *lie*. We had no intention of being here that long," Dance said. "What in Goose's name could we possibly put on with three days of rehearsal?"

Will's glance went anxiously from face to face like a dog watching people pass a biscuit tin.

"Not even that," Gilda said. "Two and a half. It had better be something we know."

Hans felt something, like a finger poking his brain. "Do you know *The Tragedy of Amaris and Arturo*?" he said.

"Ooh, that's the 'he's a fish, she's a bird' one, isn't it?" Gilda said. "I like that."

"Is that the Collinson version?" Hans said.

"Yes," said Curly.

"Oh, dear, it's a little dated," Hans said.

"Yeah, but it's a classic," Curly said. "And we know it inside out."

"If I make some slight alterations, would you still have time to learn them?" Hans said.

Dance looked at his troupe, looked at Will, and threw up his hands. "All right. I suppose we're doing the show right here."

Will beamed and clapped his hands. "Oh, wonderful!"

"But they'd better be *slight* alterations," Dance said. "What do you intend?"

"Just to sharpen it up a bit," Hans said, his eyes already going distant behind his spectacles. "Besides, you're going to have quite an audience, aren't you? A crowd of powerful Good Folk. You want to give them something a little special."

"So long as it keeps them happy until we can get out of here," Dance said. "Preferably in our original shapes."

"I'll do my best," Hans said. His fingers were already itching for a pen. He had not felt this excited about rewriting an old play since—well, in fact, he'd *never* felt excited about rewriting someone else's work. But now, for some reason, and despite the circumstances, it was all he could think about.

The Despairing Prince

HARMING PACED HIS room, thrusting his hands through his hair. Had he bothered to glance in the mirror, he would have seen that he looked almost like a woodwose himself.

He didn't have Roland. He didn't even have Kichka. Why he wanted either of them, he couldn't think, except that Roland felt like the closest thing he had had to a friend in a very long time. Not that he'd treated him like one. And Kichka—well, Kichka reminded him of Roland.

But Roland, wherever he was now, almost certainly didn't think of him as a friend. Nor did any of the women—or the various other people—he'd robbed, deceived, and left behind.

All to try and save a father who didn't even like him.

Well, and to save himself. Although Charming was seriously beginning to wonder whether he was worth saving. His earlier plunge into self-reflection had been unpleasant, certainly, but it was nothing to the

284

pitchy mineshaft of misery down which he was now plummeting.

Well? Did you plan to just never tell *her, and hope that no one else ever recognised you?* It must have been the players. Perhaps they had been performing at some town when he was there, perhaps he had even been in the audience.

Not that it mattered. His luck had finally, and utterly, run out.

Even if he used the ring to get to his meeting with Mephistopheles, what then? What if Hans and Will were right and he would simply forget that the Beast existed? What if he remembered but couldn't find the place again?

He had to earn her forgiveness, somehow. The only way he could imagine doing it was by solving the riddle, but he'd had a *month*. All his cleverness had not helped him one bit.

And now—in so many ways—his time was almost up.

The stuffiness of the room was unbearable. He tried to open the window, but it refused to move.

He clutched his scalp and groaned.

The Fairy Godmother

HE KUCHENMEISTER'S TWO stableboys were playing a game involving four stones, three sticks and a great many complex rules which changed depending on who seemed to be winning. Hooves rattled on the hardened mud of the road, and a very upright old lady on a magnificent, glossy dappled grey sat looking down at them with an eyebrow raised.

She had the look of a grandmother who changed you when you were a skinny little naked crab of a baby and is never going to let you forget it.

She dropped nimbly to the ground and tossed the reins to the nearest boy. "See to the horse, there's good lads. Clean water and good grain, I shall know if you give him anything else. Oh, and this." She handed the other boy a large chunk of cheese. "*After* he's had his grain, not before."

She straightened her skirts and strode into the inn.

They looked at the cheese, then at each other. "Cheese," one said. "For a *horse*."

"Gentry," said the other.

"Gentry."

The horse whickered as though in agreement, looking longingly over its shoulder at the cheese as it was led to the stables.

"ELEANOR EVANGELINE DE Braise! What *exactly* are you up to?" The old lady swept into the room in a rustle of green silks and a rattle of heels and pearls. She sniffed, suspiciously. "And is there an *imp* in this inn?"

Nell leapt to her feet, her eyes widening, and beamed. "Godmamma! Would you like a glass of wine?"

"Not if it's the stuff I was given last time I was in the Scatovald. Tasted like mushrooms and rusty magic. Come here, child, and give me a hug."

Nell embraced her godmother and gave her a smacking kiss on the cheek. "You look as splendid as ever," she said. "And no, this wine is excellent."

She poured her godmother a glass. "This is my godmother, Iolanthe. This is Princess Marie Blanche de Neige, Lady Bella Lucia dei' Sogni, and Doctor Emilia Rapunzel."

"Well, that's a great deal of importance in one room," Iolanthe said.

The macaw crowed, from his perch on the windowsill.

"That's Kichka," Nell offered, and the bird executed a remarkably formal bow.

Iolanthe regarded him with a beady eye, and sniffed. "He doesn't *smell* of magic," she said. "How very unusual."

"Not magic, as far we know," Rapunzel said. "Just clever."

The old woman gave a bark of laughter. "So I see," she said. "And you can come out from where you're hiding, too, imp."

"I wasn't *hiding*," Roland grumbled, shuffling into view.

"Weren't you, indeed. So, someone get an old lady a chair."

"I would if I could see an old lady," Nell said. "You're probably stronger than I am."

"That's enough out of you, you baggage. I'm older than your kingdom, and don't you forget it."

"Yes, Godmamma." Nell rolled her eyes, but pulled up a chair. Iolanthe sat on it as though it were a throne, and surveyed the company. "You, I know about," she said to Bella Lucia. "And you," to Marie Blanche. "You, I don't," she said to Doctor Rapunzel, "but you're obviously an educated woman, and probably sensible, so kindly tell me what all this is about."

THE EXPLANATION TOOK long enough for the glass of wine to be emptied, refilled, and emptied again. Iolanthe's eyes in their net of wrinkles were glittery sharp as obsidian knives. Occasionally she asked a pointed question, occasionally she muttered to herself, and when Doctor Rapunzel finished, Iolanthe leaned back in her chair, let out an explosive breath, and said, "Well. This is a proper coil of snakes."

"Do you think you can get us in?" Nell said.

"Oh, I can do better than that: I can get *invitations*. Whether I can do it without hauling you all into just such nets as you've already been tangled in, and worse—*and* myself—is another matter. I've kept my fingers out of all their poisonous pies for a long time, and had planned to do so forever. Our best chance to cover ourselves is probably if you can get the Bear Witch and the werewolf back on your side."

"That might be a problem," Marie Blanche said, her fingers drumming on her knife hilt.

"More than *might*," said Doctor Rapunzel.

"Well, sort it out. I'm sure you've the brains between you!"

"Do *you* know why Mephistopheles made that bargain with Charming?" Bella asked, tugging at a stray curl.

"Now what would *I* know about the doings of the infernal? Certainly not. I knew someone who did, but that was very long ago, and he was mortal, so…" Her mouth drooped for a moment, then she shrugged. "And I've forgotten a great deal. We all do. If we remembered everything we'd go mad. Not that some of them need any help.

"I will say, it's unlikely the gold is the point. Either he set the price as high as he did because he wanted Charming to fail, or he wanted to put him to some specific difficulty succeeding, or he wanted to set him on a certain course on the way.

"But the *why* of the bargain isn't the point, is it? You need Charming free to fulfil it, and after that, if you're wise, you'll leave well enough alone."

"Believe me, we plan to," said Marie Blanche. "For myself, I will be very happy never to see him again."

"Sensible woman."

"So what's the plan?" Nell said.

"Plan? There is no plan. Yet. I need a rest and a think. And if you have a tincture of honeysuckle about you, doctor, I'll take some of that, too."

"Yes, ma'am," said Doctor Rapunzel.

The Seething House

HERE WERE NO roses on anyone's plate this evening. Instead, there were two beautifully roasted partridges, and one sad, blackened lump.

The sad lump sat in front of Charming, who, it must be said, fitted the same description.

"It's not like the cook to make a mistake like that," Will said. "I wonder what happened." He looked oddly guilty, as though somehow it might have been his fault.

"It wasn't a mistake," Charming said. He sawed a dry fragment off the partridge, put it in his mouth, and chewed.

"I don't understand..." Will said.

"They hate me," Charming said.

"I'm sure they don't," Will said. "Why would they hate you?"

"Because I'm a terrible person." Charming picked up his glass and took a gulp of wine, grimaced, stared at the glass, shrugged, and kept drinking.

Will looked at Hans, who also shrugged.

After supper, where every dish served to Charming had been overdone, underdone, or simply absent, Will took Hans aside. "What in the name of Goose is going on with Charming? And the servants? Did he do something?"

Hans sighed. "Look, Will, I know you like him. So did I. But he's not a good person. He said it himself, though I don't know what sparked that sudden honesty. Stay away from him. There's only a little while to go."

"We don't know that, though. What if he knows he's been chosen to stay? What if…?"

"I'd leave well enough alone, if I were you." Hans patted his shoulder. "I have to go rehearse."

"AGAIN, FROM THE top, please," Dance said, tugging at his beard. "Gilda, try and remember it's not a comedy."

"All right," said Gilda sulkily, doing stretches to ease her muscles. "I still think we should keep the bit with the donkey."

"Just because you insisted we buy that donkey costume, at *horrific* expense I might add," Dance said, "doesn't mean we have to use it every time."

"We really don't need the donkey," Hans said. "Or the knife-throwing, Mouse, though I admire the skill. Otherwise, you're happy with the script?"

"Oh, *yes,*" Mouse said fervently. She looked at Dance out of the corner of her eye. "I mean… you know… it's all right."

"It's much better," Dance said. "You can all stop tiptoeing around it, you know. I know a good reworking when I read one. This is *way* better without poor old Collinson's meanderings about things that have no relevance to the plot. And it's a sight shorter, too, which under the circumstances is a blessing of which we are in dire need. Cassia… are you going to prompt? It seems apt since it's how we got into this."

"So long as I don't have to come out for the bows," Cassia said. "I don't want anyone seeing me, just in case."

"Fine. Now, places, everyone. Gilda, I can *see* that tail. Put it *away*."

An Interlude

ILL WAS ON his way back to the menagerie. It had quickly become his favourite place, even if it was too warm. At least he'd learned how to unlace his stupid complicated jacket so he could take it off. He just hoped the next one the house forced on him worked the same way.

The little monkey had taken to riding on his shoulder, with her tail wrapped around his neck. "If I have to stay here," he told her, "at least I'll have you, eh?"

He was trying not to think about Aunt Thelise, and her brusque kindness, and little Tylek who always ran up to him on his dimpled toddler legs shouting, "Unca Will! Unca Will!" and demanding to be spun about. Most of all he was trying not to think about Hedel, and her strong brown throat and her eyes and her smile and the way she made him feel special.

He was about to open the door when he saw Charming.

Charming's arms were full of roses, and he was absolutely covered in scratches, worse than he had been after he tried to escape. His clothes were a mass of rips, and his hair was full of leaves.

"What… Did you try to escape again?"

"No. Do you know where the Beast's private quarters are? The servants won't show me. I just want to leave some roses outside her door!" he shouted at the air. "And talk to her, even if it's *through* the door!"

Only silence responded.

"Why are you taking her roses?" Will said.

"Because women like roses!"

"But… they're already hers. Aren't they? So you're just giving her her own roses…"

"Oh." Charming looked down at the heaped flowers. "I suppose I am." His shoulders slumped and he trudged away, shedding the occasional petal and shred of trouser.

Will watched him go, shaking his head.

The Witch's Demand

HESE KEEP-AWAYS ARE annoying," Iolanthe said. "Yes, unpleasant," Doctor Rapunzel replied. "And there are more of them." Sparks snapped between her fingers.

They were on their way to Goldlöckchen's cottage. Marie Blanche walked a little ahead, knife in hand, casting about. Roland and Kichka had been left at the inn along with Bella and Nell, with strict instructions to stay out of mischief. The unspoken part of this was that if things went too wrong, some of them needed to still be alive and in human shape.

"I hope you're not seriously expecting us to keep those two out of trouble," Nell said, with a jaundiced look. Kichka was cackling and chattering to himself, and Roland was curled up in a corner with a book of recipes acquired who-knew-where, and pretending to ignore him.

"This situation requires delicate handling," Doctor Rapunzel said.

"So will I by the time you get back."

Doctor Rapunzel had been reluctant to bring Iolanthe either, feeling another stranger—and one of the Good Folk, at that—would further antagonise Goldlöckchen. But she had refused to be left behind.

"Feels like an itch," Iolanthe said. "Like an itch in my brain. She's not focussed on keeping fairies out, though, is she? They don't seem to trouble you much."

"I have methods." *I see clearly, I pass through.* It was harder, much harder, this time. Goldlöckchen must be pouring a great deal of her power into these keep-aways; either she would soon exhaust herself, or she was far more dangerously powerful than Doctor Rapunzel knew.

"Hah. You play close to the chest. Smart woman." Iolanthe picked a dandelion head and twirled it, sending the seeds drifting on the breeze. "But even a smart woman can be fooled by a handsome man with the right words and the wrong intentions."

"I was a girl, then, with less knowledge of the world than I thought. I am a great deal less susceptible now, I hope."

Iolanthe gave her a sidelong look. "Being susceptible isn't *always* a bad thing."

"It depends to what," Doctor Rapunzel said. "Or whom."

"True enough," Iolanthe said. "I fell in love, or what I thought was love, easier than I fell asleep, for many years; then I found the real thing, and if I'd known how much it would hurt, I'd have wished to be less susceptible, too. But I can't regret it."

"Even though it hurt?"

"It hurt because it was real," Iolanthe said. "Realer than anything I'd known. Maybe because he was mortal. And of course…" She sighed. "He was mortal."

"I'm sorry."

"Ah, it was a long time ago. Sometimes I'm surprised I remember it at all. There are things that are quite gone. Some conversations we had... But I'll remember his smile as long as I've a memory, and his kindness. He was a good man. Some things are worth being susceptible to."

"The hard thing is knowing whether something—or someone—is worth it, or not."

"Oh, yes."

THE FIRST BEARS appeared before they had gone much further. Iolanthe looked at them, and sniffed.

"Bears. Excessive, if you ask me. What's wrong with a good ward? It's not as though she can't make one."

"Wards just keep you out. They don't embody fear."

"Like that, is it?"

The bears closed up in front of them and blocked the path completely. Their heads were dropped between hunched shoulders, and they tore at the ground with their claws.

Marie Blanche stopped. Doctor Rapunzel and Iolanthe caught up to her.

"So what do you do about the bears?" Iolanthe said.

"We wait. She will know we are here by now. If I attempt to force them out of our way, not only might I fail, but it would worsen our situation. We need her in a good mood. Marie Blanche, what are you doing?"

"This is wrong," Marie Blanche said, striding towards the bears. "These poor creatures are suffering." She held out her hand and made a low grumbling noise.

The other women looked at each other, and drew slightly closer together.

"Your friend can speak bear?" Iolanthe said.

"A very little," Marie Blanche said, not turning around. "I can understand, and convey, some simple things. I know they are suffering. Trying to explain that they are suffering because of their mistress is too complicated, and will upset them further."

"No!" Goldlöckchen was suddenly there, right in front of Marie Blanche, holding out her hands as though warding off something. "No! Go away, all of you." She put a hand on each of the bear's sides, and they leaned into her.

"You are causing them pain," Marie Blanche said.

"I would never hurt them! Go away!"

"We don't want to hurt them, either," Rapunzel said. "Or you."

Goldlöckchen trembled like a pale flame between the bears. Rapunzel could feel the magic building in the air around them, making the trees shiver against the wind, and the ground move uneasily beneath their feet, like a hibernating bear stirred by ugly dreams.

"Oh, child," Iolanthe said. "Oh, child, there's no need to be so afraid. You could turn us all to ash with a word; I can feel it. But what would be the use of that?"

Rapunzel said, "Can you tell me what it is that frightens you so?"

"Why won't you just leave me alone?" Goldlöckchen said, and it became painfully, pitifully clear how young she really was, barely more than a child—a terrified, lethal child about to unleash her fear.

Rapunzel felt a jab of recognition. "May I speak with you?" she said. "Just us, alone. You may bind me, if you wish, before I go another step. I will not fight it."

"*Rapunzel!*" Marie Blanche hissed.

Iolanthe's gaze, old and sharp and unreadable, flicked from one to the other. "Are you sure, doctor?"

"Yes, if she is willing."

Goldlöckchen stood for a long moment, "Only you, no one else," she said. "Under a binding of my choosing."

"Yes."

"The rest of you, go away."

"No," Marie Blanche said. "Not without knowing what the binding is, and how long it lasts. We will not leave our friend in someone's power without being sure she will be safe."

Goldlöckchen shot her a look, riddled with complex emotions, and flicked her hand.

On the path between them, a candle lantern appeared. Its base was of blood-coloured wood, its glass thick and rippled, its frame of a metal that shimmered darkly as a beetle's wing. The candle in it was thick, but short. "She will be bound from magic until the candle burns out. No longer, no less."

Bound. A binding. Bound. Helpless. The thought was appalling. Rapunzel straightened her back. "On two conditions," she said. "That you hear me out, and that no harm comes to my friends by your hand or your will."

"Accepted." Goldlöckchen turned to Rapunzel and made another gesture, drawing an outline around Rapunzel's body, then snapped her fingers.

Doctor Rapunzel felt the binding land and supressed the sound that tried to leave her throat. Not quite well enough, judging by the concerned look Marie Blanche gave her.

She had become used to feeling magic at her fingertips, though—as a sorceress—her own art required physical ingredients and artefacts, unlike that of the fairies.

Being bound was like one of her senses being turned off. A sudden blankness, a wall where there should not be a wall.

Suddenly she was fourteen again, and helpless in the face of power.

Good, said that part of her mind that had always stood back, and watched, and calculated, and waited for its moment. *Let her see it.*

"Come, then," Goldlöckchen said.

The stumble with which Rapunzel followed her was not entirely calculated.

The bears moved aside to let them pass, and then closed the pathway with their bodies, heads hanging.

THE COTTAGE LOOKED as neat and pretty as ever, the scent of the ginger lilies catching at the heart with sweetness.

It is a lost child's vision of a perfect home, Rapunzel thought. *It is warm and pretty and sweet-smelling, clean and cared for. And safe.*

And much like mine.

She had spent her childhood in the thin charity of an orphanage, and her girlhood in a blood-coloured tower. In both she had been often cold, often hungry, often bruised, often afraid—though the fears she had felt in the orphanage were nothing to those she had felt in the tower. Her cottage, too, was warm and pretty and sweet-smelling (unless she had been talking to one of the Infernal's inhabitants) and as safe as she could make it.

She wondered what Goldlöckchen's childhood home had looked like.

Goldlöckchen waved her to a chair, and she almost fell into it.

You aren't so weak. But without magic she *felt* weak. *Don't fight it. Let her see.*

Goldlöckchen sat on the other side of the table and stared at her with those ice-blue eyes. "Well?" she said.

"I grew up in the orphanage in Finsterburg," Rapunzel said. "When I was a young girl, someone took me in. A sorceress. She promised me comfort and safety, but I had to obey without question. And even when I obeyed without question, there was no comfort, nor safety. I was beaten, and starved, and tormented. Because she loved power, she did not love me. And I was afraid of her, always afraid, but also I was very, very angry."

"What is this to me?" Goldlöckchen said. "Your candle is burning down, doctor. Before it goes out I will cast you back to your friends, and make sure none of you ever comes here again."

"Please, only listen a little longer. She meant to oust my spirit from my body and wear my body herself, until it wore out. She had done it before, over and over." She could still see the caskets lined up in Mother Hilda's treasure room, each of them containing a lock of hair, black or brown or yellow or red.

"In time, I got the chance to oust her spirit as she meant to do to me. Fear did not stop me. Fear drove me. I did it without remorse.

"Where her spirit is now, I do not know. But I know this. She was well known in the town, but not one person ever came looking for her. Not one of the men she danced with, not one of those who sent her roses and begged for a second glance, not one of the townsfolk who owed her for favours done and spells cast, not even the man she planned to marry, came looking for her, to see if she were sick or needed help. When I appeared with her books and her name, *no one* asked what had happened to her. Not one. Do you know why?"

Goldlöckchen shrugged and looked aside.

"Because the only thing they remembered was fear. Even those who were fascinated by her, even those who thought they adored her, what they really felt was fear. She couldn't hide what she was, not really, not for long. But if all you have is fear, who will be there for you if you need help? In the end, there are pitchforks, or there is silence."

"I have my bears. I have my brother. I don't need anyone else."

"You are driving your bears beyond their limits," Rapunzel said, as gently as she could. "And your brother, even if he comes safe home; he travels, does he not?"

"Of course he does! He's clever, he's interested in things, I don't *trap* him here."

"No, of course you don't, because he is your brother and you love him and you know that he needs a life of his own, out among people. But things happen to travellers. Not just bad things. What if he wishes to marry, and set up his own home, but does not, because he fears what you will do?"

"I would *never* hurt Hans!"

"But would you hurt someone who took him from you? Even if he wanted them to? Or would you just make them afraid you might?"

"No… no. Of course I wouldn't."

"But can *he* be sure of that?"

"Are you saying my brother is *afraid* of me?"

"I am saying that fear is a weapon that will turn on the wielder. I am saying that using fear to keep you safe will never rid you of your own terrors. Perhaps my captor, too, long ago, was terribly afraid. Perhaps she, too, let fear drive her until using it was all she knew. And it left her with nothing and no one on her side."

An Interlude

OR, DEAR, YOU'VE properly got ants up in your underthings, haven't you?" Roland said, watching Nell pace the room, her eyes clouded with worry. He had abandoned the recipe book and was hanging upside down from one of the windows, looking more than ever like a gargoyle, though one designed by a carver who had perhaps eaten slightly too many of the wrong sort of mushroom. He was using the eye not occupied by Nell to watch Lady Bella, who had gone down to the stable yard to practise her swordplay. "Ooh, nice lunge."

"What do you expect?" Nell snapped. "They've walked into the maw of a powerful and apparently thoroughly unstable witch, just to try and coax a little help out of her, our other potential ally is now running scared, and we've dragged my godmother into Goose knows what kind of mess. And we're running out of *time*."

"Well, yeah," Roland said. "They should have taken Lady Bella."

"They *couldn't*. She's all we have left if something happens to them."

"So we're left sitting on our…"

Kichka screeched and fluttered his tail.

"Shut it, you irritating flying paintbox," Roland said.

"Stop it, the pair of you," Nell said, massaging her brow. "How is throwing insults—and yes, Kichka, I can tell even if I can't understand you—helping anything?"

"It passes the time," Roland said. "I'd still rather be doing something useful."

"Like what?"

Roland shrugged. "Anything."

Nell looked at him. "Roland, is it true you want to run an eating-house?"

Roland looked around and glared, particularly at Kichka, who was cleaning his feathers and ignored him. "Well don't just *tell* everyone."

"If you're serious you're going to have to get used to people knowing about it. In fact if they don't, you won't have any customers. Which is sort of the point of an eating-house. Why make food if no one's going to come eat it?"

"I s'pose. So?"

"So come with me," Nell said. "We're going to the kitchens."

HANS PASSED THE library on his way to bed. Seeing the door open and a light on, he glanced inside.

Huddled in one of the chairs, entirely surrounded by books, as though he were using them to build a fort around himself, was Charming. He had a vast ancient volume open on his knee and was squinting at the tiny, faded text, muttering and taking notes. The room was too warm, and desperately stuffy, but the windows of the manor now resisted every effort to get them open.

He heard the floorboards creak and looked up, with desperate hope on his face, only for it to drop away at the sight of Hans.

"May I enquire…?" Hans said.

"Some of these books have riddles, and stuff about magic. I should have looked before, but I… Well, I *did,* a bit. Not enough. There might be a clue in here, about the riddle, don't you think? Surely, *somewhere.*"

He looked so desperate Hans almost felt sorry for him, but the man was as much of an actor as those he'd just been dealing with. Who knew if either the hope or the desperation were even real? And if it was, surely, it was only hope and desperation for himself, for a last chance to get free before whatever was going to happen, happened.

"I have searched this library quite thoroughly," Hans said. "And I have some practice at it. I have found nothing. I think we simply have to wait it out."

Charming shook his head and went back to his book, not even looking up when Hans left.

THE DAY DARKENED. Settling birds rustled in the trees. Marie Blanche grew impatient, and paced, glancing now and again at the lantern with deep dislike. Sometimes she approached the bears, but they looked away and would not communicate with her. She picked up a stick and started to cast through the undergrowth, poking at ferns and turning aside leaf litter.

"Restive, aren't you?" Iolanthe said. She had conjured

a small cushion and settled herself on it. "I'm too old for resting my backside on a mossy bank, these days," she said. "The damp gets in my hips."

Marie Blanche ignored her, poking and prodding and staring. Then she turned and came back. "There are wolf tracks here," she said. "They become the tracks of men, going towards the cottage." She looked extremely grim.

The Strangers Came Calling

OWER IS NOT 'nothing,'" Goldlöckchen said.

"No, but it doesn't care about you," said Rapunzel. "I would never tell a witch to give up her power; this world is dangerous, and power is useful. But there is more than one kind of power. Making alliances is powerful, and having actual friends is powerful, too. A village full of people who are terrified of you is powerful, certainly, but will they have your back when the witch-burners come to town?"

"I don't need *them* to protect me from witch-burners. I can burn witch-burners."

"And what about a more powerful sorcerer? Someone your wards don't work on, and your binding doesn't work on? Or someone who knows your true name?"

"How could they possibly help me then?"

"You never know. People are remarkably resourceful. *You* were resourceful enough to get yourself and your brother away from your father, and how much power did you have when you did that? Why deny yourself something that might be useful?"

Goldlöckchen looked at the table, and rubbed her finger over a knot in the wood. "What do you want, sorceress?"

"I want your help, and your bears' help, to get that wretched man out of the mansion, by midnight tomorrow night. If we can get your brother out as well, of course we will."

"I have sent someone to get him out already. I *told* you."

"So I understand, but I don't yet see him here."

"Those stupid players. I should never have trusted them."

"You sent a group of players?"

"They had a fairy with them, in the form of a cat. She persuaded me."

"Ah."

"You think I was stupid." A cold, resentful flicker in those blue eyes.

"I think you were very worried for your brother. And I have found players to be extraordinarily useful in the past. My fear is that we have no time. We are coming up to a point where whatever is going on in that house is playing out. *Someone* is going to be chosen, for whatever it is, and whether it is Charming, or the wolf-clan's boy, or your brother, once it is done it will be hard to undo. Will you tell me what happened, to make you so angry?"

Goldlöckchen looked at the table again, staring deep into the grain, as though she could disappear into it and pull it shut behind her.

"There were men," she said, so quietly Rapunzel could hardly hear her. "There were two men. I was in the garden, and I saw them, standing in the trees and watching me. I don't know how they got past the wards, and the bears. They were watching me and *grinning*." She shuddered, so violently the legs of her chair rattled against the stone flags.

"They looked like him. Like my father. And I... I froze. I couldn't do anything. I just stood there. Then one of the bears smelled them and came running and she roared and they didn't move and... she caught one of them. The other turned to a wolf, and then I knew what they were. Then another of the bears came. They drove them off. I wish she'd *killed* him," she said. "They just stood there and *grinned* at me and I couldn't *move!* I couldn't cast or *anything!* If it hadn't been for the bear..." The air shuddered and glimmered, and a small whirlwind caught up some twigs and leaves that had blown in the door, and whipped them about.

"Oh, my dear," Rapunzel said, mentally cursing the two weres. "Oh, my poor child. Listen—hush—listen. I can help you. I can help you not to freeze. Will you let me help you?"

"CANDLE'S GONE OUT," Iolanthe said.

Marie Blanche glared at the tiny orange glow that was all that remained. "Then where *is* she?"

"There," Iolanthe said.

The Changing Prince

HEN HE NEXT heard the floorboards creak, Charming did not even look up. "You might help me *look*, Hans. You might have missed something."

"Oh, I doubt Hans missed anything," the Beast said. "He's quite astute. Of course, we all missed *something*, didn't we?"

Charming leapt to his feet, books tumbling everywhere. "Beast…"

"Some of the books are quite valuable, don't forget those," she said. "That one by your feet, with the gilded cover, is probably worth more than half the rest. You don't want to be too loaded down, I'm sure."

"I wasn't… I'm trying to solve the riddle!"

She looked at him and laughed. It was not the laugh he was used to, low and with a pleasant huskiness, but a sharp, ugly cascade of barks and yips. "Solve the riddle!" she yelped. "Solve the riddle! *You!*" And before he could say another word, she was gone again.

311

He almost ran after her, but by this point he was fairly sure the servants would set tripwires for him if he tried. They had turned against him. No new clothes had been set out for him, he was wearing those he'd worn to pick (or wrestle) the roses, though he had replaced the completely destroyed shirt with a limp, yellowed one he had found at the bottom of a chest in his room.

Perhaps if he could solve the riddle, the servants would forgive him, too.

What's happened to you, Charming?

He honestly wasn't sure. Somehow, he had come to care what people he'd never met thought of him. More, he'd come to care for what the *Beast* thought of him. Even if she never saw him again, if he was dumped back in the forest with no memory of her whatsoever, he hated the thought that all *she* would remember was a man who had planned to rob her. And it wasn't even *true*.

(That part, admittedly, stung. For once he was innocent, and here he stood, accused.)

Maybe all this brooding was just knowing his own death—or something equally unpleasant and possibly a lot slower—was likely to happen very soon. People did start contemplating what they'd done with their lives when they were about to die, or so he'd heard.

And he cared for the Beast, ridiculous as it was. She was a beast, of course, but he *liked* her. Or he had. He contemplated the wound on his hand, far deeper than the scratches from the roses, where she'd caught him with her claws.

There was a sort of stillness in the air, like a held breath.

Yes, he still liked her, but damn, he would make her regret thinking so badly of him. Somehow he would find a way to prove his innocence, even if by then he was far away, or dead, and then she'd be sorry.

The held breath released in a mournful sigh. Charming felt a cold draught on the back of his neck, turned his collar up, and went back to reading.

What the Sorceress Learned

HE BEARS LIFTED their heads, shook themselves, and drew apart, allowing Doctor Rapunzel to walk between them.

"You're well? You're safe?" Marie Blanche demanded.

"Yes, thank you." She looked drained, her already pale skin almost luminous in the darkening forest, her hands, still faintly shining with the aftermath of sorcery, trembling faintly but constantly.

Marie Blanche offered her a flask of water, and Rapunzel drank gratefully. The bears turned and walked away, their great shaggy hindquarters visible for a few moments before the woods hid them.

"Well, what happened?" Iolanthe said. "Took it out of you, whatever it was."

"We have her agreement to aid us."

"Hmm. And what did you have to give for it?"

"Little enough," Doctor Rapunzel said.

"Doesn't look like it," Iolanthe said. "Oh, well, don't mind me. It's no skin off my nose if you overspent your skill, so long as you're back on form tomorrow."

"I will be," Doctor Rapunzel said, and then collapsed into the leaf mould.

MARIE BLANCHE SUPPORTED Doctor Rapunzel back to the Inn. Iolanthe followed, muttering. "Don't be expecting me to turn anything into anything," she said. "No fruit into coaches and such. I don't do that anymore."

"I did not expect it," Marie Blanche said. She looked sharply at the older woman. "Why, could you?"

"Well, of course I *could*. I was famous for it."

"I was not aware," Marie Blanche said. "If you *could* assist, in any way, that would be helpful."

Iolanthe grumbled, but propped up Doctor Rapunzel's other side.

Before long, Doctor Rapunzel was fully conscious, and eventually removed herself from their support, or tried. Marie Blanche kept hold of her, gripping her arm firmly. "You are too thin," she said. "You have been working too hard, and not eating enough. No wonder you collapsed. When we get back I will tell the kitchen to make you a posset, and you will drink it."

"Yes, Mamma," Doctor Rapunzel said, drily.

They approached the inn to a strong smell of burning, but at least, as Rapunzel pointed out, none of the building was visibly on fire.

Kichka flew out of an upper window, chattering.

"Oh, it appears Roland burned a pie," Marie Blanche said. "That would explain the smell."

* * *

"CAN YOU TELL me what you did?" Marie Blanche said.

Doctor Rapunzel was leaning back in a chair with her fingers smeared with salve, a wet cloth (pungent with herbs) on her head, and a hot tisane (pungent with brandy) at her elbow. An empty bowl of posset stood on the table. "I gave her some tools to protect herself. The sort of thing that normally takes months of training. She is disturbingly adept. But I hope that now, she will be less... volatile."

Rapunzel knew she had mishandled the girl, badly, to start with. Whether she had done enough to make up for it, she was not sure; but enough, at least, to get them through tomorrow. *Tomorrow*. She groaned inwardly. "We have yet to deal with Red Cap."

"Bella and I are about to leave. You are exhausted. Stay here. Nell, keep those little wretches out of her room, and make sure she eats a good supper."

"Not pie," Doctor Rapunzel said.

"It won't be pie," Nell said, narrowing her eyes at Roland. "There is no pie. We're lucky there's still a kitchen. I had to give that poor cook so much gold... And she's still never going to forgive me."

"Yeah, but I know what I did wrong," Roland said.

The Wolves and the Diplomat

ELLA LUCIA AND Marie Blanche approached
the clearing, shadowed by the wolves that had
followed them since they entered the fringes of
the forest. The trees cast long shadows, the afternoon was
well advanced and the sun lowering redly in the west.

The leaf mould was damp with dew, already smelling
of autumn. The memory of her fight with Red Cap—
Thelise—made Marie Blanche shiver. She clenched and
relaxed her fingers, heard Bella take a slightly shaky breath.

"You'll do well," Marie Blanche said.

"I hope so," Bella said, shoving a curl behind her ear.
"But when I've negotiated before—Well, Papa and Mama
have always been there to advise me, not to mention a
dozen councillors and who-knows-who-else."

"None of them were there when you dealt with the
villagers."

"I suppose I hadn't had time to think about it. I just did
it."

So just do it again. Marie Blanche realised this was

317

probably not helpful or encouraging. "My mother always told me, put your hands to what is in front of them. Sometimes what's in front of them is not something you ever wanted, or saw yourself dealing with, but you do it nonetheless, because you must. When I learned to negotiate with the dwarven tribes, I was a great deal younger than you are, and knew far less than I thought I did. Even so I managed not to lose trade, or spark a tribal war. And I have none of your gifts."

"I rather hate the gifts, sometimes," Bella muttered. "I know, I know how ungrateful it sounds, but I never know if it's *me*. Would I be anything at all, without them?"

"Don't think of them as part of you, then," Marie Blanche said. "Think of them as tools you've been given. Would you throw away an excellent sword, simply because you never asked for it?"

"Huh. I never thought of it like that." Bella straightened her shoulders. "Shall we?"

They walked forward.

MARIE BLANCHE DID not want to be jealous. It would, in any case, be ridiculous to be jealous.

She told herself this in her sternest, most no-nonsense inner voice, as she waited for Bella's usual effect to flood out around her like sunlight, brightening the faces of everyone who approached.

But most of these faces were not human. Almost all of them were in wolf form, all were wary.

Bella stood, calm, as the pack approached, her hands held out low and open.

As they got closer, hackles dropped, and muzzles softened, but they still kept their distance.

Thelise, in human form, came last, stepping lightly and holding herself ready. She nodded to Marie Blanche, then her gaze fixed on Bella.

I will not be jealous.

"You're the fey-touched one, then," Thelise said.

Bella bowed. "Bella Lucia dei' Sogni, at your service. And you are Lady Thelise Fournier, the leader of these people. I hoped we might speak with you."

"I don't go by that name, here," Thelise said. "Red Cap will do."

"My apologies."

"No matter. Come to the hall. We'll have this discussion where everyone can hear, if you please."

Thelise, or Red Cap as she was currently insisting, was chilly and distant, not precisely rude, but definitely not in the mood to be cooperative. Whether it was her mood that was affecting the pack, or the other way around, Marie Blanche could not be sure, but there was a definite feel of rather too many tensed muscles and bared teeth around them.

Bella's low, musical voice, calm and sensible and soothing, barely needed actual words to suggest that everyone should just listen and it would all work out for the best.

But even with her skills, she was working against the tide.

"Unless you can get an agreement from the witch that neither she nor hers will harm me or mine," Red Cap snapped, "there's no deal. I don't trust her."

"I do understand," Bella said. "Could I speak to the person who was hurt? Just so I have a clear understanding of what happened."

One of the wolves leapt to its feet, and began to shift. "Claus!" Red Cap snapped. "Clothing!"

The wolf looked shamefaced, exactly like a dog that has been caught doing something it shouldn't, and slunk out of the hall towards one of the huts as fast as it could slink.

Bella attempted to draw Red Cap out, and Red Cap gave abrupt answers, hardly looking at Bella at all. Marie Blanche knew Bella had that effect on some people, rendering them completely tongue-tied. Part of her wanted to drag Red Cap aside and say... something, she wasn't sure what.

Shortly after, Claus appeared, in human form and in a pair of approximately clean and reasonably mended breeches, and a shirt that was as white as could be expected, given the circumstances. In the open neck of the shirt, the end of a thick, shiny scar could be seen lying across his shoulder like rope.

Bella smiled at him. "How is your injury now? Can we offer any help?"

Claus blushed and swaggered. "I'm all right," he said. "I'm strong, me."

Another wolf grumbled, and Claus ignored it, staring at Bella. The other wolf got up and went to the hut.

"I'm sorry that happened," Bella said. "Could you tell me more about it?"

"Well the thing is," Claus said, "we went out to have a sniff about."

"Hunting." Kurt emerged from the hut in slightly more battered versions of everything Claus was wearing. "I'm his brother," he said. "I was there too. We were hunting. And that's *my* shirt. Your ladyship." He bowed. Claus glared at him, and also bowed.

"Yes. Hunting. And no, it isn't."

"And did you have any luck?" Bella said.

"Nah. Looking for deer, found a trail but it faded out, so we went a bit further. Used to be plenty of deer, but…" Claus shrugged. "Guess they know we're here by now."

Red Cap shifted in her seat, and glanced over at a young woman nearby, who was frowning.

"That must be frustrating," Bella said. "Especially if you know people are depending on you for the food you bring."

"Yeah, well, you know," Kurt said. "We mostly find *something*, this time of year. And we've got plenty stored."

"I see. So the deer trail ran out, and you went a bit further, to see what you could find, yes?"

"Yeah."

"Was that deep into the Scatovald? I hear it can be very dangerous. Were you not worried about that?"

"Nah, I wasn't worried. Takes a lot to frighten me," Claus said.

"And me," Kurt said. "I mean, I'm not letting anything stop me going where I want to go."

"Nothing? Not even if it's raining, or muddy, or snowing?"

"That's just being uncomfortable, isn't it? Wears off."

"How uncomfortable are you prepared to get, in the service of your pack?"

"Oh, pushed through the worst of it, we have, haven't we, Claus? Blizzard, hail, them bloody wards…"

Claus yelped. Kurt snapped his mouth shut and looked sideways at Thelise.

"Ah," Bella said.

"Wait," Thelise said. "You went through the wards? You *knowingly* went into the witch's territory?"

Kurt pointed at Marie Blanche. "She hasn't found Will

yet, has she? She wasn't even looking for him, she was looking for someone else. So we went to have a sniff about."

"You went to have a sniff about."

Clause spoke up. "We were doing all right, only the wind changed."

"When you say 'doing all right'…?"

"Kurt had this really good idea, see, that we'd pretend to be from the village. Thought she might talk to us if she didn't know who we were. And we got pretty close to the cottage—it's *fancy*," he said darkly. "Only then… the wind changed."

"The wind changed." Red Cap was rigid with anger, a barely held-back growl evident in her voice. "And the bears smelled you. You do *remember* they've a better sense of smell than we do? No? You do realise that they'd have known what you were the second you got close enough *whatever* direction the wind was in? *Long* before you'd have had a chance to talk to the witch?"

Bella sighed. "She saw two strange men, standing outside her garden, staring at her. I'm afraid they scared her very badly."

"*They* scared *her*? What did they do?" Thelise turned a look on the men that sent a whimper around the watching circle.

"We didn't do nothing! Only she didn't *look* like a witch, did she?" Kurt said. "She wasn't more than a cub. Skinny little twig of a thing, I could have blown her away with a breath. I saw her and I said to Claus, '*That's* who we've been scared of, all this time?' So I guess I smiled because it was funny, and so did he, and…"

"And then a bear came and nearly tore your brother's head off his shoulders. Did you *forget* about the bears?"

Claus dropped his gaze. "Well, it was still a good idea," he muttered.

"It was a *terrible, stupid* idea, and you are lucky you and your brother and half the pack are not *dead*."

"But she…"

"Quiet! I. Do. Not. Care. You *idiots* put us all in danger. What if she'd come here? What if she *did* have Will, and decided to punish him for your idiocy? Did you injure the bear?"

Kurt puffed out his chest, but quickly deflated at the look she gave him. "No. But…"

"If you use that word one more time I will have your hide. Did you do anything else you haven't told me?"

"I don't think so…"

"You had better be very sure, Kurt. And you, Claus. *Very* sure." She stared, and waited.

Both men were staring at the ground. They shook their heads.

"Get out of my sight, the pair of you. Do *nothing* until I call for you again, to tell you how you will be punished. Go!"

The twins slunk off.

Red Cap shoved her hands through her hair, and looked at Bella and Marie Blanche, then at the pack. "All of you, stay calm. Don't do anything stupid. Anything *else* stupid. We are going to my hut. Hedel, please come with us."

The young woman nodded and joined them.

They left the hall. The rest of the pack, in subdued silence, watched them go.

"In here, you may call me Thelise. I should have known better than to trust what those two told me," she said.

"But… It's the pack. Trusting them before outsiders becomes part of the air we breathe."

"That is not confined to wolf packs," Bella said.

Marie Blanche, while extremely relieved at the turn of events, felt slightly agitated that there were so many people here in the hut. She knew she was being ridiculous, no doubt people were in and out all the time. But it had felt private, when she and Thelise were there alone, like somewhere that belonged, briefly, just to the two of them.

"This is Hedel," Thelise said.

Bella and Marie Blanche bowed to her, and Hedel, a little self-consciously, bowed back.

"I plan for her to be my successor as leader," Thelise said. "You noticed, didn't you?" she said to Hedel. "When they changed their story."

"Yes," Hedel said. "Hunting rabbits to hunting deer. Perhaps they thought deer sounded more impressive."

"I am sorry you have been put to so much trouble," Bella said.

"Hardly your fault two of my pack are raging idiots with more balls than brain," Thelise said. She relaxed back in her chair, lean and lithe and looking more than a little exhausted. Marie Blanche wanted to send everyone else away, and give her tea, and make her rest. But that was not why they were here.

"Tell me your plan," Thelise said to Bella, "and we will see what we can do."

Marie Blanche told herself not to be ridiculous, again, that it was Bella she turned to. Bella was the one who had drawn out the truth, after all. Bella was the one who was here to negotiate, being the best at it. And it was not Bella's fault that she was as breathtaking by firelight, in worn britches and a simple doublet, as she would be dressed for a ball and lit by a thousand candles.

Marie Blanche would not entertain any more stupidity, she told herself firmly, watching Thelise relax, an occasional smile flickering over her mouth as she talked to Bella. Not a bit of it.

"I BELIEVE MARIE Blanche has a proposal for you," Bella said. "Which may help inform your decision as to whether you wish to help us."

"You do?" Thelise turned to her. "What might that be?"

"Firstly, I am willing to put my lawyers at your disposal. I am certain that, given time, they can discover irregularities in your cousin's inheritance of your lands. In the meantime, they can investigate every aspect of the estate, and, in the manner of lawyers, make his life both difficult and expensive.

"Some of the dwarven tribes are considering expanding their mines in Ariens. I can ensure that any deals he may wish to make with them are not to his advantage. While this is going on, life on the estate may become harder for those who work there, so, if you wish, the servants and farmworkers can be found places on my own lands. It may also be possible to discourage any new workers from finding their way to his employ. Eventually, the estate will simply not be worth his time."

"I see," Thelise said.

"I admit, that may all take some years, and will not improve the condition of the estate. More direct methods may be employed."

"Oh?"

"We have resources," Marie Blanche said. "An eye for an eye, or a curse for a curse."

"Ahem," Bella said. "I'm not sure…"

"I would *like* your approval, Lady Bella," Marie Blanche said, "but I do not *need* it."

"I will consider your proposal," Thelise said. "In the meantime, yes, we will help retrieve your wayward prince. In return for one thing."

"And what is that?" Marie Blanche said.

"When you have dealt with your prince, come hunting with me." Thelise grinned at her, both wolf and woman, and Marie Blanche felt her cheeks burning, and could not help smiling back.

Preparations for a Ball

HARMING DRAGGED HIMSELF out of the library past midnight, went to his room and drifted in and out of sleep. He finally fell asleep properly, only to find himself standing on Devil's Head, sitting in one half of a giant pair of scales while Mephistopheles towered over him.

Black dogs with amber eyes ran back and forth with their mouths full of gold, pouring it into the other side of the scales, but no matter how much gold they poured, Charming's side remained firmly fixed to the ground. Mephistopheles bent, inhumanly flexible, until his mouth was near Charming's ear. "Your soul is just too heavy, my boy," he said, and laughed, and laughed, and laughed until Charming jolted awake, sweating and nauseated.

He could hear the sounds of vigorous cleaning and birdsong. The water in his ewer was cold, and yesterday's clothes had been left where he had dropped them. He opened the window further, hoping to clear his head, and maybe to spot Kichka flying towards him, somehow bearing news of how to solve the riddle. Where *was* Kichka? Had there been an early frost while he slept, and now the poor creature was lying dead on the forest floor in a puddle of bright feathers?

The ball was tonight. His date with Mephistopheles was at midnight.

He dressed in the clothes, made a vague pass at combing his hair, and left his room.

He paused in the doorway. Sunlight poured through the windows of the passageway, lighting honey notes in the newly polished floors. As he moved through the manor, everywhere gleamed and glittered. Closer to the kitchens, he could smell cooking, though his stomach cringed from the thought of breakfast. Coffee, however, might help him think.

Will and Hans were already seated in the small dining room. Judging by the barely-touched plates, neither of them had much of a taste for breakfast either.

There were no roses lying by anyone's plates.

Hans looked at him over his spectacles and nodded. Will attempted a smile, which fell away quickly.

"Cheer up, fellow inmates," Charming said. "At least two of us are going to get out of here today."

But his words fell flat, even to his own ears. He managed at least to get a decent, if lukewarm, cup of coffee by pouring it himself before some invisible servitor could snatch away the pot and fill it with tepid cow spit, or whatever they had decided his punishment should be today.

"They must have been cleaning half the night," Will said. "I came out to get some air well before dawn and there were already brooms sweeping and polishing cloths flying about. I mean, I know they *weren't* doing it by themselves, it still looked like it. I didn't even think the place was that dirty!"

"That's balls for you," Charming said.

Will looked glum. "This is all bad enough without anyone expecting me to dance fancy. I can hop about to a fiddle, but doing like they do in those pictures..." He gestured to a painting that showed rows of folk dressed in the height of last century's fashions, lining up and pointing their toes at each other.

"Come, Will," Charming said, pushing back his chair. "You wouldn't do a bout with me, but I can at least show you a few steps. And neither of us will be in danger of accidentally stabbing the other. What do you say?"

"Oh, no, I..."

Hans rose from the table. "I must see how the players are getting on." He left.

"I think Hans is worried," Will confided. "He's not usually so, I don't know..."

"Abrupt? Nerves," Charming said. "Like the rest of us." He held out a hand to Will. "Will you? Hans has his players to occupy his mind, and I am desperate for something to occupy mine. Teaching you the steps of a basic basse dance will be as good as anything."

He exerted as much of his charm as he could summon, and Will pushed back his chair, albeit reluctantly.

"I'll probably tread on your feet," Will said.

"Unlikely, I promise you. And if you do, it's my punishment for being a poor teacher."

As he guided Will, taking it slowly and repeating everything over and over, he could not help thinking of the Beast, and how much she seemed to love dancing. He pushed the thought away, but as he said, "No, try like this. Ta da *da,* ta da *da*... see?" and as poor Will, teeth gritted, clomped solemnly and sweatily through the steps, the shine of the Beast's eyes, her unexpected grace, and her breathless laughter kept drifting through his mind.

Once Will had refused any more teaching, claiming that he had learned as much as he ever would and needed a breath of air, Charming set out to prowl the manor in search of the Beast.

He opened doors at random to be met with the whirl of polishing cloths and swoop of brooms, or else gleaming silence. The main doors remained firmly shut, as did the doors to the menagerie and the ballroom and the great dining hall. Some, he knew, led only to pantries or servants' quarters. Others which had formerly been locked now opened under his hand; he found an armoury, but the weapons were mostly very old and poorly kept. No armsmen in the manor when the curse came down, perhaps.

There was one gallery of middling paintings, and one full of rather better tapestries, none of which held his interest for more than a moment. There were empty bedrooms, the beds stark without sheets or coverlets.

Eventually he came to a pair of heavy double doors of blackened and riveted oak. Something told him that these led to the Beast's private rooms: a trace of scent, or a whisper in the air, something.

He knocked.

There was no answer.

"Beast?"

Could she even hear him, through these doors? They were old and solid and unmoving.

He leaned his head against the dark wood. "Please, I know what you think, but it isn't—I didn't... I came here by accident. I didn't know about your treasure. I just got pulled in, like the others. I want to free you, you understand? I really do."

Was she even there? She probably thought he'd gone— well, of course she thought he'd gone. Why would she believe he was still here, when she'd given him the magic ring with her own hands?

"I'm sorry," he said. "I never meant to hurt you. Really. I'm sorry."

In all his career, had he *ever* said that, to any of the women—or men—he had calculatedly and knowingly betrayed? Possibly. Had he ever *meant* it? Possibly, but never quite as much as now.

There was no answer. Had he even really sensed her there, or was it just his own wish for some sort of absolution?

He was too depressed to look up at the flicker of colour at the window, and Kichka's shrieks went unheard.

The Fairy Ball

HE LONG SLOW dusk of a late summer evening rolls slowly across the lawns of the manor. The roses release their heaviest, sweetest perfumes. One by one, the elegant wrought-iron torches bloom to life, along the driveway, along the paths of the gardens, shedding a dancing golden light and their own complex and exotic scent, resins mixed with spices from lands far away.

One by one, the windows of the manor wake with light—though they still don't open, locked as tight as a chest full of treasure.

Inside, thousands of candles blossom, in holders of polished brass and crystal and silver, and in the great heavy chandeliers of wood and iron that brood far above the shining floors.

Garlands of roses swoop everywhere, in every shade, white as snow, red as blood, from the first innocent blush of an infant's cheek, to the lush garnet of the wines for which Charming's home country of Floriens is famous;

to the rich, dark carmine of a poisoned apple, or a poisoned heart.

The grey mist swirls, thins, dissipates; and the forest crowds around the manor's neglected lands.

In their rooms the three men find their clothes laid out. Hans has ice-blue satin, the colour of his eyes, and a mask that turns the upper half of his face into that of a snarling bronze bear. He blinks at the stranger in the mirror, and thinks of his sister, and shivers.

Will finds satin grey as winter, grey as moonlit fog. Invisible hands help him dress, gently, and someone pats his arm in a gesture intended to be comforting. His half mask is silver, a wolf. Seeing it in the mirror gives him more comfort than the invisible hands can offer. His family *will* come for him, or he will go to them, one way or another. Wolf or human, they are his pack.

And Charming finds black. Black as ravens, black as funerals, touched here and there with gold. His mask is a harlequin's simple domino, also black, with gold at its corners. Hands tug at his hair, impatiently brushing out the tangles and fragments of leaf, and it spills to his shoulders, like gold coins spilling into a darkness that can never be filled.

One by one, the doors open. One by one, the men emerge, and walk the gleaming corridors beneath the whispering torches, to wait in a small chamber that leads to the grand ballroom.

HANS ARRIVED FIRST, and as the others approached he turned, and jolted with surprise as the tray in front of him, bearing a glass of wine, grew hands to hold it, and arms in blue livery, and all at once a thin young man with a pale face who blinked and shivered as he solidified.

Then they were everywhere, the silent and invisible servants, still mostly silent, though perhaps, when they were out of sight of those they serve, they took the chance to speak.

Charming felt a clutch in his gut at the sight of them. Five years. Not as long as Bella's servants were held in an enchanted sleep, but long enough, to walk these halls and gardens like ghosts.

He smiled at the young man who served him, who only ducked his head nervously and scurried away to some other duty.

"Oh!" said Will, at the window. "Look!"

"The other guests, I suppose," Hans said.

And here they came, in coaches of fantastical design, some rumbling along the ground and some floating in the air, drawn by wyverns or leopards or serpents, or gleaming black horses with seawater dripping from their manes. Alongside them came their own servants, in livery of green and gold, in livery of silver and purple. They were all sizes, from tame pixies no longer than Charming's middle finger, to hulking domesticated trolls with jewelled collars around their thick necks and puzzled, angry eyes.

"Awake the house!" went up the cry. "And open for the feast!"

With music, and laughter, and chatter, and the flitter of wings and the rustle of fine silks, here were the guests on the eve of the full moon, the eve of the equinox, pouring in through the gates of the manor and the wide open doors, and the rosebushes swayed and bowed before them.

* * *

"Well," Charming said. "That's quite a crew. I think I'm going to need more wine."

Will seemed almost stunned, frozen in place and open-mouthed. Hans's posture was wary, but less rigid; he had at least been to a ball or two in his time, Charming thought, though probably not one like this.

Poor Will, on the other hand... Charming clapped him on the back. "Drink up, my lad. One way or another this will be over soon, eh?"

Will gulped his wine, and nodded.

"I wonder where the Beast is," Hans said. "Isn't she the hostess?"

Charming looked through the openwork panel in the door at the guests now beginning to spread across the floor and fill the gallery, tilting their masks and whispering together. Two fairy women stood near each other in the gallery. One had silver hair that fell to her waist. She was dressed in nothing but cascades of shimmering purple jewels on silver chains. The other wore her green hair piled high over an elaborate golden frame, and her gown was of living flowers and butterflies in all shades of yellow and green. These two were surrounded by servants, and sycophants who leaned in to hear each word and laughed excessively at every remark. "I suspect that those two consider themselves the hostesses," Charming said. "The Beast is a piece in their game, whatever it is. And so are we. I *object* to that."

"I have to go," Hans said. "Set up for the play."

Will smiled. "Now *that* part I'm looking forward to."

* * *

KLUTZ THE HOBGOBLIN, his knobbly root of a face contrasting strangely with the splendour of his purple and silver livery, called on his friend Piddish to take his post, and snuck out of the revels, cup in hand. He headed for the stables, where he planned to parade his new position before his friends, who were still stuck caring for the selkies, which were vicious, and bit.

Before he could reach the stable yard, a figure loomed out of the shadows and he found himself staring into the face of an old woman with glittering dark eyes. "Who're you?" he demanded.

"Never you mind," said the old woman. There was a thud, and Klutz's unconscious form disappeared around a corner.

A moment later a young man emerged, tugging at a set of purple and silver livery that was too short in the legs, too long in the arms, and too tight everywhere else. The old woman tutted, and flicked her wand at him. Klutz's face, near enough, blinked at her, and the livery seemed to fit—or at least, no worse than it had fitted Klutz.

"I still can't *breathe*," the young man grumbled. "Who *wears* this stuff, anyway?"

"I've only given you a light glamour," Iolanthe said. "I've too much to do. Don't leap around too much and don't stand still for too long and you'll do."

"Leap? I can hardly *walk*."

"You're walking pretty much the way a hobgoblin walks anyway, so that's all to the good. Now get back in there before you're missed."

"Klutz? Klutz!" Piddish appeared in the doorway. "Hurry *up*, I need a slash!"

"Coming," not-Klutz said, and hobbled away.

Piddish headed for the garden, and his inevitable fate.

"Not *another* hobgoblin," Iolanthe moaned under her breath. "We need some more who look at least *mostly* human, or we're in trouble!"

GOSSIP AND CHATTER and flirting. The ballroom a glorious kaleidoscope of figures and costumes both gorgeous and fantastically, wonderfully ugly. Here a silvery banshee, her long white hair floating around her in whirling clouds; there a cloud of tiny pixies, their membranous wings jewel-coloured as stained glass. Here a hulking figure with a headdress—or were they his own antlers?—branching impossibly wide, eight foot across, and nearly brushing the heavy chandeliers.

A great fountain, carved of rose quartz, had appeared at one side of the ballroom. In its bowl merfolk and nixies, their scales rippling with cold rainbows, exchanged gossip and insults, and watched the goings-on of the dryfolk with cold, serpentine eyes. Music, silvery and insinuating, filled the air, but no musicians could be seen.

The manor's house servants in their plain blue livery moved flinchingly among the crowd, keeping their eyes down. The fairies' servants ignored them, except to order them about; the higher folk seemed unaware that they existed at all.

And in the very centre of the room stood the small stand of plain white marble. On it now lay a silver dish, heavy and ancient, carved about the rim with dancing, gambolling figures of imps and fairies, bears and wolves. In the centre of the dish rested a single rose, a perfect bud, just ready to unfurl.

Tables had been set up below the gallery, draped in

cloth of deep purple and emerald green. They groaned beneath the weight of enough food to feed the town of Felendstadt for a year—though some of it they'd be ill-advised to eat. Airy spun-sugar fantasies of ships and castles and eagles and dancing nymphs; great haunches of blood-dripping meat. Heaps of pomegranates and figs, bowls of apple blossom and the whites of dragon eggs whipped with saffron cream. Huge jugs of wine and nectar, tiny jugs brimming with heady tinctures of bluebell and aconite.

At the far end of the room, a stage had been erected. Compared to the fountain, the garlands, the feast tables, it was a crude thing; but crimson velvet draperies hid a multitude of sins.

Hans bowed his way towards the purple-garbed fairy. Stares and whispers followed him.

"Why, it's one of the chosen," Ione said, as he knelt before her.

Hans graciously begged her permission to put on a play for the guests' entertainment.

"A play?" Ione said. "Oh, how delightful, I haven't seen such a thing for many a year."

The green-and-gold fairy, Giadia, pouted. "There won't be time," she protested. "And where is the girl? Is she sulking? I shan't allow it."

"It's but a short play, great lady," Hans said. "Just a little treat, for your amusement."

"*If* it's short," she said, waving Hans away. "Someone fetch the girl."

But the girl had not waited to be fetched. With a brassy flare of trumpets, the Beast made her entrance.

Her gown was cloth of gold, looped and ruffled, draped with chains of rubies, extravagant, excessive. Gold shoes with pearl and ruby buckles peeped beneath the hem, cascades of rubies hung from her hairy ears. She held her head high, a gold domino perched above her snout, as though so small a thing could hide what she was.

She didn't choose that dress, or that mask, Charming thought. *The fairy who cursed her did, as a humiliation.*

But the Beast walked as proudly as though this was all her choice: the dress, the ball, the guests, the garlands. He felt a stab of admiration, or pity.

A troll, sweating and constrained in his green-gold livery, flung open the door to the room where Will and Charming waited, and they emerged, to stares, and whispers, and speculation. Charming heard Will swallow, and put his hand on the boy's shoulder. "Chin up, Will. They look fancy, I know, but I bet not one of them can build a table or cook a meal like you, eh? Useless, the lot of 'em."

Will gave a choke of laughter, and relaxed a very little.

The room was so full, Charming thought, it should be hot and lively, but somehow it still felt cold; and you could *feel* the silence, the clock's graveyard ticking, beneath the chatter and the music. The bears and wolves on the wall-plaques were frozen in plaster, the fluttering cherubs on the ceiling had absent, empty eyes.

THE FLOOR OF the stables was now rather full of unconscious bodies, of various kinds, in various states of undress. "How are we doing?" Thelise said.

"Probably as many as we can manage," Marie Blanche said, tapping her knife hilt. "Any more will be risky. Most of the rest don't even look *slightly* human. Even Iolanthe's had to go in."

"Well, once we get them out, my pack and the bears can—" She snapped about, quick as a whip, at the sound of growling behind her. "*Quiet*. We are working *with the bears*. If you don't like it, you may leave. And form your own pack, if you've the strength."

The young she-wolf lowered her head and grumbled, but lay down, putting her head on her paws with an ostentatious, whiny yawn.

Thelise glared at her for another moment and then turned back to Marie Blanche. "They're all overwrought. I shall be glad when this is over."

"We all will."

CHARMING MADE HIS way around the room, bowing and flirting and—well—*charming*, trying to move towards the Beast; but wherever he was, she somehow wasn't. He felt eyes on his back everywhere, but *she* was always looking at anything but him.

A fairy in a peacock mask, her crow-black hair piled in a towering extravaganza in which tiny lights shifted and glimmered, gestured to him imperiously. He made his way towards her. Her gown was a foam of sea-green gauze, and a dozen tiny pixies, dressed as skuas, held up her train.

The orchestra struck up the first notes of a galliard. Will should manage at least some of the steps, Charming thought. The fairy looked at him expectantly, and he had no choice but to offer her his arm.

"So, will *you* be the one, I wonder?" she said, as the dance began. Her eyes in the mask were merry, but he thought that they too were like the sea, shifting and untrustworthy. "I have a wager on the matter."

"Then you probably have a better guess than I," Charming said, smiling and moving expertly, his tone light.

"What, none of you have worked it out? But it's so obvious!" She giggled like tinkling ice, and tapped his arm with her fan. "Well, perhaps you will. There's a little time yet to midnight."

He saw Will over her shoulder, valiantly plodding through the steps with a slender fairy. She was half his height, but rendered twice his width by a construction of red silk that spread great petals around her, making her narrow, birdlike face the centre of a giant flower. He could not tell if she was wearing a mask, or if she really was beaked and feathered.

Charming caught a glimpse of a golden gown, but before he could pursue the Beast again, the music ended, and a voice rang out.

"Ladies, lords, and all assembled," said one of the actors from the stage. "We present, for your entertainment and delight, *The Tragedy of Amaris and Arturo*."

The crowd rustled and turned, and focussed on the stage. This was new, this was something different. The endless hiss of gossip quieted, and the play began.

Amaris was slight and frail, but burned with passion like a glass of phosphorous.

Arturo was lean and tall, and full of his own alchemical explosiveness.

They loved, they quarreled, they bathed each other in nectar and tore each other to shreds with words. They were adoring and vicious by turns. The audience gasped and applauded at every particularly adept turn of phrase. (Though some of them frowned, and looked, for a moment, as though they were trying to remember something: something they'd heard, perhaps, or seen, or felt, a very long time ago.)

Amaris was a queen, and Arturo a king. Their countries suffered, falling into starvation and disrepair as their rulers could think of nothing but each other, for good or ill. A peasant waylaid Amaris and pleaded with her to turn her thoughts to her people, and his simple, honest entreaties made some of the audience sigh and wipe their eyes.

Arturo's mother fell at his feet, and begged him to remember his responsibilities, and her speech to her son stirred the hearts of every wayward offspring present who was capable of being stirred. (Even Charming— still trying, as subtly as possible, to work his way to the Beast's side—heard a phrase or two that made him wince and think of his own sainted mother. And the actor's voice sounded a little familiar, but he had other things on his mind).

And finally the court wizards, fed up of the whole business, turned the two quarrelsome lovers into a fish and a bird, so that they might cease the ruination of all their lands. Only for one day a year, on the equinox, would they regain their human forms, to see each other again. Tragic speeches were given, a little moral rhyme topped off the whole, and the players took their bows.

For a moment there was a silence that rung strangely. The players glanced nervously at each other.

Then, applause exploded all around. The audience showered them with gifts (although who knew how many of those jewels that landed on the stage would still be jewels the next day?).

The players bowed, and bowed again, and the curtains closed.

"Quite unexpected. I didn't think Ione had such imagination," said one of the court fairies, a pearly-skinned fellow with sheaves of green-gold hair, tugging pettishly at one of the garlands. A crimson petal detached and floated to the floor, where it lay like a drop of blood.

"You think it was Ione's doing? I'm certain it was Giadia," his companion said. He had a fox mask, and his legs were like the hind legs of a roe deer. He peered at the dancefloor through a jewelled lorgnette. He had no need of it, he simply liked the style. "Come, let's go tease the little wolf-mask, he's *so* unsuitable, I quite adore him."

"I'M UP IN a minute," Bella said, mask in hand, as she stepped down from the horse-drawn carriage, which smelled of metal and ink and burned feathers. "Are you going to be alright?"

Doctor Rapunzel, her fingers flickering with magic, rubbed her sore eyes and shook her head. "It's this *wretched* forest. And everything else. So much wild magic... If only we had those blasted boots! I've still the cloak of feathers, but it's old, and unless the wind favours us it's unlikely to be fast enough. I have one more thing to try."

"If only Kichka had been able to get in, at least we could have prepared Charming."

"Even if he had, the blasted man would probably have some plan of his own. It might actually be better he doesn't know."

Kichka perched on the box, bobbing up and down, watching the lights and the moving shapes through the windows. He poked his head down into the carriage.

"Not yet, Kichka," Bella said. "Go back to the inn, if you wish. I know you don't like it here."

Kichka shook his head emphatically, chattered for a moment, and settled on his perch.

"Thank you, Kichka, it's a comfort to know Emilia will have such a fine protector."

GOLDLÖCKCHEN STOOD BETWEEN two of the bears, her fingers twined in the rough comfort of their fur, watching the lights, hearing the music. Silhouettes moved past the windows. She searched them for any figure that might have been her brother, but though some looked, briefly, almost human, none of them were his dear familiar shape.

But it wasn't just Hans she looked for. She was studying the manor, and the spell that surrounded it. It might be diminished for tonight, to allow the guests in, but it was still there. She felt out for its construction, its shape and edges.

THE MUSIC STRUCK up again. The clock hands crept around its face, a javelin and a spear.

Will was backed against a wall, surrounded by the Good Folk, trying to answer their barrage of questions without making a complete fool of himself, wishing Charming or his aunt Thelise or *anyone* were here to stand between him and their sleek smiles and greedy, searching eyes. He was grateful for the mask, even though it narrowed his vision.

Only the watchers at the door noticed the final carriage—desperately, almost unfashionably late—

rolling up the driveway. It was an elegantly simple vehicle, drawn by two excellent but perfectly mundane chestnut horses.

The driver, who was small and slightly oddly shaped, leapt down and set the stool, flung open the door and bowed the occupants out.

"I thought the mortals' play was amusing," Ione said. "I do love their burning passions, it all seems so *important* to them." She pressed a finger to her perfect lower lip. "It reminded me of something, though I don't know what."

"*I* thought it very insolent of them to put on an entertainment at *our* feast."

"Well, then, why did you change the spell to let them in?"

"I did no such thing! I thought *you'd* decided to add pieces to the game!"

They looked at each other, flat-eyed as snakes. Ione glanced at the clock.

Giadia scanned the floor. Charming, in his black, was easy to spot, waylaid in the middle of the floor by one of Ione's hangers-on. *There is one.*

And where…? Ah, there, in his ice-blue, bowing at congratulations on his skill, how delightful a play, how oddly moving…

Two.

And there, with his back pressed to the wall and one of her own followers flirting with him—she would have to be punished for that—the wolf-masked boy.

Three.

All there, all accounted for. "So someone else has decided to join the game," she said. "But all our pieces are still in play, my dear. Let's see how this turns out."

*   *   *

A MOMENT LATER, two figures entered the ballroom. The older woman, magnificent in scarlet and jet, her mask a black rat, imperiously handed two slips of violet cloth to one of the guards. The other, younger, was dressed in the blue of a midsummer sky, delicately threaded with shimmering gold. Her mask was of gold filigree. A mysterious and beautiful stranger!

All around the murmur rose, like the chatter of sparrows as they settle into their hedgerows for the night.

"So she came! I didn't think she'd come."

"Why, poor Iolanthe, so *old*. That's what getting entangled with mortals does to one."

"And has she brought the goddaughter? It must be her, surely. What *is* she playing at?"

"Oh, Iolanthe thinks herself too good for our games nowadays, my dear. Probably the girl begged to come. When else will she get the chance?"

"NOT ONE CLUE?" Charming said, exuding every bit of allure he could drag up, making the most of his eyes, tossing his hair, injecting his voice with velvety promise.

The fairy laughed at him and trembled her gleaming wings, which rippled with subtle colours like the inside of a shell. "Naughty boy. That would be against the rules!" She leaned in close, confiding. "But I'll tell you this... you're the last batch. She's reached the end. Not that solving the riddle is even the important part. But if it doesn't happen by midnight..." She kissed her fingertips and blew—*phoo!*—as though scattering some light and fragile seed.

"If what doesn't happen?"

She shook her head at him, smiling in a way that made his hands clench.

"What happens at midnight?"

"Why, she dies, of course."

"*What?*"

His exclamation was so abrupt, so loud and harsh, that people turned to look, and the winged fairy pouted, and flittered away before he could stop her, to perch on one of the candelabra and tease a tame troll by dropping sweetmeats on his head.

CHARMING HAD FINALLY managed to get close to the Beast, and was attempting to get her attention. She was listening with apparent fascination to a being even taller than she, with human arms, legs like some huge ancient deer long gone from these forests, and vast branching antlers. He was quite blatantly flirting with her.

"Beast!" Charming said.

The great creature looked at him and sighed. "I suppose I must relinquish you," he said. "Or Ione will not forgive me. Ah, I wish things were otherwise, my dear. Fare thee well! Or as well as possible, under the circumstances." He kissed her paw with too much relish for Charming's taste, and moved away.

The Beast, with obvious reluctance, turned to Charming. "Why are you still here?" she said. "Have you not taken enough?"

He opened his mouth and realised he had nothing to say, no slick excuse or easy flattery. Before he could force words out, the music struck up again, and she was gone. He tried to go after her, and knocked into the white marble pedestal. The rosebud had opened in the heat of the room, and was now a full-blown bloom, its scent so strong that for a moment his head swum.

AND NOW, AGAIN, the music. And in front of him was some woman in blue who seemed vaguely familiar. He didn't want to dance, he didn't want to do *anything*, but his hand was in a light but firm grip and he was led onto the floor.

Step and turn and step and turn.

Whispering rose around them like the wind in the trees of the forest. *The goddaughter? What is she doing? Surely she can't think…*

Oh, she's just desperate, silly child… Silly little mortal girl, she should have taken her chance when she had it…

Step and turn and kick and turn and Charming paid little mind, he was such a practised dancer he didn't need to, his gaze still searching the room for the Beast. There she was, dancing with Will! He must get her attention, somehow, as soon as the music stops…

IONE AND GIADIA watched from the balcony as the long-since-rejected goddaughter danced with Charming. "Some move by Iolanthe, do you think?" Ione said, her amethysts clinking as she swayed a little with the music.

"A very clumsy one," Giadia said. She glanced down at her dress and frowned. The butterflies were dying already. She waved a hand, and they livened up, fluttering. They'd all be dead before sunrise, but she'd have changed costume by then.

Charming and the woman in blue disappeared behind a pillar.

CHARMING LANDED ON the floor with his dancing partner on top. He was in no state of mind to enjoy this, and scrambled unceremoniously out from under. "What the *Goose?*"

The goddaughter…

"Bella—?"

The ballroom is gone. He was in a place he did not recognise, surrounded by bags of flour and onions.

The gold filigree mask rose, and there was Nell, rolling those lovely brown eyes, looking resigned and somewhat harried. "I suppose I should be used to you not recognising me by now. Get your royal backside out the doors, Your Highness. You've got places to be."

"But I can't! I have to go back!"

"*There's* gratitude. If you don't get moving, you are going to *die,* in case you hadn't remembered, and you won't be the only one. If you've left a fancy trinket or two behind, you can forget them. We're not here to help you rob someone else." She put her hands on him and shoved. "Will you *move?*"

He was too shocked by the turn of events at first to realise that Nell, for all her toughness, was not actually strong enough to shove him towards the door. He stumbled blindly on until she said, "Take him, quick. I have to get back." She dragged her mask back on and scurried for the stairs.

"Roland?"

The imp was in the doorway, looking at him with implacable cynicism. "Yeah. Don't ask me why. Come on."

"I can't!"

"You *can't*? After the ladies—*and* me, I might add—went to all this trouble to save your arse, you *can't*?"

"Roland, please, I *have* to go. I will get to the mountain, I *vow*, but I have to get back! She's going to *die!*"

Roland stared at him. "You actually mean it, don't you? Listen, you got about three minutes to midnight, and if you ain't out I'm coming in after you, and dragging you out by whatever bits I can grab, get me?"

"Yes! Thank you, Roland!" He bolted for the stairs.

Roland shook his head, and looked back at the courtyard where the coach waited, with Doctor Rapunzel and a cloak of feathers. "I'm an idiot," he said. "What am I?"

AFTER A PAUSE *almost* long enough to be indecorous, the lady in blue and her graceful black-clad partner swept out from behind the pillar again and rejoined the dancers. The rising tide of gossip subsided a little.

Will saw the Beast approaching him through the crowd, and practically flung himself at her as the music began again. He heard those around him laugh, but hardly cared. "Dance with me?" he gasped.

"Of course, Will."

She sounded so sad.

"I'm sorry," he babbled. "I'm a terrible dancer. Charming tried to teach me, but…"

"Don't worry," she said gently. "It doesn't matter in the least." She took his hand in her paw and led him onto the floor.

* * *

THE DANCE WENT on. Two figures in blue and black. Two in grey and gold—the Beast was leading, her wolf-masked suitor even clumsier than she, how amusing it was!

Hans leaned against the wall, not dancing, watching the others. The murmuring was like the sea.

The music changed, and the lady in blue took Will by the hand, and the Beast was face to face with a familiar figure in a black domino, edged with gold. She looked down. She frowned. "Wait…" she said. "You're not…"

"No, I'm not," the dancer said. "But please do me the honour?"

Something about that voice was very persuasive, and besides, the Beast thought, what does it matter now?

The lady in blue edged Will across the room, and around behind the pillar they went…

And they didn't come out.

WILL FOUND HIMSELF on the floor of the undercroft. The mask rose and there, in the blue dress, was Hedel. For a moment he just held her, looking into her eyes. "I knew you'd come for me," he said.

"Of course we did. Come on, let's get out of this place."

They scrambled for the door.

"These clothes are *ridiculous*," she said, as they ran. "Yours are worse than mine!"

"I can't *wait* to take it all off," Will said. "You might have to help."

Hedel grinned. "I'm sure I can manage that."

*   *   *

"No no no no…" Nell muttered, desperately shuffling along the wall. "They were supposed to *wait*…"

A figure in grey satin grabbed her arm. "Sorry," he growled. He was taller and skinnier than Will, his hair was not curly enough, his 'mask' was only there if you didn't look too closely, but he was the closest they had.

Nell used language more appropriate to a kitchen than a ballroom as they shot out from behind the pillar and spun out across the floor. "Where's the other two?"

"They're ready." He jerked his head and she saw a couple, a glimpse of ice-blue showing beneath one cloak, beneath the other the hem of a no-colour dress that would change at need, to match Hans's partner, but Hans wasn't *dancing*. "Godmother!" Nell hissed frantically.

"All right, all right, child, I'm doing what I can, I'm an old woman!" Iolanthe swept past her, majestic, and said to Hans, "Young man, I've someone for you to dance with. Indulge an old woman."

Somehow he found himself taking hands with a young woman in a dress whose colour he couldn't quite make out, and being whirled, with a slightly disconcerting strength, around behind a pillar.

Up on the balcony, Ione and Giadia caught this byplay and bristled—but then, it was only foolish old Iolanthe, now being led through the pillars to a chair by a young man in ice-blue satin and a bear mask. Perhaps she still hoped for a suitor for that uncooperative goddaughter of hers…

HANS LANDED ON a sack of flour, which burst, clouding the air, covering him and his dance partner in white. They choked and flailed. The young woman tore off her mask. She was stocky and bronze-haired under the flour, and he had never seen her before in his life. She gestured, coughing. "Door. Run."

"But I... What...?"

"*Run*," she growled, showing too many teeth, and his legs had made the choice before his mind could catch up.

The Clock Strikes Twelve

HARMING PLUNGES THROUGH the crowd, searching.

Thraangggg.

The first bell of midnight rolls across the room.

Everything stops. The dancers stare and whisper. Even the splash of the fountain is suddenly muted, as the naiads and the merfolk go still and watch.

Thraangggg.

A wolf-masked figure strides onto the floor with Nell...

A bear-masked man stands clasping the waist of a figure in scarlet satin...

Thraangggg.

The Beast sways, and crumples, the skirt of the ridiculous dress puffing up around her, as though she lies in the heart of a great gold flower.

Thraangggg

Her black-clad partner looks around frantically. "Someone, water!" And it's a woman's voice, clear and musical.

Ione rises. "That's not the Prince."

Thraangggg

One of the blue-liveried servants, who have been ignored all evening, runs up with a glass, and drops to his knees at the Beast's side.

Thraangggg

A second figure in black barges through the avidly watching crowd, and hurls himself across the floor, skidding to a halt next to the Beast.

Thraangggg

"Oh, you *idiot*," Nell says. She plunges back into the crowd, searching for Iolanthe.

Thraangggg

The Beast looks up and sees two black-clad figures, side by side, but looks at, focuses on, only one. "You..." she says weakly.

Thraangggg

"Me," Charming says, pulling off the mask. "No tricks, no lies. Just me. I love you."

The gossiping and laughter stop in an instant and a shocked hush falls on the crowd.

Her vision is blurring, her ears hear the sound of the sea. Did he really say that, or was it just her own last desperate hope?

Thraangggg

"*Please* don't die, I love you."

"Really?" she says.

Thraangggg

"No trick, no lie."

"I love you too."

* * *

THERE IS A glimmer in the air, as bright as day. The very stones of the manor shiver to their foundations. Every banner in the house whips in an unheard and unfelt wind.

In the garden, all the roses shudder at once, sending petals flying on the breeze, and then are still.

And there, lying on the floor in a ridiculous, extravagant dress, is a lean, red-headed young woman.

SHE TAKES A deep breath and slowly pulls off her mask, to stare Charming square in the face.

"You should see," she said. "I'm not pretty. I never was."

Thraangggg.

Charming's eyes caress her freckles and her square jaw, and he smiles. "You look lovely to me," he says. "I hoped your eyes would be the same, and they are. You're probably still taller than me, though. I shall learn to live with it."

GIADIA AND IONE, up on their balcony, look at each other, and smile.

Some of those around them, seeing those smiles, feel a cold breath of unease; but they hide it beneath smiles and laughter and applause.

"What's your name? Your real name?" Charming says, ignoring the cheers, the applause, the laughter.

"Gabrielle. Gabrielle de Villeneuve."

"Charmed," he says. "*Utterly.*" And he kisses her hand.

A small footman in ill-fitting blue livery and an overlarge wig pulled down almost to his nose sidles up to Charming's elbow and yanks on his sleeve. "We gotta go," he hisses. "*Now.*"

Charming kisses Gabrielle's hand once again. "I *am* coming back," he says.

And he turns the dark, oily-looking ring on his finger, and disappears.

"WHERE IS HE?" Ione hisses, her violet eyes suddenly slit-pupilled and blazing. "Where is the Prince?"

Giadia gives a trill of laughter. "*Such* a pity, and you worked so hard to bring it all together! Well, my dear, I'm sure we'll find another game soon enough."

"There are two pieces still in play. I'll find them, if I have to scour this forest from end to end!"

Ione sweeps away, trailing purple sparks, summoning her sycophants, her servants, and her hounds.

HANS RUNS FROM one set of teeth only to find himself suddenly surrounded by a lot more of them. "You're the Bear brother?" someone growls out of the darkness.

"Er... yes?" He has long known there are wolves in this forest, but he's never seen them this close, or this many. And he's never seen their leader, human but definitely wolfish, whose hair, in the flickering torchlight, is too close to the colour of blood for comfort.

"Go with them," she says. "They'll cover your scent, and keep the hounds off you."

"Hounds?"

"*Go.*"

GOLDLÖCKCHEN SEES THE young couple running towards her. She knows what to expect, draws on what the doctor taught her, slows her breath and stops her fists from tightening too hard in the bears' fur. "You're Will? And Hedel? Go with them."

"The *bears*?"

"They'll see you safe. I'll meet you later." She slips away into the wood, pale and slight as a will-o'-the-wisp.

"Will she be all right?" Will says. "She's…"

"That's the *Bear Witch*," Hedel says. "I think she'll be fine."

ROLAND, GRUMBLING HIS way back to Doctor Rapunzel, saw Giadia waving to Ione as she entered her coach. "Don't sulk, my sweet!" Giadia called. "The game's not over yet!" Dead butterflies dropped behind her as her coach rose into the air.

Ione paused for a moment, then shrugged, and laughed, that tinkling, silvery laugh, her gown of amethysts glimmering with the movement. "You're right, even if you *are* stupid," she said. "I'll hunt down the other two, *and* him. One way or another, he'll be back. I'll make sure of it."

Roland stood very, very still until Ione turned away to snap out more orders at her servants.

Then he ran to the carriage where Doctor Rapunzel waited. He opened the door, and jumped in, and said, "Let's get out of here."

"Roland? What happened?"

"Charming got hold of a magical transportation ring and has nipped off, presumably to the Devil's Head Mountain to keep his bargain, 'cause he might be slimy, but stupid he ain't. Oh, and he fell in love and broke the curse. Ione's sent hounds after the other two, like you thought one of them might if they didn't get their way. And everything's fine and dandy and can we *go*?"

"What else?" Doctor Rapunzel said, looking at him closely. Kichka put his head down through the roof and regarded him upside-down. "Roland?"

"I found out who's conspiring with Mephistopheles, that's what happened. I'd know that voice anywhere."

"You heard them *here*? What was a denizen of the Infernal doing at a fairy ball?"

"It wasn't one of my lot," Roland said. "It was Ione. Of the Good Folk. And I don't know what that means, but it feels to me like very bad news."

GABRIELLE SAT, LOOKING at her hands, then wonderingly, around her. The blue-liveried servant held out the glass of water, and she got to her feet, and took it. The dress, now, was at least a foot too long—but Charming had been right, she would still be a fraction taller than he.

The garlands began to disintegrate, petals, leaves, then whole flowerheads, whole strands, dropping towards the floor, disappearing before they got there. The remains of the feast vapourised in puffs of smoke and strange-scented vapours. The crowd of fairy folk, now the entertainment was over, dispersed like leaves on an autumn wind, streaming out of the doors and windows and up the chimneys. The fountain and its occupants dissolved away. One of the last to go was the tall wolflike fellow in the red jacket, who grinned at Gabrielle, kissed his fingers to her, and swept away.

The rose lying on the pedestal had turned to a single great carved ruby, glimmering in the last of the candlelight.

Gabrielle picked up her hem. Her final dance partner pulled off her mask, revealing an extraordinarily beautiful young woman with olive skin. She took Gabrielle's arm, and said, "I'm very sorry, my dear, but he does that."

"So, only true love could break the curse," another woman remarked, her hands on her hips as she regarded the scene. "Frankly, I would not have thought him capable. But life is full of surprises, is it not? This time he may actually come back."

"He'd better," Gabrielle said. "Who... who are you?"

The dancer in black held her hand to her chest. "Of course! Where are my manners? My name is Bella Lucia; my friend here is Marie Blanche. We came here"—she looked around her—"trying to right a wrong. I'm afraid we don't know *you*, though."

Gabrielle looked down at herself, and around at the ballroom now rapidly emptying, the candles guttering in their beds. "I'm... I don't know. I don't know what I am. Steward?" She looked around and spied a lean older man with sharp, intelligent features and long silver hair. "Oh, Matthias, I'm so glad to see you."

He reached out his hands and clasped hers. "My Lady, I..." He swiped at his eyes. "Forgive me..."

"It's *your* forgiveness I need. Please bring everyone— all the staff, I mean."

They filed in, in little clumps, two and three and five, and stood, like her, staring at each other and at their own hands.

"I am so *sorry*," Gabrielle said. "If I'd known, if I had any idea..."

"It wasn't your doing, Highness," said a pink-faced, middle-aged woman in a grease-spotted apron. "It was *them*."

"But you've been robbed of your lives for so *long*..."

"It could have been worse," Bella said, gently. "When my palace woke, two hundred years had gone. At least most of their families will still remember them. You are free. You are all free. Try to be happy."

Gabrielle looked at her, then at the empty ballroom. "Yes," she said. "Frederich? Pawel? If you're not too tired... something merry, please. The merriest thing you know."

And flute and fiddle struck up, and everyone was pulled into the dance, and Gabrielle de Villeneuve spun and whirled in the midst of them all, with the hem of her too-long dress caught up in her hand and her red hair flying like a flag of battle, and danced, and danced, and danced.

GOLDLÖCKCHEN THE BEAR Witch began to weave a spell. It was a spell of hiding, and confusion. It didn't surround the manor this time, but a small cottage, and the land around it, and a nearby settlement with its huts and hall and beehives.

There was no curse, here. Only safety, and protection. Those who meant well could pass freely, but those who meant ill would not find either place at all.

IONE'S HOUNDS FUMBLED and whined, casting for a scent that turned back on itself or trailed off altogether. Ione cursed and shrieked and eventually, as the dawn began to lighten the tops of the distant mountains, summoned her coach and her servants and her hounds and sped for home, chasing the night across the treetops.

The Cat and Her Company

HE NEXT DAY...

    "I'm *starving*," Gilda complained. "I'm wasting away."

"Rubbish, you've got more muscles than the bears," Mouse said. She was flicking one of her knives into a tree and pulling it out again, over and over.

"It's those flowers. They smell like cake, and it makes me hungry."

"Everything makes you hungry," Curly said. "You've already eaten everything I brought with me."

They were standing in the clearing by Goldlöckchen's cottage. Mouse bit her lip. "D'you suppose...? I mean, we didn't really *do* anything."

"We tried," Curly said. "Not our fault it didn't work." He cast an anxious look at the sky but it remained cloudless, and without thunder.

They waited. Two bears sat either side of the door like monuments to patience.

After a period that was probably not as long as it

seemed, the door opened. Dance emerged, his beard jutting triumphantly, with several rolls of parchment under his arm, followed by a slight figure in a dress of brown velvet and battered boots. She had short, sleek, tabby-striped hair, bright green eyes, and an air of self-possession.

"Is that...?" Mouse said.

"Hello, darlings," said Cassia.

"It worked, then," Gilda said.

"Mostly," Cassia said, with an exasperated sigh. "Apparently I may become a cat again under stress. And my hair did *not* look like this before."

"Well, since we didn't *actually* get her brother back," Dance said, "I don't think you've much to complain of."

"Nor have you. Enough plays for a *year*, there."

"What about the information?" Mouse said. "She wanted a piece of information."

"Oh, that." Dance shrugged. "She said she's sure Cassia will think of something."

"She seems to have relaxed," Cassia said, "now she's got that rather delicious brother of hers back. I was rather hoping we could persuade him to come with us, but..."

"Us?" Dance said. "Who said anything about *us?*"

"Oh come on, you know you want me along. I'm ever so useful."

"For what, exactly?"

"You never know. *And* I'm decorative."

"Hmm. We'll give you a lift to the next town. After that..."

Cassia grinned, and headbutted Mouse's shoulder affectionately.

* * *

(NOT LONG AFTER, in another part of the forest, on a day of fresh breezes and quick-moving cloud shadows, a woman strode through the forest with a bow in her hand and a wolf at her side...)

(NOT LONG AFTER *that,* in a nearby town, a small, oddly shaped figure in a tattered green coat could be seen looking at a grimy, neglected inn with a speculative glint in his eye...)

BUT THIS PART of the story ends, or begins, as so many do, with a man, on a mountaintop, preparing to meet a devil.

The End

Acknowledgements

THANKS TO MY amazing, ever helpful and creative editor, David Thomas Moore, and the team at Solaris, and to Dave and Sarah E for constant encouragement, support and occasional necessary arse-kickage. This book would not exist without them.

About the Author

Jade Linwood was raised in Oxfordshire, with books, cats and apple trees.

Jade has lived in Dorset, Wiltshire, Wales, Cambridgeshire and London, and has travelled to Venice, Paris, Rome, Athens, Jordan, and Egypt's White Desert. Jade has competed in swordfighting competitions, been a member of a travelling theatre company, flown on military transport and was once offered a part in *The Bill*.

There are still books, cats, and apple trees. Everything else is mutable.

FIND US ONLINE!

www.rebellionpublishing.com

/solarisbooks /solarisbks /solarisbooks

SIGN UP TO OUR NEWSLETTER!

rebellionpublishing.com/newsletter

YOUR REVIEWS MATTER!

Enjoy this book? Got something to say?

Leave a review on Amazon, GoodReads or with your
favourite bookseller and let the world know!